Nightmare Scenario

Hazel Clarke

Nightmare Scenario

SALAD
PAGES

A NEW AGE OF BOOKS

Salad Pages Ltd.
89 Leigh Road, Eastleigh,
Hampshire, England, SO50 9DQ

Published by Salad Pages Ltd.
© Salad Pages Ltd. 2019
The author asserts the moral right to be
identified as the author of this work.

A catalogue record of this book is available
from the British Library
ISBN: 9781913067007

Printed and bound in Great Britain
by Clays Ltd, Elcograf S.p.A

For my mum, for always loving and supporting me no matter what.

THE RULES

The rules for each Nightmare Scenario are as follows:

1. A scenario must be played every night.
2. The scenario cannot be changed once accepted.
3. The scenario will be proposed at sunset. The Player can turn it down.
4. The scenario can only be played between sunset and sunrise in accordance with the time displayed on the Hourglass.
5. If the Player refuses the scenario, they will be forced to play it half an hour before sunrise.
6. The Voices can help the Player during the scenario.
7. Details of how to win the scenario must be given truthfully by the Voices.
8. Each Level increases by 10XP e.g. to attain Level 1 the Player needs 10XP, to attain Level 5 the Player needs 50XP etc. XP is reset to zero upon attainment of each Level.
9. The Voices can decide if the Player must get to a certain Level by a certain date.
10. If the Player does not achieve the set Level by the set date, the Voices can hurt the Player or force the Player to hurt someone else.
11. The Voices are allowed to access the Player's fears for the scenario.
12. None of the scenarios can be repeated.

CHAPTER 1

'Scenario: the android clown from Anna McCann's ninth birthday party is behind you. Get home without turning around to look at it. You also lose if the clown touches you. Do you accept the scenario?'

I grimaced as the buzzing in my head started again. I checked the time on my Hourglass – 19:27. It was sunset.

'Do you accept the scenario?'

'Can we just wait a few minutes until I finish work?' I whispered. There were only a few customers left in the café, but I didn't want to draw attention to myself by letting them hear me.

'Do you accept the scenario, Gracie?'

'One minute, Eros.' I could practically hear him tapping his foot inside my head, already impatient despite only having given me the scenario 30 seconds ago. I didn't want to make him angry again. I made my way behind the counter to where Miss Leyshon, my boss, was making coffee. I waited while she bashed the portafilter into the machine with more force than necessary. 'Miss Leyshon?'

She glanced up at me, one eyebrow raised. 'What?'

8

'I don't feel very well. I was wondering if I could go home early tonight? I only have 15 minutes left of my shift.'

She clicked her tongue against the roof of her mouth. 'If you have to. I'll be docking your wages, though.'

'Thank you!' I smiled in relief. I grabbed my coat from under the counter, putting my arm in the wrong sleeve as I hurried out of the door.

'Do you accept the scenario, Gracie?'

'Yes,' I said. It wasn't like I had much choice. Sooner or later I would have to play. A yellow hologram popped up in front of me. A box with the familiar word "Scenario" typed neatly inside it. "Yes" and "No" buttons hovered just below.

'Please confirm your choice.'

I pressed the "Yes" button and the hologram disappeared. A high-pitched screeching noise started some way behind me. I recognised it immediately. The sound of metal grating on artificial skin. I shut my eyes trying to stop myself from reliving Anna McCann's ninth birthday party, but it was already too late. I could hear the echoes of my friends' screams from all those years ago, the crunching of party hats and presents as we all ran, terrified of what could happen. Of what did happen. I needed to see if it was real, to make sure the thing making the horrific sound was actually there. But how could I check if it was there without turning around? I lifted up my left wrist. My Hourglass lit up. The skin it was surgically attached to illuminated a gentle emerald green. 'Front camera,' I instructed.

The screen flipped from the normal clock to the camera and I held up my wrist so it was angled over my shoulder. Standing behind me, fake flesh stretched and rotting over his metal frame, was the android clown that murdered my entire primary school class nine years ago. To my relief, the hologram flickered and disappeared for a moment. He wasn't real. This wasn't real. All I had to do was get home without turning around. As far as other scenarios went, this was a piece of cake.

Terry tutted. 'We didn't think you'd do that. We should make these scenarios harder; don't you think, Eros?'

'Definitely. I bet you can't wait to play the scenario we have planned for you tomorrow night.'

'But tomorrow's my first day at Uni,' I said, trying not to whine. The last thing the Voices needed was an excuse to make these scenarios even worse for me.

'We don't care. Isn't life meant to be unfair?'

'Leave her alone, boys. Gracie, you're doing great.'

I smiled and lowered my Hourglass. 'Thanks, Psyche.'

Unlike Eros and Terry, Psyche was kind and talked me through the scenarios so I wouldn't get too scared. Terry flicked my frontal lobe and I flinched. 'What was that for?' I asked, unable to hide my agitation this time.

'She's not as nice as you think she is,' he hissed. 'But you better get moving. Or we're going to have to order Mr Android Clown here to speed things up.'

I checked the front camera again and saw that the clown had moved closer. Unfortunately, I got a better look at it. The clown's eyes were made of glass and one was shattered beyond repair. The other one had the lens intact, but the fake eyeball was broken and kept rolling around in the socket. The clown had no eyebrows and the hair on top of its head was almost gone, apart from a few loose strands that swayed back and forth in front of its broken eyes. But that wasn't what disturbed me the most about its appearance. The clown's paint-chipped face was splattered with blood. I knew it wasn't real, but it scared me.

I took a deep breath and made my way down George's Road, passing the terracotta coloured apartment blocks and old terraced houses. I could see a group of boys huddled around an entrance to an apartment block, laughing and joking with each other. They stopped when they saw me drawing closer, but they didn't move. They couldn't do anything whilst wearing the Hourglass.

'That's it, keep walking. Don't let them scare you.' I thanked Psyche once the boys were out of earshot and carried on walking, trying to ignore the grating of flesh on metal behind me.

'Can I ask you a question, Gracie?'

'What is it, Eros?'

'This android clown... after the murders, did they destroy it?'

I licked my dry lips and stuffed my hands into my coat pockets. 'I don't know. No one told me.'

'You thinking what I'm thinking, Eros?' Terry asked.

'Yeah. I say when tonight's scenario is over, we go out and find the killer android and make this scenario real.'

I took a shaky breath. 'Please, don't do that. It was a horrible experience.'

'Why do you think we want you to play it, hm?' Eros whispered. It felt like he was hovering close to my ear. His voice was husky and sinister, and it made me shiver.

'Ignore him, Gracie. They won't be able to do that.'

'Says who?' Eros interrupted, scoffing at his wife.

A few streets later I turned the corner onto Hillmarton Road and took a deep breath in when I heard what sounded like the puncturing of skin behind me. 'What's it doing, Psyche?'

'The android? Can't tell you, sorry.'

I raised my Hourglass again. 'Front camera.' The screen flipped and I watched as the android clown tore holes in its clown suit, ripping the fake flesh underneath the rainbow coloured fabric with its sharp fingers. I felt bile rise up in my throat, remembering how the blood of my friends ran down those metal appendages, pooling in the joints before dripping down onto the grass of Anna's back garden. I needed to stop looking. I brought my wrist back down and dug my hands further into my pockets. Just one more street to go and I would be home. I could do this.

Hillmarton Road was pretty much deserted. The only movement besides the flickering lampposts, were leaves dancing across the flagstones in the wind.

'Oh, I have another question!' Psyche said.

'What?'

'Dust is made of human particles. You know, like dead skin. Do you think there are some dead skin bits on you from when the android clown killed those kids?'

I almost stopped walking. I had to swallow down the lump that had formed in my throat. 'Let's not talk about that,' I laughed. I don't know why I laughed. Maybe to try and lighten my mood, but it wasn't working.

'I told you she's not as nice as she seems,' Terry hissed.

I ignored him and continued down the tree-lined Hillmarton Road. In the distance, standing under a broken bus stop, was a man dressed in white, looking not all that dissimilar to a member of the Ku Klux Klan. He moved towards St. Luke's, the only church left in Holloway, and as he approached the entrance he took a graffiti can out of his pocket. I watched as he sprayed a bright white dolphin onto the large oak doors, his hand shaking and blood dripping quietly onto the pavement. I wanted to turn back. Walking by an Irukian was something people without a brain did, but the distant whirring of the killer android forced me to carry on.

As I approached the church, the Irukian stopped spraying and dropped his can, then turned to face me. I couldn't see his eyes beneath his hood, but through his jacket, a bloody outline indicated where his Hourglass had once been attached to his skin.

'What are you doing here?' he asked. I didn't reply. I just kept walking. One more street to go and I would be safe. 'You're wearing an Hourglass. Let me help you get it off.'

I broke into a run. I couldn't turn around to see if the Irukian was following me and I didn't have time to check my Hourglass. I just kept going. The sound of the android's skin ripping got louder as it sprinted after me. The sound reminded me of that day in Anna's back garden when I watched the android impale each of my classmates on its razor fingers and tear the skin from their bodies. Now the clown was running after me again.

'Hey,' Eros said, interrupting the gruesome memory, 'did you know that androids are designed to run faster than humans? Even the first models, like your clown here.'

I ignored him and sprinted onto Hungerford Road. I could see my house a few doors down, the brickwork covered in ivy and moss, the outline of the building silhouetted against the moon. The android clown's jerky footsteps had quickened behind me. My legs were tired and started to burn.

'Psyche!' I shouted, not caring if any neighbours could hear me. 'I can't do this!'

'Yes, you can. Just a little further.'

'Isn't there a way you can get it to slow down?'

'No. You know the rules.'

Rule 2: The scenario cannot be changed once accepted.

I used the last of my energy and slammed into the grey front door of my home.

'Congratulations. You won the scenario. You gained 28XP. You are now Level 50.' There was an explosion of fake confetti in front of me that dissolved into the air. I hoped the buzzing would stop now the scenario was over but it persisted. That meant Eros, Psyche, and Terry had decided to stay with me for the rest of the night. I shuddered then turned around, checking to see if the android had really gone. There was nothing there, just the red post box that stood on the pavement opposite my house.

I let out the breath that I didn't know I had been holding, then pressed my Hourglass to the front door and entered the hallway. The lights in the house were thankfully on. Once I had stopped panting, I made my way to the kitchen where I could smell cooking.

Mum was in front of the stove, stirring a pan of soup. She was wearing a pink flowery apron over her pristine white work shirt. She turned around when she heard me enter but her stony expression didn't change. 'What's the matter with you? It looks like you've seen a ghost.'

'It's nothing,' I told her as I unzipped my coat. She raised an auburn eyebrow at me and waited. I sighed. 'I was just thinking about the android clown from Anna's birthday party.'

She tutted loudly. 'Why would you do that?'

'I don't know. Sometimes I get reminded of it.' She shook her head impatiently and turned back to the stove. A "normal" mother might have said that I shouldn't feel bad and she was glad I was alive, but I was used to her dismissing me.

'Did you eat at the café?'

'No. I wasn't hungry.'

'You need to eat. I'll make you something.'

I narrowed my eyes. I couldn't remember the last time my Mum had made anything more than a cup of tea or a bowl of soup. Did she even know how to? 'You'll make me something? Not Macy?'

'Macy's already in sleep mode for the night,' she said with a shake of her head. 'What do you want to eat?'

'Noodles are fine.'

She nodded and searched around in the cupboards, then brought out a pack of instant ramen. 'Go and have a shower first. You stink of coffee.' Her words were cutting, but she had a point.

I left the kitchen and headed to my bedroom. Dad was leaving tomorrow for a four-month tour in Egypt which was probably why Mum was almost being "motherly". Maybe she was trying to show me I had two parents that cared.

I passed the basement entrance and could hear Macy whirring and clicking six feet below me. I stopped walking and glanced at the closed door. It was always locked, even when Macy was out doing her chores. It wasn't even an electronic lock like the rest of the doors in the house. It would be easy to open but I couldn't bring myself to go inside. Some things were worth staying secret.

'You know…' I squealed as Terry began one of his quizzical tangents.

'Gracie?' Mum shouted from the kitchen.

'I'm fine!' I shouted back. I hurried into my room, slammed the door and threw my coat on my unmade bed. 'What do you want?' I asked. Terry's outbursts made me nervous. I switched on my light, then drew the curtains so no one on the street could see me talking to myself.

'You should take a look around the basement. Could be cool.'

'Really? That's all you wanted to say?'

He chuckled. 'I'm not supposed to be comforting. Hey, since I'm inside your head, do you think I could give you brain damage? Eros wants to do it, but he's not sure how to.'

I shivered at the thought of the Voices tampering inside my body and looked in the full-length mirror on the back of my door. Floating above my right eye was Terry's blue and white hologram tugging on my auburn hair, trying to work out how to braid it. He was still in his school uniform, his top button undone and his hair dishevelled.

'I'm not going in the basement,' I told him as his hologram flickered.

'Aw, come on. Who knows what your Mum's keeping there? You said she's never let you go down. I think it's time you should.'

'I don't want to,' I whispered. I felt weak and tired.

Terry smirked, then yanked on my hair hard so my head jerked backwards. I bit back a cry. 'You will if we tell you to,' he hissed. Then he flickered and disappeared.

My hair fell back into place and my eyes began to fill with tears – not just from the pain Terry had caused my scalp.

All the fear and anxiety I had experienced in the last hour came rushing out. I bit my lip and slumped down on my bed. It was a relief to get off my feet and be on my own. The stillness was soothing, but in the shadows of my room, I started stewing on Terry's words. He did have a point. We had moved here five years ago and Mum had not once, not even on the day we moved in, allowed me or Dad to go into the basement. What was she keeping down there?

CHAPTER 2

I sat up with a groan. Last night, after Terry disappeared, the Voices had stayed silent but the buzzing had persisted. I knew something was coming. They were quiet as I showered and ate dinner, but Eros made an appearance as soon as I got under the covers. For five hours, he sat in the rear lobe of my left hemisphere and flicked my skull every five seconds. I couldn't shout at him to stop. Mum and Dad would hear and explaining what was going on in my head was something I didn't want to do. Why give Mum another reason to dislike me? Things were tense enough between us already. I had a feeling Dad would be understanding and try to help but I couldn't be sure.

It's not that mental illness was a taboo topic in our house, but we didn't have any reason to talk about it. I didn't know what Dad thought about people hearing voices, but the general public consensus was that it wasn't a good thing. I figured it was best not to tell anyone. Letting Eros flick me was easy to put up with – at least he hadn't scared me or told me I was worthless. That was an improvement. But it probably wouldn't last long – he'd be back on top form tonight when all the Voices would re-appear.

My head pounded as I thought about what they had planned for me next. Would these scenarios ever end? Surely, the game would get harder the more I played. But I had to play. The only way to stop the Voices and their antics would be to get cured of this schizophrenic-come-psychotic thing. But I'd have to tell someone about it first. I wasn't ready to face that. Not yet.

My stomach felt knotted. I wasn't looking forward to the first day of university. I hadn't wanted to go in the first place, but Mum said it would be good for me no matter how tough I found it. She had suggested London University as it was close by and I could live at home which seemed a good option. I knew the first day was going to be difficult, but it would be harder now I was so tired.

I got dressed, pulling on the first things I came across in my wardrobe. I ran a brush through my hair before looking at my disappointing appearance in the mirror. Creased t-shirt, stained jeans and frizzy auburn hair. It could be worse.

I left my room and went down the hall into the kitchen where Macy was cleaning the dishes from last night. Her third eye saw me and she let go of the bowl she was washing. As she turned to face me, her hands dripped water onto the floor. Her purple irises were wide, the same size and shape as mine. Her blonde hair was also the same length and style. Dad had ordered Macy to be made to look like me, hoping

I would be scared less if she looked familiar. If anything, Macy's appearance had the opposite effect. We had roughly the same height, build and face shape, but purple eyes weren't exactly normal. In the middle of her forehead, was an imprint of a rose, the logo of the manufacturer Jangmi, but it just looked like an oddly placed tattoo. There was no artificial flesh plating on Macy's neck so the wiring that powered her was visible, including a thick cord which flashed with blue light every few seconds. If she ever did attack me, all I had to do was damage it and she'd shut down for good. I didn't know what the cord was for, but that's how I stopped the android clown – eventually. When it was too late.

'Miss Thrace. Good morning. What would you like for breakfast?'

'Toast is fine, Macy,' I told her as I sat down at the kitchen table. She nodded, head moving up and down at a stuttered pace. Macy went over to the counter to reach for the bread. 'Macy, dry your hands first.'

She tilted her head to one side and her neck crackled with static. 'Well done, Miss Thrace! Kitchen safety must always come first.'

I rolled my eyes as she took two slices of bread from the packet and pressed a button at the top of her thigh. Two slits opened in the side of her abdomen and she placed the bread inside.

'Your toast shall be prepared shortly, Miss Thrace. What drink would you like? Can I interest you in a banana milkshake?'

'Erm… go on…' I was intrigued to see how she would prepare this. Since when had Macy been able to make banana milkshake? She placed an empty dish on the table in front of me, then poured in some milk and yoghurt. She grabbed a banana from the fruit bowl and added it to the dairy concoction with the skin still on. 'Macy, don't you think you should peel that?'

She ignored me and lifted up her right hand, then her fingers and thumb transformed into spinning blades. I ran from the room, only just making it into the hallway before there was a loud splat. I peered back into the kitchen, rolling my lips together to stop my laughter. Macy was entirely covered in milk and bits of banana – so was the floor, the table and a good portion of the wall.

'What's happened?' Mum shouted from her bedroom.

'Erm… Macy's… well…'

Mum grumbled and came downstairs, glaring when she saw me. 'Where is she?' I pointed into the kitchen and Mum stomped down the hall, black work heels clicking against the laminate floor. As I watched her face morph from annoyance to complete despair, I couldn't hold my laughter in any longer. 'Macy! What were you doing?!'

'Good morning, Mrs Thrace. What would you like for breakfast?'

My Mum groaned 'What I *want* is for you to tidy up this mess. Which reminds me, I'm fed up of the spiders that keep coming up the plughole in the shower. Get rid of them.'

'Yes, Mrs Thrace.'

Dad came downstairs, smiling when he saw me. 'Gray? What's going on?'

'Mum's sorting it.' I bounced over to him, our identical green eyes meeting. 'What time did you come home last night?'

'Not until half eleven. Sorry, darling. I know you wanted to spend time with me before I left.'

I shrugged, pretending I didn't mind. Dad was probably feeling guilty about leaving me with Mum again and I didn't want to make it harder for him. 'It's fine. You'll get some time to come home at Christmas, right?'

'I should do. Even VIRENT must have Christmas day off.'

'Jake!' Mum screeched and Dad smiled.

'Yes, dear?'

'Come and help clean up!'

Dad rolled his eyes and smiled. 'You know, I fell in love with your mother for how loud she could shout.'

'Yeah, right.'

I followed him into the kitchen where Macy was already on her hands and knees cleaning up the mess, while Mum stood by the door in her clean IrukaTech uniform. Dad grabbed some paper towels and started on the wall. I went over to the sink and put my hands in the water to find the cloth Macy was using earlier.

Gracie.

I gasped and let go of the cloth, then glanced around to see if anyone else had noticed the voice. It had sounded muffled and distant, but surely someone else had heard it. Dad and Macy were still cleaning. Mum was staring at me, brown eyes narrowed. 'What's the matter, Gracie?'

'Nothing.' I wrung out the cloth and started wiping the yoghurt and milk on the table. A new voice? But it was daytime. The Voices didn't come out until sunset. What were they playing at? Was this a new tactic to scare me at university? It was going to work. I wouldn't be able to handle this.

'Oh, Gracie.'

I turned to look at Mum, confused by her disappointed expression, even though it was the most common look she wore whenever she was around me. 'What?'

'Are you wearing *that* for your first day at university?' I nodded and turned back to the table. 'If I give you money for a taxi, would you consider changing?'

'No. There's no need. Iliana and I are walking to Uni together.'

Mum tutted. It didn't matter that Iliana had been my best friend since high school, Mum never passed up an opportunity to make sure that I knew she disapproved of her. There was a knock on the front door and Mum went to answer it, muttering under her breath as she left the room.

Mum returned a moment later with Iliana, who smiled when she saw me, her straight brown hair swished as she moved. Her hand that carried her Hourglass was tucked deep into her pocket. She gave me a quick once over with her umber eyes and shook her head. 'Really? That?'

I glared at her. 'If it really means that much to you, feel free to pick something else for me.'

'Happy to.' She smiled and left the kitchen.

Mum just shook her head at me. 'You'll change when *she* wants you to?'

'Yes. Because she's not *you*.'

Dad laughed and Mum scowled at him before stamping out of the room. Dad always knew how to diffuse an argument between Mum and me. I was going to miss him. The thought made me feel a bit numb and empty. We cleaned up the rest of the mess, then Dad took the cloths and went outside. I followed, wanting to spend as much time alone with him as possible before he left. I closed the French doors that led outside from the kitchen and stood on the patio, watching as he pegged the cloths up. He was dressed in his green t-shirt, camo pants and boots. He always looked impressive in his uniform. Being part of the Android Disposal Unit was an honourable position. It was a specialist skill, to repair broken androids and deal with rogue robots that VIRENT sent out, under difficult combat conditions. He was a really good engineer but wasn't bothered in the least that I hadn't chosen to study Electronic Engineering. He knew how much I hated androids, despite how good with machines I was. He was proud of me for getting onto the Creative Writing course. Unlike Mum.

'Hey.' Dad gave me a big bear hug. He always had a kind smile. 'I'm really sorry we couldn't spend more time together, Gray.'

'It's fine. It's just unfair that you don't get much time off.'

'I know. By the way…' he trailed off, glancing back through the French doors for a moment. 'I know how difficult Mum can be sometimes with you, but just go easy on her. She does care.'

'Yeah. Right.'

'I'm serious. She does. So, while I'm gone can you at least *try* to get on?'

'You should talk to *her*, not me.'

'And I will. But I'll feel better knowing you're trying too.' I stayed silent. The sound of Macy clattering dishes echoed faintly from the kitchen. Our compact garden would otherwise have been quite peaceful. 'That android gets more and more clumsy. I'll take a good look at her when I'm back. Which reminds me, when I'm not here, Mum's the primary user of Macy, but you should know how to handle Macy too. If at any point you need to override her, the activation phrase is "ring a ring o'roses".'

I raised an eyebrow. 'Really? The nursery rhyme you used to sing to me? That's original.'

'Hey, don't insult the activation phrase.' We both smiled and Dad's Hourglass beeped, reminding him it was time to get to the base. 'I would say ring me tonight, but I don't know if I'll be able to answer it. I hope your first day at university goes well.'

I sighed. 'I don't really want to go.'

He put his hands on my shoulders and knelt down a little so our eyes were level. 'I know, but I think this will be good for you. It'll help you get out of the house more and give you some direction, even if it's only for three years. And maybe whilst you're there, it can help you decide what you want to do next. Yeah?'

'Alright. Good pep talk.'

'What can I say? I'm not bad at this "Dad" stuff sometimes. And if Mum really is a nightmare, you can always hide in my shed.'

I laughed as I glanced at the tiny cabin toward the bottom of the garden. 'I think I'll just stay at Iliana's.'

We hugged, said a final goodbye and he jogged back inside. Through the French doors, I watched him pick up his rucksack. A few moments later, the front door banged shut… and he was gone. I carried on standing in the back garden. It was quiet. I already missed him.

Iliana had arranged an outfit on my bed. This time it was a white blouse with a flowery skirt, tights, boots and a leather jacket. 'Iliana?'

She crawled out from the other side of the bed, my makeup bag in hand. 'Why don't you keep this on your desk like a normal person?'

'Because the desk is my writing space.' We both glanced over at the cluttered table. My Orca tablet was in the centre as well as notepads, books and various other bits and pieces scattered in no particular order. Post-it notes lined the cream coloured walls.

'Your desk looks like a bomb site.'

'It's creative.'

'It's a mess.' Iliana unzipped my tiny makeup bag and emptied the contents onto my bed as I got changed.

'What are you looking for?'

She didn't reply. Instead, she rooted through the pile of expired makeup until she found my concealer. 'Bingo.'

'You know that thing is really old.'

'Chill, Gracie, it's not for my face.' She uncapped the tube and smeared the concealer around the blood-coated skin on her wrist – the wrist she had hidden in her pocket earlier. A couple of weeks ago, Iliana got drunk at a party. She tried, yet failed, to cut her Hourglass off. It's a criminal offence, so she couldn't go to a hospital to get it treated without being arrested.

'I ran out of concealer this morning and I didn't want your Mum to see it. She'd make hell for me if she found out.'

I smiled and put on the last of the clothes Iliana had picked out for me. Mum had always been very proud to work for IrukaTech, which was understandable in a way. IrukaTech was the largest technology company in the world. It was also very powerful. It had been 24 years since IrukaTech had started making the Hourglass and a law had passed through Parliament making it compulsory for everyone to have one surgically attached to their skin from birth. "For the safety of the masses" was the message we were used to hearing. No official person ever used the word "spying" – the Hourglasses were for "surveillance only".

Iliana had always hated technology and anyone telling her what to do, so forcing her to wear a watch that tracked her every move wasn't exactly what she wanted.

'I don't need another reason for your Mum to hate me. She was foul this morning when she let me in. She wouldn't say anything. She just kept glaring at me.'

'She glares at everyone. I think the only person she doesn't glare at is Mr. Izumi.'

Iliana laughed and picked up her bag from the floor. 'I reckon they're having an affair.'

'What?'

'It makes sense. A good match, I reckon. They're both serious and frigid.'

'My Mum is definitely *not* having an affair with the owner of IrukaTech. Can you even imagine that?'

Iliana pulled a face. 'I don't want to, to be honest. It sounds gross.'

'Not in that way. I mean that it would be bad for his reputation and the company. My Mum's married and Izumi's whole image is built on how much he still loves his dead wife.'

'I still think it's a possibility, though.'

We went down the hall towards the front door but just as I reached for the handle, Macy appeared out of the kitchen with a plate of toast in her hand. 'Miss Thrace, Mrs Thrace insisted upon you eating your toast before you left.' I sighed and took the plate from her, munching on the sour bread as quickly as I could. I was surprisingly hungry after missing out on Macy's milkshake. 'Good morning, Miss Lopez. How are you today?'

'Alright.'

'Macy,' I said between bites, 'we're going to be late for enrolment.'

'In that case, I suggest you eat your breakfast on the way, Miss Thrace. You will get some nutrition and have a healthy walk.' I stared at Macy with one triangle of toast suspended between my lips. Sometimes I really regretted Dad getting the 'housemaid' android model that spouted all this health and safety stuff.

'Miss Thrace, Mrs Thrace asked me to remind you about lunch at Tower 142. Please text her the time you shall be free. Good luck on your first day.' Macy turned to walk back to the kitchen, but completely misjudged it and walked into the wall before correcting herself. I shook my head despairingly and carried on eating. We really needed to get an upgrade.

Neither of us spoke until I had finished eating, which I was glad about. London University was only a few streets further than the café, meaning we walked the same route that I had taken last night with the android clown. I was still a bit shaken but at least the Voices wouldn't appear until sunset to torment me about it. There was white graffiti covering the church doors of St. Luke's. The Irukian's work was shaky and I could only just make out the symbol of a dolphin he had painted. There was also dried blood on the pavement, but Iliana didn't notice it.

'How come you're going for lunch at your Mum's office?' Iliana asked. 'I thought you hated IrukaTech.'

'I do, but she asked me weeks ago. It's not often she asks me to spend time with her. Since Dad left today, she might be nice to me. I'll be at work later, though.'

'Oh, good. I'm rostered to start at 2pm but I won't make it until 3pm. Can you let Miss Leyshon know? I think she might fire me today.'

'Well, maybe if you turned up for work on time...'

'That's rich. She'll be after you next if you keep leaving early.' Iliana dug her elbow into my ribs playfully and I laughed uneasily. Sunset was only going to get earlier now summer was over. We walked down Caledonian Road, an Airground train hovering above us. It sank down to street level, stopping outside what had been the Underground station, before VIRENT's bombing spree had destroyed most of London's Underground rail network. The old station entrance looked sad and dilapidated. That's what 22 years does.

Up ahead was the university. Its navy banners hung out of the windows of the tall buildings to welcome new students. An android stood at the entrance to the university library, arms outstretched, ready to give an uncomforting welcome. 'This way for enrolment. We're delighted to welcome you to London University. This way for enrolment. We're delighted...'

Iliana and I entered the large library with high white ceilings and raspberry coloured chairs behind every

sk. Some older students were already getting
eir first assignments of the year. The human
were pushing trolleys of books around, an android
ng them, ready to levitate each volume back to the
ct floor and shelf. I watched one of the androids as it
ted up five tiers of the library, climbed over the railing
put the book on the shelf and then descended to the
ground floor. 'Woah. That is the best use of an android
I've ever seen,' Iliana said. 'You should replace Macy with
a university model.'

'You hate androids.'

'I do. But they're not going away anytime soon. At least
that one looks useful.'

We joined a queue behind the other first years at the
library help desk. Five university model androids with
Orca tablets from IrukaTech were lined up ready to enrol
us. Iliana was called over by a male android. His fringe
drooped down into his magenta eyes. I was called over to
the android next to Iliana's. This android was female with
a dyed lilac bob and false lashes, as if the university had
dressed her up to appeal to eighteen-year-old first years.
She wore a navy t-shirt embroidered with the university
logo. 'Welcome to London University. My name is Plexi and
I shall be enrolling you today. Please tell me what course
you are registering for.'

'Creative Writing.'

She nodded in the same way Macy did, her neck faltering
and crackling with static. She touched a couple of icons

on the Orca then looked back up at me with a fake smile programmed onto her metal lips. 'Please hold out your Hourglass so I scan you in.' I did as she asked and the Orca tablet beeped when it came into contact with my Hourglass' ID code. '"Miss Grace Thrace". Is that correct?'

'It should be "Gracie".'

Plexi nodded and re-entered the information. She turned to the help desk and picked up a stack of papers which she handed to me. 'Miss Thrace,' she smiled again, her eyes wide and fake eyelashes fluttering, 'welcome to London University. I hope you enjoy your three-year course in Creative Writing. Your student ID has been uploaded to your Hourglass.' A piece of paper printed out of the side of Plexi's abdomen from the same place Macy's built-in toaster was located. 'This is your timetable. Your first class will start in half an hour in the Grad Hub. Please do not hesitate to ask me or another android for directions. Have a nice day.'

Iliana was by the first row of computers reading through her timetable. She looked up when she saw me and sighed. 'We've got so many classes.'

My timetable showed we were only in university for two classes each day. 'It doesn't seem like a lot, Iliana. We get loads of time off.' Iliana looked sceptical as she crumpled the timetable into her bag. I sent Mum a quick text on my Hourglass. A small part of me was slightly looking forward to lunch with her. There was a possibility – a very small possibility – she might *try* to get on with me while Dad was away this time. I couldn't help hoping, even though it was unlikely. 'I'm going to go to the toilet before we go to the Grad Hub in case we get lost. Coming?'

'Na, I'll wait here for you.'

The toilets were tucked away in the corner of the building. When I was only a few feet away from the door, one of the university androids rushed over to me. 'I am sorry but the toilets are currently out of order. We have called for a maintenance android to fix the flooding.'

I looked down at the grey carpet the android was standing on, which was completely soaked. Some water was still escaping from under the toilet door.

Can you hear me, Gracie?

I froze. It was the same voice I heard this morning when I was by the sink in my kitchen. It was louder this time and it was definitely a man's voice. He was older than Terry, as his voice didn't squeak and crack with puberty. He wasn't like Eros either, whose voice was posh and punctuated. This voice moved over the words like water, but still sounded broken, as if English wasn't his native language.

'Are you okay?' the android asked.

I nodded, still spooked by the new voice. I made my way back to Iliana, who was studying her Hourglass, probably trying to find the Grad Hub on her map app. 'Hey.'

Iliana turned to me, one slick eyebrow raised. 'That was quick.'

'They were out of order.' I glanced down at the floor, my hands shaking slightly. The buzzing had started again and, teamed with the bright lights of the library, it was making me see multi-coloured shapes in front of my eyes.

'Why doesn't that surprise me – the place is run by androids. Anyway, I found the Grad Hub on my Hourglass. Let's go.'

CHAPTER 3

Iliana and I sat on the back row of the lecture theatre, the other students chatting around us. Iliana was talking to a smart-looking guy seated in front of her. I didn't join in, despite her imploring glances to encourage me into their awkward first conversation. I couldn't stop thinking about the new voice. It didn't have an accent I recognised. It had only appeared when I was near water. This morning I had my hands in the sink and then I stood in the floodwater from the toilets. But why was it appearing now? Eros, Psyche and Terry had materialised at the same time, several months ago when I was still in college. Why now?

A university android model walked into the room, her hair styled into a French twist and a rose logo protruding from her forehead. She smiled at us as she took her place behind the podium at the front of the lecture theatre. Her synthetic teeth matched the brilliant white walls of the room.

'Good morning, students. Welcome to London University. My name is Miss Dyna. I am the head of the Creative Writing course. You shall have me for the module called "Introduction to Writing". You shall meet the other tutors as you go to each of your classes. But before we get started with the curriculum, it is university protocol to break the ice.' I rolled my eyes. The way androids were programmed to adopt sayings was cringy. Then again, hopefully this model wasn't going to be as literal as Macy and *actually* give us some ice to break. 'Students, please split into groups of three. A list of questions will be sent to a group member's Hourglass.'

The girl in front of me turned around. Her eyes were a vibrant blue and her blonde hair was set in perfect corkscrew curls. She smiled at Iliana and me, then her neck crackled with static. My eyes widened in alarm. Why was there an android in our class? Androids weren't allowed to take part in any kind of education, for the simple reason that all the knowledge they needed was already pre-programmed.

'My name is Maida Paddington. Please may I form a threesome with you two?'

Iliana snorted and everyone near us turned around to look at her. 'Sorry!' she spluttered. 'Of course, you can be in a group with us.' Iliana sniggered as her Hourglass beeped. She clicked on the message she had been sent. 'Alright, I've got the questions. Number one – what's your name? I'm Iliana Lopez.'

'Gracie Thrace.' Maida smiled at both of us. She appeared normal but I was close enough to hear something inside her head whirring. Macy had done the same thing when we first got her. The mechanisms in her head would hum as her artificial brain input my family's names and the layout of our house as new data. Maida's head made exactly the same sound.

'Okay, next question,' Iliana said, showing no sign that she had heard anything unusual, 'what do you like to eat on toast?'

'Not burnt android circuits,' I joked.

Maida looked at me, her smile now almost as fake as Miss Dyna's. 'How humorous of you. My favourite thing to eat on toast is strawberry gam.'

'Gam?' Iliana asked, eyebrows raised. 'Don't you mean jam?'

'Ah, yes. You are quite right. How fortunate am I to have made friends with the two most humorous people on the course?!'

She smiled at both of us and I smiled back, unsure what to say. Maida's head made the whirring noise again, probably inputting how "jam" was pronounced. As we continued to answer the questions, I kept my eyes focused on Maida. She smiled and laughed at appropriate times and didn't spew out unnecessary information like other androids. Her voice was a little higher pitched than Macy's and wasn't as robotic, but her speech pattern was the same. I shuffled a little closer towards Maida to look at the skin around her neck. There were no wires showing and her skin moved normally. Macy's artificial skin was made from leather, dyed to match the skin colour Dad had ordered. From far away, it looked realistic.

'Yes, Gracie?'

I looked up, surprised at how close I was to Maida. 'Oh, sorry. I must have been daydreaming.'

Maida nodded and her neck crackled with static again. She turned around in her seat as Miss Dyna called us to quieten down. As she explained what we'd be studying in our first term, my gaze fell back to Maida. Her hair was so long and thick with curls that looked a little too sleek and perfect to be real. Was I reading too much into this? I shook my head, there was no use getting jealous about another girl's hair. Maybe if I actually brushed mine properly, I would have glossy locks like Maida. With a sigh, I took my notepad out of my bag and jotted down the details of the coursework. Some students shot scornful side looks at the pen and paper I was using. Everyone else had an Orca on the desk in front of them, so it was clear that Iliana and I were the only anti-tech people on the course. We did use Orcas when we had to. We weren't as bad as the Irukians who basically wanted all technology to be wiped out.

Miss Dyna's information dump came to an end and she sauntered to the front of the platform, her arms raised theatrically. It was a bit over-the-top. 'I hope that you shall enjoy your time here at university. Your first assignment, which shall be due by this time next week, is to write a 100 word short story that falls into the romance genre. More details will be sent to your Hourglass. Have a good day.'

Everyone packed their things away and left. Hardly anyone spoke to each other. I stayed in my seat and watched Maida. I didn't understand – her movement fluctuated between fluid and mechanical as she put her Orca in her bag. She didn't turn to look at me or Iliana as she left the room. She just kept walking without showing any sign that I had been staring at her. Androids were built with some amazing abilities and one of those was a third eye. It wasn't visible to humans, and I wasn't sure how it worked, but androids were supposed to know exactly what was happening in the room, even if they had their eyes closed. It was probably why androids made such great teachers. They knew exactly who was talking or texting or doodling. You couldn't get anything passed them. If Maida really was an android, surely she would have known I was staring at her. Maybe she didn't even know she was an android? Could that happen?

'Gracie?'

I jumped a little and looked around. Iliana and I were the only people left in the lecture theatre. 'Where did everyone go?'

'Class is over. They all left. Are you okay?' Iliana asked, looking concerned.

'Errmm… yeah. I think so.' My eyes landed on Maida's seat and I bit my lip. 'What do you think of Maida?'

'She seems alright. A bit posh.'

'Did you hear static crackling around her neck and the whirring inside her head when she processed new information?'

'No…' Iliana raised an eyebrow at me. 'Are you trying to tell me that she's an android?'

I nodded as we left the lecture theatre, my eyes darting around the corridor to look for Maida or any of the university model androids. 'It's plausible. Right?'

'It's really not, Gracie,' Iliana said firmly. That was the end of it. I felt a bit foolish. Iliana checked her crumpled timetable and groaned. 'Japanese Language next.'

I smiled and hooked my arm through hers as we exited the Grad Hub. 'How come you're doing that? You can already speak Japanese because of your Mum.'

'I know, but she wants me to do it, so I have the qualification. She either wants me to be a Japanese-British diplomat like her, or to get a job at an international firm to gain worldwide experience. A firm similar to IrukaTech, I suppose.'

'You'd get paid a lot if you worked for IrukaTech. My Mum does alright.'

'Yeah, and your Mum is Izumi's kiss-arse, no offence.'

I laughed. 'None taken.'

'I couldn't stand working for them anyway.'

'This isn't going to be another Hourglass rant is it?'

'They force this watch on us at birth, which we have to pay for and if we don't have one, we're viewed as less than human. They're toxic. Dad hated working for them.'

I shrugged. I knew Iliana was right of course. Iliana's Dad, especially where IrukaTech were concerned, was an understandable sore spot for her. He'd met Iliana's mother when she was training at the Japanese embassy in Spain. It was a whirlwind romance and he moved back to England with her, when she got a job at the Japanese embassy in London. He started to work for IrukaTech. He eventually became a manager in the Procurement Division, in charge of gathering rare earth metals used in IrukaTech's devices. The mines were all in Asia and he had to make occasional trips to oversee mining operations. Safety standards were not what they should have been and accidents were not uncommon. Iliana's Dad got trapped when a mine shaft collapsed. Iliana had never gone into the details of her Dad's death, but it was no surprise that Iliana hated IrukaTech with a passion.

'What do you have next?'

'Ermmm...' I fished around my bag for my timetable and found it curled around my water bottle. 'Electronic Engineering Enrichment in the Tech Centre.'

Iliana smirked. 'Oh, Gracie, your mother will be so proud of you.'

I smacked her shoulder and she laughed as we walked arm in arm back down Holloway Road. 'I'm doing it for Dad, not for her.'

'I know.' She smiled at me and I ever so slightly tightened my arm around hers. Without Iliana, I'm not sure I could have got through today. 'Meet me in the library after your class quickly, just to let me know how you've got on.'

'Will do.'

The Tech Centre was on the corner of Hornsey Road. A 13-storey hulking modern mass of metal and glass. The

sleek design screamed of IrukaTech. At the front of the
building was a row of perfectly straight trees and a set of
small fountains that spurted water into the air every five
seconds. Stamped onto the paving slabs at the entrance
was a dolphin – IrukaTech's logo. So they had built the
building. As I walked by the fountains, some of the fine
spray splashed me a little. It felt refreshing and cool.

Gracie?

I flinched at the sound of the new voice. The annoying
buzzing followed and my stomach began to churn. I wasn't
used to the Voices harassing me during the day and even if
the new voice had appeared at night, I still wouldn't have
dealt with it well. My hands felt tingly and numb, but I
wiped the water away as calmly as I could. Thankfully the
buzzing stopped.

The Tech Centre lobby was sleek with grey pillars,
black linoleum flooring and metal tables with yellow
chairs. Mounted on one of the glass walls was a Baiji – the
television that IrukaTech made – and a pristine Orca lay
neatly on every table. Everything was so clinical and exact.
There was no mistaking the fact that IrukaTech controlled
the Electronic Engineering department – just like they
controlled most of our technological innovations.

'Are you lost?' I turned around, expecting to see one of
the university model androids and was pleasantly surprised
to meet a guy about my age. His crew cut hair was blonde,
fading to brown at the roots. His basic black v-neck tee hung
loose and the muscles in his arms bulged a little where they

crossed over his chest. He looked fairly plain and ordinary, like he blended in well.

'Errmm… yes. Sorry.'

'It's alright,' he told me kindly. He had a patient smile. 'What room do you need?'

'Oh, errmm…' I got my timetable out again. 'TC104.'

The boy's smile got wider. 'Electronic Engineering Enrichment? That's my class. It's this way. I'm Joe, by the way. Joe Armstrong.'

'I'm Gracie Thrace.'

'That's a pretty name.' I felt myself redden slightly. I wasn't used to compliments, of any kind really. It was a nice change from the things Eros and Terry called me. Maybe Electronic Engineering Enrichment would turn out to be a good choice if everyone was this friendly. I followed Joe up a set of smart spiral stairs and towards a classroom situated in a corner of the building. One wall was made entirely of glass and looked out onto the rest of the university campus. It was an impressive view. The classroom had five identical rows of benches, each filled with engineering equipment and computers.

A couple of guys were sitting on the backbench and Joe guided me over to them. 'This is Diego and Owen. Guys, this is Gracie.' The two boys nodded but neither looked up at me. They were engrossed in some video on their Orca tablet. One kept periodically pushing his glasses up the bridge of his nose like a nervous twitch. The other had a messy brown mop of hair and a gnawed yellow pencil tucked behind one ear. Although he was scruffy, it was reassuring to see someone else use some non-tech apparatus.

'What are you studying, Gracie?' asked Joe.

'Creative Writing.'

'Good choice. We're all third year Sports Science students.'

'I didn't realise this class was for third years.'

'It's supposed to be for anyone. Not sure if it'll be much good, though. I've heard the lecturer is rubbish.'

A few more students came into the room, as well as the aforementioned lecturer. I expected him to be an android, but his body didn't click as he moved to the front of the class. He was older though, probably about mid-sixties with pale wrinkled skin and thick-lensed glasses. He stooped behind the front bench, eyes passing over each of us. He looked disappointed.

'Right, well, we'd better get started.' His voice was tired and despondent. 'My name is Professor Long. This is Electronic Engineering Enrichment. There's some equipment on the benches. This first class will help me assess your level of ability. It will also test your creativity. Split into groups of four and make anything you want. I'll check your work at the end.'

Professor Long heaved himself onto the nearest stool and pulled a novel from his bag, ignoring all of us. A small smile graced his face as he began to read. He was a little… odd.

'Is he okay?' I whispered to Joe.

He shrugged. 'Apparently he's always like that. I've heard he's been at this Uni since he graduated. I guess I would be like him too if I had been teaching the same class for 40 years.'

'We should still try to make something, though.'

'Do you have anything in mind?' Joe asked as I got out my tool kit. I often kept it handy. Carrying a tool kit was something that Dad advocated and it seemed a good idea.

I shook my head and the boy with the pencil behind his ear, either Diego or Owen, spoke. 'What about a stun gun to stop rogue androids? With a masking device so the android's third eye won't register it.'

'You know, you can just hit their neck hard and they'll shut down permanently,' I said.

All three guys looked at me curiously. 'I've heard of that happening once,' Joe said, 'but I didn't know if it was true or not.'

I smiled at him, realising he had probably heard about it in the news when he was younger, when the killer android clown had been in the headlines. He was only two years older than me, so he probably didn't remember the specifics – how the android malfunctioned, how over twenty children died, how I was the only survivor of the attack. 'Yeah, it's true. Just hit it.'

Either Diego or Owen sighed. 'That's the only idea I had.'

'No, we can still do it,' I said, feeling guilty for putting his suggestion to shame with just one sentence. 'If an android is malfunctioning badly, it may be too dangerous to get near enough to hit their neck. We can make it look like one of those guns from old science fiction television shows, so it would be retro and collectible, too.'

The three guys stared at me and I couldn't help but feel I had seen them somewhere before. I thought back to last night, when those boys were watching me during the scenario, the ones huddled together in the apartment block entrance. I didn't see their faces. I suppose it could have been them. Or maybe not. I was getting too suspicious and jumpy.

, 'I think it's a good idea,' Joe said, his smile wide and bright. 'Let's work together on it.' I returned his smile. These three definitely weren't the boys I saw last night. They couldn't have been.

For the rest of the period, we continued to work on the stun gun. Eventually, Professor Long did a circuit of the room, half-heartedly reviewing each group's progress. It was difficult to gauge what he thought of our work. He gave little away and soon retreated back to his stool and book. The lesson ended five minutes later.

'Off you go. Come back next week.' His monotone voice was depressing. He didn't move from his stool and continued reading. I stared at him for a moment. I didn't particularly want to be at university, either in Creative Writing or in Electronic Engineering Enrichment, but at least Miss Dyna had taught us something. I wasn't going to get into debt by at least £30,000 and not learn anything. I made a fuss of packing my things away. As soon as the other students left, I walked over to the front where the Professor was engrossed in *1984*.

'Professor Long?'

He glanced up quickly, but hardly registered me. 'Hello,' he said, turning back to his book. 'What do you want?'

I clicked my tongue against the roof of my mouth. 'I just wanted to ask if you were okay? I couldn't help but notice that you didn't *actually* teach us anything.'

Professor Long stared at me for a moment, brown eyes narrowed. 'What course are you on?'

'Creative Writing,' I replied, a little confused by his avoidance of my question.

'Ah, the arts. The only area which the androids have not superseded us, even though it's 2047. When I was your age, we could barely get a machine to make a decent coffee. Now, they can do almost everything. Soon, they'll even be able to feel emotions. In a few years, humans will be obsolete.'

I was clearly wasting my time. 'Right. Thanks for speaking to me. See you next week.' I glanced at the floor as I left the room, feeling a little awkward and even more annoyed.

Joe was leaning against the glass wall opposite the classroom door, a bulging gym bag slung over his shoulder like it weighed nothing. 'You okay? Got the answers you needed from the Professor?' he asked, registering my confused expression.

'Not really. It's a waste of time talking to him.'

'Yeah. Thought as much. My housemate had him for class last year and was always complaining. We'll get used to him.'

We left the monstrous building and stepped into the September sunshine. It was nice to feel some warmth on my face. We passed the fountain and I looked away from the water. No voice this time. 'I need a caffeine hit after that,' Joe said, darting a diffident look in my direction. 'What do you say?'

'Huh?'

He smiled. 'Do you want to go and get coffee or something? If you don't have class, that is.'

'Oh, errmm…' I bit my lip, not really knowing how to reply. 'Sorry, but I have to go and meet a friend, then I'm going out for lunch with my Mum. I'm really sorry.'

Joe held up his hands, his lips and brown eyes simpering with mirth. 'Chill. It's fine. Another time?' I nodded and he walked off. I watched him for a moment. It felt nice to be asked out for a change, even if it was by someone who had a fairly plain appearance. The day was looking up.

CHAPTER 4

I got back to the library and found Iliana at one of the study tables. She had her head in her hands and a university model android was making its way over to her.

'She's alright,' I said, and it hovered back to its human librarian counterpart. I sat down next to Iliana and shook her by the shoulder. 'You okay?'

She sat up and shrugged, tears in her eyes. 'The android was racist to me in Japanese Language class.'

'What?! Which one?'

'It doesn't matter.'

'What did it do?'

'I don't want to talk about it.'

'Iliana, come on.'

'I said, it doesn't matter.'

'Yes, it does. You know as well as I do, androids aren't programmed to be racist. That means someone tampered with it.' I thought back to the android clown but shook the memory from my head.

'Just leave it, Gracie. You're being paranoid. It was using racist words to the Asian students, too. It wasn't just me.'

'That doesn't make it okay.'

'Drop it.'

I sighed. 'Only if you're sure.'

'I am. How was Electronic Engineering Enrichment?'

'Kind of boring. We had a human teacher, but he seemed depressed. I also met this guy called Joe. He asked me out for a coffee.'

Iliana grinned at me, tears gone from her eyes. 'And you said…'

'I said another time. I told him I needed to meet you.'

She tutted. 'You could have just messaged me. I would have been fine with it. It's about time you had a boyfriend.'

'I think I'll be okay for now.' I stood up and pushed my chair back under the desk. 'I'll see you at the café later. Don't be too late.'

'I will!' she shouted after me.

The train was already at the platform when I arrived at Holloway Airground Station. I always felt sick whenever I used the Airground. When the train was at ground level it hovered two inches from the pavement, but as soon as the doors shut, it levitated ten feet above the ground and I couldn't handle it. I had lived in London my entire life but I still wasn't used to the Airground. I stared straight ahead, not glancing out of the window or talking to anybody, keeping my eyes focused on the blue fabric seats. When the train descended to Liverpool Street Airground Station, the queasy feeling in my stomach left and I jumped off.

The IrukaTech British Headquarters had always unnerved me. It was 142 floors of glass, metal and technology shaped into a prism that dominated the London skyline. Through the floor-to-ceiling windows, I could see Mum in the entrance foyer, white lab coat pristine and her heeled foot tapping impatiently next to a security android. I went through the automatic doors and she stomped over to me, heels clacking on the foyer floor.

'Come on. My lunch break ends in half an hour and I'm not being late.' She didn't give me chance to reply before she took off towards the swanky cafeteria behind the escalators. There were a few IrukaTech employees inside, already on their lunch breaks, all sat alone and doing work on their Orcas. Mum took a seat away from the bar and read the menu on her Hourglass without even looking up at me.

'Aren't you going to ask about my first day?' I said as I sat down opposite her.

Mum sighed and lowered her Hourglass. 'How was the Electronic Engineering Enrichment class?'

'Kind of boring. The lecturer was rubbish. The Creative Writing class was interesting.'

'You mean easy. Creative Writing isn't going to get you anywhere.' She looked back at her Hourglass and tapped out her meal choice on the touch screen. She glanced up at me, both eyebrows raised now. '30 minutes, Gracie.'

I bit my tongue, stopping the retort I wanted to dish out. Dad wouldn't be home until Christmas, so I had four months to spend with Mum and it would be better if we didn't argue the entire time. I ordered food on my Hourglass and then we sat in silence waiting for it to arrive. I shifted around in the red wingback chair, watching as the android waiters prepared the food behind the bar.

'We're having problems with them,' Mum said shaking her head.

'What do you mean?'

'The android waiters. They're clumsy. They keep dropping food.'

'Then order replacements,' I told her with a shrug.

'They only need fixing.'

'Doesn't *IrukaTech* have someone who can fix them?'

She scowled at me, mouth open, ready to throw a retort back, but her face suddenly brightened up. 'Oh, Andy!' I turned around and saw Mr. Izumi approaching our table. I had to admit his sharp designer suit looked impressive. His greying black hair dangled down in front of his light blue eyes.

'Sharon, how are you?' His voice came out in a weird hoarse whisper that hadn't changed since I had known him as a little girl. I'd heard him speak Japanese on the phone once or twice – his voice had sounded rapid and much deeper. But his English was slow, sensuous and kind of creepy.

'Fine, thank you.' Mum grinned at him, blushing a little. I had never seen her look at Dad like that.

'And how are you, Gracie?'

'I'm good.' I smiled at him, unnerved by his smirk.

'How is your first day at university so far?' he asked, pulling up a chair from another table.

Mum replied for me. 'She had a fabulous morning. Her Electronic Engineering course is going so well already. You know her teacher called her a mechanical prodigy?' I guess the truth was too disappointing for her.

'Of course she is with her parentage.' Izumi turned back to me, smirk morphing into a slimy smile. 'Just let me know when you want a job and it's yours.'

'Thanks,' I replied, as non-committal as possible. I found him creepy, but he was always kind to me.

An android waiter came over to the table with two plates of plain baked fish with steamed white rice and vegetables. There was also a glass of water for me, but my Mum's drink was nowhere in sight. Mum sighed and Izumi stood up.

'I'll get your drink, Sharon. Come with me, Gracie. I have something for you.' I followed him up to the bar and watched as a slow android made a cup of tea for my Mum. Izumi rested his elbows on the marble top and reached into his blazer pocket. He produced two tickets. 'These are for you, Gracie.'

The tickets looked impressive – all shiny and black. In the centre, embossed with gold, was IrukaTech's logo and the text:

Join us to celebrate
IrukaTech's 25th birthday
Friday 22nd November
at Tower 142

'This is a big celebration for us. All employees and family members are invited. These are gold standard tickets for special guests we consider to be the company's rising stars of the future.'

'Thank you, sir. Why are there two?'

'I want you to bring a date.'

I laughed and shook my head, holding one ticket out to him. 'I don't have anyone to bring.'

'Well, keep it, just in case. Ichigo is coming and she will be delighted to see you there.'

I inwardly shuddered at the mention of Izumi's daughter. She was several years older than me and was head of the global communications department, despite only knowing English and a smidgen of Japanese. She had always disliked me. She'd brought up the android clown too many times in my presence just to get a reaction. 'I'd rather you have it back. If it's not an electronic pass, I'll more than likely lose it.'

Izumi just smiled. 'You won't, Gracie. Besides, I thought I'd go with a paper format this year. It seems more luxurious, don't you think?'

I shrugged. He was no doubt right, but I was probably still going to lose them. The cup of tea arrived and we returned to the table. Mum was stuffing something into her lab coat pocket.

'I'll see you in the development lab, Sharon,' Izumi told her, smiling at us both.

'Yeah, see you, Andy.'

I took a sip of my water and its sourness made me grimace. Mum looked at me, unimpressed. 'What's wrong now?'

'It's nothing. The water tastes a bit odd.' I smiled at her and started to eat.

'Oh, that.' Mum tutted. 'IrukaTech are trying a new filtered water. Better for the environment apparently. It's not been very popular, though.'

Can you hear me now, Gracie?

I only just managed to stop the shriek that wanted to bubble over my lips. The new voice was getting clearer and louder each time it spoke, but no one in the cafeteria seemed to notice. Everyone was eating their meals and going about their own business. Some were sitting alone, absorbed by their Orcas. Some employees sat around tables of two or three speaking quietly to each other. No one but me seemed to hear the hushed voice with the foreign accent. I concentrated on my food. During the meal I could feel Mum watching me, eyes narrowed and barely eating a thing. She tutted as I finished my fish and I looked up at her. 'What?'

'Drink some more. I would like the rest of the staff to see that this new filtered water is acceptable.'

Not wanting to argue with my Mum in public, I grimaced but held the glass to my mouth and downed the whole thing. I pressed my lips together as I forced myself to swallow it all. I waited, but the voice didn't say anything else.

Mum sighed and stood up. 'Go on. I know you're dying to leave.' She walked me to the automatic doors at the entrance but she didn't look at me once.

'Thanks for lunch. I think.'

Mum's Hourglass beeped and she huffed when she read the screen. 'I don't have time for this.'

'What is it?'

'The manager at the Waterloo Station IrukaTech store needs some paperwork dropping off. Why is everyone so disorganised?'

'I'll do it if you want,' I told her with a shrug. I had half an hour before my shift at the café started, so I had time to kill. It couldn't hurt to get in her good books.

Mum hesitated, weighing up her options. 'Alright then.' She went to the nearest service user android and a screen popped out of its torso. Mum typed in her login details and pressed print. A document slowly dispended from the silver android's side slits, then the android sealed the document in a crisp white envelope. Mum typed something quickly into her Hourglass and handed me the package. It was still warm. 'I've messaged Geoff, one of the company drivers. He'll take you down to Waterloo then to the café. Make sure these are given to Tom Dean, the store manager. Understand?'

'I can do that.'

'Good. Geoff will be outside in a minute in a black car.' Then she walked away from the automatic doors and onto the escalator without saying goodbye or even turning back to look at me. Not that I had expected her to really.

I left the building just as a black car pulled up to the kerb. The front driver side window wound down and a bald man poked his head out.

'Miss Thrace?' he asked. I nodded and climbed into the back of the car. It was exactly what I expected from IrukaTech, plush leather heated seats and a mini bar embedded in the middle. 'Can I interest you in a beverage, Miss Thrace?'

'No, thank you.'

He smiled at me in the rear-view mirror and pulled away from the kerb. I leaned back in my seat and watched as London passed by the window. The Airground trains came close to some of the buildings but never hit them. Everyone walking past on the pavement had an Hourglass attached to their wrist, some carried Orcas. IrukaTech's technology was everywhere.

Geoff drove over London Bridge so I had a good view of the Thames. Each year the water got dirtier and even more disgusting. A group of activists used to stand along the Millennium Bridge, protesting about excess android oil being tipped into the river. Jangmi quickly silenced them and they were never seen again. It wasn't worth fighting the change and, more often than not, people didn't know who to address to make things better. Jangmi's operations had become a lot more secretive. No one knew who ran the company and no one was allowed into any of the Jangmi factories. You ordered an android and it was delivered to your doorstep. There were no refunds, only upgrades. I didn't trust them, but Jangmi and the government had made us all so reliant on these machines that people just accepted the way things were done.

'Sorry about this, Miss Thrace. There's a bit of traffic,' Geoff said as the car slowed down halfway over London Bridge.

'It's fine.'

This is much better. Can you hear me?

I froze.

You can definitely hear me now; I know you can.

I uttered a small gasp. It was only just audible but Geoff glanced at me in the rear-view mirror. 'Are you alright Miss Thrace?'

'Yeah.' I couldn't muster any more words. My whole body became rigid. I waited.

Aren't you going to talk to me, Gracie? It's rude not to say hello. My name is Kai.

The car started moving again and I stayed as still as possible, staring out of the window to conceal my face from Geoff.

How was your first day at university? I think yours went better than mine did.

The buzzing in my head got louder and I gripped the door handle to stop myself groaning.

But I guess that's just how first days are. Everyone gets a different first impression. And my first impression of you isn't very favourable, I'm telling you that now.

Geoff pulled up outside Waterloo Station and I practically leapt out of the car and ran up the stone steps.

This is really rude.

I leant against a shop window and pretended to use the voice activation on my Hourglass. My arm was trembling. 'Hello,' I finally said.

Well, now you reply. Why were you being so rude?

If Eros had said that, it would have made me flinch, but Kai's voice was a lot softer and didn't sound malicious. It almost made me want to relax a little. But I didn't. It wouldn't help my sanity to start getting comfortable around the voices in my head.

'I'm sorry,' I said, barely moving my lips, 'but it's weird to talk to you when other people are around.'

Why is talking to people weird?

'It's not. But you're not real, so it's weird talking to you.'

Kai was silent and I took the opportunity to enter the station, heading for the IrukaTech store by the ticket machines.

I am real.

A hologram flickered to life in front of me. A young man in full colour. I shrieked in fright and dropped the envelope, which caused some people in the station to turn and look at me. Embarrassed, I knelt down and picked up the package, then entered the IrukaTech store.

Stop being rude and look at me.

'I did look at you,' I whispered.

No, you saw *me, you didn't* look *at me. What colour is my hair?*

'Does it matter?' I muttered as I stepped up to the Hourglass counter in the shop. Everything in the shop – from the clean-cut metal to the glass décor – was the same style as Tower 142. IrukaTech projected this clinical look in every single part of the company and their shops were no exception. There wasn't a piece of wood or plastic in sight. Even the counter I leant on to support my unsteady arms was made entirely of glass.

'Can I help you?' a woman asked from behind the counter. She was wearing the signature white lab coat of IrukaTech.

'I've been sent from Tower 142. I need to give this document to Tom Dean.'

'I'll just go and get him.'

The employee disappeared into the back of the shop. I waited at the counter but jumped a little when Kai decided to appear opposite me.

What do you think?

'What do I think about what?' I tried to speak without moving my lips again. There weren't any customers in the shop, but still, I didn't want to draw attention to myself.

Am I rendering well?

'Can you leave me alone?' I whispered. I didn't need this. The Voices in my head were enough. I stared down at the counter, watching as the Baiji inside it played an animated demonstration of how the Hourglass was connected to the arteries in the wearer's body to keep it charged. It was a little gruesome, but a helpful distraction.

What's wrong?

He reached across the counter and laid his hand on mine. I jerked it away and stared at my hand with wide eyes. I felt him. The skin he had touched felt warm. I ran my fingers over the spot just to make sure I wasn't imagining it.

'How did you do that?' I asked, still staring at my hand.

Do what?

'You made my hand warm,' I stuttered. 'I… I felt you. But… you're not real. You shouldn't be able to do that.'

I don't know. Anyway, am I rendering well?

I hesitated, then slowly looked up. He wasn't British, so I was right about that. His hair was black and silky. His skin was pale. As I surveyed his face, his eyes struck me most of all. His irises were blue. A bright, beautiful, mesmerising blue. I'd seen blue eyes before, plenty of them. The majority of the people I knew had blue eyes. But not like this. I had never seen eyes like this. His irises contained flecks of black that made them pop and I had to force myself to look away. 'Are your eyes supposed to be that colour?' I asked, staring at his forehead.

What's that supposed to mean?

'Well, I thought all Asian people had brown eyes.'

I'm Japanese. There are exceptions to the rules, you racist.

He glared at me and I bowed my head in apology. 'Sorry.'

And you're bowing to me. Wow. Thanks. Why don't you just commit seppuku too, whilst you're at it?

'Miss Thrace?' I turned and saw a middle-aged man waiting next to me, his white uniform embroidered with the words "Store Manager".

'Hi. My Mum, Sharon Thrace, sent me to give you this document.'

'Ah, thank you.' He took the sealed envelope from me. 'Your mother, Sharon… what a fabulous lady.'

'If you say so.' I smiled at him, but it probably looked more like a frown.

'Thanks for this. I'll contact your Mum to let her know I've got it.'

I nodded and left the store. Kai walked beside me as I made my way out of the train station.

Do you not like your mother?

I opened my mouth to answer his question but I managed to stop myself. I couldn't get comfortable around him. 'Does it matter?'

Alright, no, I suppose it doesn't.

'Then why did you ask?'

Calm down.

'You don't know anything about me.'

Well, actually, I've been with you since the banana milkshake incident this morning, so I know a thing or two. I'm just trying to be nice.

I glanced at him and sighed. At least he was friendly, unlike Eros and Terry. Psyche was nice too, but she was only around after sunset. 'No, I don't like my Mum. Do you like yours?' I asked.

I don't know. She's dead. My housekeeper looks after me. But I don't like her. She spikes my food.

'What?' I turned to look at him, confused. He just shrugged and stuffed his hands into his pockets, crumpling the hem of his blue shirt.

She says she doesn't, but I put a camera in the kitchen. She does it every night to my rice.

'You eat rice every night?'

I wouldn't have said my diet is the most important thing to take away from this conversation.

We got back to the car and both climbed in. Kai sat in the front next to Geoff. 'To the café, Miss Thrace?'

'Yes please.' Geoff nodded and drove off, back over London Bridge and towards Holloway Road.

Aren't you going to ask me what she spikes my meals with?

I glared at Kai and shook my head subtly enough so that Geoff wouldn't see. Kai watched me over the top of the headrest. His blue eyes were shining a little too brightly and they were starting to unnerve me. I shifted my gaze back to the window and he tutted.

Back to ignoring me, then? It's no use. You'll like me eventually.

CHAPTER 5

I dashed inside the café and Kai followed me.

Do you sell rice here?

I shook my head and went behind the counter. I dumped my bag and coat then grabbed my striped apron.

That's terrible. Every café should sell rice.

'Maybe in Japan, but not here. Don't get in my way. Or better yet, leave,' I said. Kai was actually quite amusing, but the longer he stayed, the more relaxed I would get around him and I didn't want that to happen.

You're so rude.

'But you're not real, so it doesn't matter.' Kai snorted and sat on top of the cake counter, swatting away any flies that got close to the food. There weren't any customers, so I started washing the cups and plates already in the sink, then hung them up on the Welsh dresser to drip dry.

'You came back then.'

I looked to my left and saw Miss Leyshon leaning against the counter. She'd probably just taken a quick break in the flat above the café whilst it was quiet. 'Yeah, I'm sorry for leaving slightly early yesterday.'

She frowned and put the cups I'd already washed back in the sink. 'These aren't good enough. Wash them again.'

'Yes, Miss Leyshon.' I didn't have the energy to argue with anyone after the unpleasant lunch I'd had with my Mum. I was feeling drained and still had a horrible scenario to come later. I navigated between the sink, Welsh dresser, oven and coffee machine attempting to clean in the cramped preparation space behind the sandwich and cake counters.

'Will Iliana be turning up on time?' Miss Leyshon asked from the front of the shop, where she was wiping down the circular tables.

'She said she may be a little late.' I went back to washing up, my back to the door as the bell above it dinged.

'Gracie?' I turned around and saw Joe from Electronic Engineering Enrichment and another guy who looked about the same age as him.

'No wonder you didn't want to have coffee with me. You're probably sick of the smell of it.'

'No, it wasn't that. I just didn't have time, that's all.'

I glanced at Kai and saw that he was glaring at Joe, leaning forwards on the cake counter so he could sniff him.

He smells weird. Like the stuff my housekeeper spikes my food with.

I ignored him and smiled at Joe and his friend. 'What can I get you?'

'Errmm…' The other guy looked at the menu boards pinned to the back wall. 'I'll have an espresso, please.'

'Not much choice, is there? I'll just have a water.'

I nodded, ignoring Joe's dig, and started to make the drinks as the bell dinged again and Iliana came swanning into the café.

'I'm on time!' she exclaimed, grinning at Miss Leyshon. Miss Leyshon uttered an exasperated sigh and went back to cleaning the tables. Iliana glided behind the counter, dumped her stuff and grabbed her apron.

'Iliana, this is Joe from my Electronic Engineering Enrichment class.'

'Ah, so you're the one who asked her out. Very nice. I told her she should have said yes.'

I scowled at Iliana. 'I didn't say no. I said another time.'

Joe smiled awkwardly at the two of us. 'It's fine, really. This is Chris, by the way,' gesturing to the guy next to him. Chris was a few inches taller than Joe, with black hair and grey eyes, but wasn't as well built.

'It's nice to meet you,' said Iliana. 'Do you do Electronic Engineering Enrichment, too?'

'No. I'm studying Biochemistry. Third year.'

Iliana grinned at him. 'I love Biochemistry. It's so interesting.'

I shot Iliana a suspicious glance. She was awful at anything to do with science and had never taken an interest in it. 'Right. Anyway, you make an espresso and I'll get Joe some water.'

'Yeah, in a minute.' Iliana waved me away and she stayed at the counter to chat with Chris.

She's flirting with him.

Kai scooted over to me and took a seat on the Welsh dresser. I said nothing, hoping if I ignored him he would get the hint and go away. I took a glass and turned the tap.

Can I fill it up?

'You're welcome to try,' I said. Maybe if he failed, he would get annoyed with himself and leave me alone. Then again, he might get annoyed at me and make the buzzing in my head even worse.

Before I had the chance to tell him I changed my mind, he took the glass from me and placed it under the flowing tap, but as soon as it started to fill up with water, the glass slipped from his hands and I caught it.

'Thanks, but I don't think holograms can hold a lot,' I told him, trying to downplay the little success he had. The Voices could touch me, but none of them had managed to transfer any body heat, and none of them had managed to pick up real objects. Why was Kai different? I tried not to shudder, not wanting to show him how much he was freaking me out.

'What are you talking about?'

I turned around and saw that Iliana, Joe, and Chris were all staring at me, eyebrows raised. 'Oh, nothing. I just like talking to myself.' I turned back to the sink and felt my face heat up. I was almost caught out. I couldn't let that happen again. What would those three do if they found out I could hear voices?

You're a liar.

Instead of replying, I just scowled at him, then filled up the glass. I turned back to the front counter and handed Joe his water. 'Sorry about that.'

'It's no problem.' He smiled. 'So, do you fancy catching up sometime soon then? Somewhere that doesn't sell coffee.'

I forced myself to smile back at him. 'I'll have to let you know. I'm very... busy.'

'Then let's exchange numbers.' Before I could even open my mouth to reject his suggestion, Iliana yanked my arm forwards and pressed my Hourglass against Joe's, then put her own against Chris'.

'This way I can let Chris know if you're just bailing on Joe to do more writing,' she said with a wink. If she was going to tell a lie to justify getting someone else's number, then she should have at least come up with something more imaginative.

'Are you two going to get some work done?' Miss Leyshon barked from the front of the shop, where she was wiping down the last table.

'Sorry, Miss Leyshon,' we both chimed.

The boys paid for their drinks and went to sit down, leaving Iliana with a wide grin on her face. 'You know what this means, right?'

'Errmm... no?'

'Shopping! Joe's clearly interested in you and Chris is going to ask me out.'

'Really?'

'I'm always right about these things. So we're going to need something to wear on our dates. We'll go after work.'

I bit my bottom lip. 'I don't know…' I tapped the touch screen of my Hourglass and brought up the weather app. Sunset was going to be at 19:25 – a few minutes earlier than last night. We finished our shift at five o'clock and Iliana never took too long shopping since she looked good in everything. I should have enough time to get home before the scenario needed to start. 'Alright then.'

Iliana squealed and hugged me. 'Thank you!'

'Gracie, Iliana! Do some work!'

'Sorry, Miss Leyshon!'

As soon as the clock hit five, Iliana picked up our bags and coats and dragged me down to Holloway Road Airground Station. Kai followed us onto the train and swung on the strap hangers by the carriage doors as Iliana rambled on about what she was going to buy.

She never stops talking. Is she always like this?

I just nodded. I couldn't reply properly when there were so many people around. Not that I wanted to anyway. We got off the Airground at Holborn, changed onto the Central Line and left the Airground two stops later at Oxford Circus. The street was as busy as always, despite it being a Wednesday evening.

Iliana led us across the street and down into what once had been Oxford Street's Underground Station. It had been 22 years since the VIRENT bombing spree on the

Underground and now some of the bigger stations and tunnels had been refurbished into shopping centres. The success of the Airground diminished the need to rebuild the stations to serve their former purpose.

Where is she going?

Kai walked closely beside me as I crossed the road. I sighed and decided to reply. I figured it would be okay if I only spoke to him a little. 'The Underground. She loves the shops down there.' I followed Iliana down the tiled steps. The roof of the tunnel was curved, like when it had been in operation to accommodate trains. Most of the tiles were still on the walls. The sign for Oxford Circus was semi-destroyed and metal benches, that were once on the platform, now lined the Underground shopping avenue. The Underground features were part of the shopping centre's charm. A piece of London history that now served a very different function.

I went in and out of shops following Iliana as she tried on dresses. I almost convinced her to buy one until she changed her mind at the last moment and flitted into the next store. We walked down to the last shop, which was at the far end of the disused tunnel.

I do not like shopping with girls.

'Me neither.' I wanted to laugh. Kai was nice, in comparison to the Voices. He was funny too, in a weird way. But at the end of the day, he wasn't real. My sanity was already at breaking point and I was certain that becoming friends with someone who wasn't real wouldn't help.

I was pulled from my thoughts when Iliana gasped and both Kai and I looked over at her. She was gazing at a purple dress hanging on a mannequin in a shop window. 'I've found it! I'll just go and try it on. You can wait out here if you like.'

'Thank God.'

She disappeared inside the final shop and Kai wandered further down the tunnel. At the end of the passage was a metal gate and darkness beyond. I followed him. It was quiet and I was glad no one else was around. Most people were on their way home from work and their shopping would have to wait until another day.

Why are these stations not used anymore? Kai scrunched up his eyes as he peered into the blackness.

'VIRENT's attacks. They bombed shopping centres and transport networks throughout the country.'

Why?

'To protest. VIRENT have always been anti-tech and anti-commercialism. The bombings hit what they saw as iconic symbols of corporate capitalism and the people and transport services that help make them function. It's ironic really, they describe themselves as anti-tech yet they use robots to wage warfare. If they…'

'Ow!'

The shriek came from behind the gate. I quickly switched on my Hourglass' torch and shone it down the tunnel, trying to see where the voice had come from.

'Hello?' I asked, trying not to be too loud in case other shoppers were listening.

'She's heard us now!'

Rocks and other rubble fell behind the gate and I saw two boys run off down the tunnel. People weren't allowed to go in the disused Underground tunnels. They were still unsafe and some of the electric train rails hadn't been deactivated fully.

I looked back at the pile of rubble just behind the gate and saw a little girl crouched behind it, trying to hide. Her face and dress were dirty, but that wasn't what alarmed me. She wasn't wearing an Hourglass. Her wrist was bare. There wasn't even a scar where it should have been. It was completely clean. I glanced at Kai – even he was wearing an Hourglass in his hologram. Everyone had one. We had to. I turned back to the little girl but she was already dashing down the tunnel. I switched off my torch and turned to Kai.

Are people allowed to go down there?

'They're not.'

My Hourglass lit up to indicate 'call mode' and Iliana's face appeared on the screen.

'Gracie! Where are you?'

'Sorry. I just went for a walk. What is it?'

'I found a dress for you!'

We both turned and in the distance saw Iliana on the doorstep of the last shop she had gone into, paper bag in hand.

'It's fine, I don't need one. Hang on, I'll come and meet you,' I said.

As we approached, Iliana grabbed my hand and pulled me into the shop. Under the bright lights of the boutique, Iliana held up a knee-length dress. It was yellow with tiny white flowers decorating the skirt and the waist was adorned with a brown leather belt.

'Joe will love you in this.'

'I'm not trying to impress him. I'm really not that interested in him.'

'What! Did you see his muscles?'

I nodded and glanced at Kai who had followed me into the shop. He wasn't as well defined as Joe, but he was nicely toned and it suited his lithe body.

'They were okay.'

'Just go and try it on.'

She stuffed the dress into my arms and shoved me in the direction of the changing rooms. As I turned my head, about to argue with her, I caught a glimpse of the time on her Hourglass – 18:54. Only 31 minutes until sunset. I felt the pit of my stomach convulse and I clenched my fists to stop my hands from shaking. It would be okay. Maybe the scenario wouldn't be that bad. Maybe Eros and Terry would go easy on me since there were so many people around. I squeezed my eyes shut as I remembered their threat from last night. I was awful at trying to kid myself.

'Actually, you know what, I love it,' I told Iliana with a fake smile. 'I'll go and pay for it.' I skipped past her and put the dress on the front counter. Kai came over to the till.

That was odd.

'Yeah, well, I need to get home before the scenario starts,' I whispered.

I paid the retail android for the dress and made my excuses to Iliana, then I practically ran from the shopping centre and jumped onto the next Airground train to Caledonian Road.

You know, I'm pretty sure almost everyone in London just saw you sprint through the busiest street in the city.

Kai sat opposite me on the Airground carriage, swinging his legs. I glared at him, unable to answer because of the businessmen and women surrounding me. The journey seemed to take forever. When the Airground finally got to Caledonian Road I checked the time on my Hourglass again – 19:20. Five minutes to go. I managed to run all the way home and slam the front door shut just as the buzzing started and Eros spoke.

'Scenario: the floor is made of lava. If you touch the floor, you lose. Do you accept the scenario?'

I breathed a sigh of relief. I had been building myself up all day, expecting to have to escape a panic room or have to face the android clown again. But I could handle this one. I dashed along the corridor and into my room, then jumped onto my unmade bed. 'I accept.'

'Please confirm your choice.'

The two yellow boxes floated in front of me and I pressed the "Yes" button. A red layer of hologram settled on the laminate floor of my bedroom with several pixels missing.

I kicked off my shoes, then threw my bag to the floor, unable to stop the smile spreading across my lips. 'I thought you said that this was going to be a really hard scenario. I think I've already won this one, Eros, don't you?'

Eros hummed, not replying properly, and Psyche laughed. 'Yes, you've won, as long as you don't stand on the floor until sunrise.'

'Easy. Thanks, Psyche. I wish all the scenarios were this straightforward.'

'Sorry Gracie,' Psyche replied, 'no can do.'

Rule 12: None of the scenarios can be repeated.

Kai's hologram wandered into the room with no shoes on his feet.

Sorry, I had to take off my shoes before I could come inside.

I smirked and he glared at me.

Racist.

He sat down on the bed and glanced around my room. My double bed was in the centre, the sheets crumpled and messy, much like my desk opposite. Clothes were spilling out of my wardrobe and chest of drawers. Mum always moaned at me for writing story ideas on post-it notes over the walls, but it was the way I liked it. Kai was scrutinising every corner of my bedroom. Finally, he turned to me. His face was stony and serious, as if someone had taken all his rice from him.

Do you like Joe?

I frowned. 'Why does it matter to you?'

Kai stared at me, eyes narrowed, but not glaring. After a few seconds, he floated towards my face and disappeared.

'Kai?'

There was no response. He'd gone.

'Aw, did you lose a friend?' Eros asked, manifesting in front of me. He flickered for a brief moment. His blue and white hologram was dull to look at – nowhere near as nice as Kai's. Eros wasn't wearing an Hourglass, though. He had curly hair and a pair of feathered wings that reached his knees, along with a chiton. Greek Gods probably didn't have portable technology that was powered by your blood.

'He's not my friend,' I whispered. I'd been too smug and clearly I'd pissed him off. After four months with the Voices, I had learnt to keep my guard up around them, but Kai had made me relax. I had to be more careful.

'You're right,' Eros said, then floated closer to me. 'The only friend you have is Iliana, and I'm not even sure she wants you around. She probably feels sorry for you because the rest of your friends got murdered by that clown.'

I scowled and looked away from Eros, not wanting him to see the tears gathering in my eyes. It would only egg him on. 'Iliana doesn't know about the android clown,' I said quietly.

'I'm sure it can be arranged…' He chuckled, then disappeared.

The buzzing stopped. I let out a shaky breath and rubbed my forehead. The Voices had gone again, but they would be back soon. They never stayed away for long and whenever they came back, Eros and Terry would have a new way to torment me. With a sigh, I flopped back on my bed and brought my Hourglass up to my face. I stared at it for a moment, then said, 'Search – schizophrenia signs.' It had been four months since the Voices first appeared and had started making me play the scenarios. I hadn't told anyone, nor had I ever researched what might be happening to me. I shrugged them off as stress-related. I assumed they would disappear once I relaxed over the summer. However, the arrival of Kai made me realise I was not improving. If I wanted the Voices to go away, if I wanted to get better, then I needed to understand and accept that I might have an actual condition.

The results popped up on the small square screen and my eyes scanned over the list of symptoms. Hallucinations, yep, delusions, nope, muddled thoughts, no, and changes in behaviour… did running home so I wouldn't have to play a scenario in public count? It probably wasn't schizophrenia.

'Search – psychosis signs.' The browser reloaded. Hallucinations, check. Delusions, negative. Not psychosis either. I bit my lip as I stared at the screen. What the hell was wrong with me then? I didn't know any mental illnesses that involved hallucinations and hearing voices but no other signs. Unless the hallucinations counted as delusions? Attempting to self-diagnose myself wasn't getting me very far. But could I speak to anyone about the Voices? Even a trained professional? I didn't feel ready.

I groaned and shouted for Macy. She came into the room a few moments later, food splattered on her cheek and some flour embedded in her Jangmi rose stamp. 'Welcome home, Miss Thrace. How may I be of assistance?'

'Could you make me some food please?'

'Of course. What is it you wish to eat?'

'Errmm… I don't know. Just make me whatever we have in the fridge.'

She smiled at me, showing her mechanical, perfect pearly whites. 'Then I shall make you a banana milkshake.'

'You know, I'll actually have some pasta and a glass of milk. Normal milk. From the fridge. Don't go and milk a cow.'

'How humorous.' Macy's laughter chimed off the mouth box circuits in her throat, making a tinny sound. Then she left the room, her shoulder connecting with my doorframe and sparking. "How humorous" – Maida had said the same thing earlier in class. Androids were the only ones who talked like that. Maida had to be an android, there was no other explanation for it.

REPORT ON PARTICIPANT 1 OUT OF 4: Miss Gracie Thrace

10/09/2047	Observed talking to herself after sunset on George's Road – presumed to be taking part in a scenario.
	Seen talking to an Irukian.
	Observed running down Hungerford Road.
11/09/2047	Observed in a café on Holloway Road talking to someone at the sink.
	Seen running back home again from Caledonian Road Airground Station.

It is my opinion that Miss Thrace has continued playing the nightmare scenarios but there is a new voice. One which appears in the daytime. The voice also appears to be tangible to Miss Thrace and she does not seem to be scared of it, unlike the other voices, but more data collection is required.

CHAPTER 6

I had been staring silently at the blank screen of my Orca for ages, not knowing what to write for my 100 word love story. It was due tomorrow. Mum had barely spoken to me this week whilst I was at home. I was trying not to think of Dad much, but it wasn't easy. The less Mum spoke to me, the more I missed him. Kai had kept me company though.

Why don't you write a story about Japan?

I jolted, not expecting Kai to start talking or the buzzing to kick in. I took in some deep breaths then glanced around the room. I couldn't see him and realised that he was just using his voice this time, instead of appearing as a hologram.

Are you ignoring me again?

'No. What do you want, Kai?'

I just thought I'd drop by for a chat.

'Drop by? Where have you been? Getting drunk off sake?'

Racist.

I smiled. We'd slipped into a comfortable routine. I kept forgetting he wasn't real. 'So, how come you've decided to appear now?'

Just felt like it. Besides, you need help with your story. What genre has it got to be?

'Romance and only 100 words long.'

Hmmm… years ago in Japan, the soldiers used to give their wives the second button from their uniform because it was closest to their heart. Boys sometimes give the second button from their school uniform to the girl they like. Maybe you could write about that?

'That's actually not bad.' I started typing, keeping a close eye on the word count in the bottom of the screen. 'Have you ever given your second button away to someone?'

Yes.

I stopped typing. 'Oh.' I felt a bit disappointed. 'Who did you give it to?'

My Aunty.

I laughed and carried on writing. 'I thought you were going to say you'd given it to your girlfriend.'

I've never had one.

'I've never had a boyfriend either.'

Joe could be?

I shrugged, reading through what I'd just written. 'He just asked me out once.'

Will you go on a date with him then?

'No. I don't want any complications at the moment. Handling whatever is going on inside my head is enough right now.'

I'm sure someone finds hearing voices an attractive quality.

'Me, too. Someone like Chuck Broon.'

Who's that?

'He lead a cult in America and convinced some of the members to murder people.'

Kai hummed. *He sounds perfect for you.*

'I'll keep that in mind.' I gave my short story another once over then sent it to my Hourglass. 'Thanks for that, Kai.'

It's what friends are for.

My fingers hovered over the trackpad. 'I hate to break it to you, but you're not actually real.'

Kai manifested in front of me. His expression was firm and his blue eyes serious.

I'm as real as you.

'So, you have a heartbeat?' I asked.

He looked away from me. *No. Do I need one to be real?*

'It definitely helps.'

Do I have to be real to be your friend?

I glanced up at Kai. 'No, but... whatever is going on in my mind, you're part of it. I don't think being friends would be a good idea.'

Why not?

'Because I don't plan on being like this for the rest of my life. What would be the point in becoming friends with you if I don't even want you in my head?'

He frowned, almost looking upset, then disappeared.

'Kai? Look, I'm sorry, but I hear voices and it isn't fun in the slightest. I can't go out at night because of the scenarios and I can't make new friends, just in case someone finds out. The way the Voices make me feel… I have zero self-esteem. And on top of that, I'm not even sure what is actually wrong with me. I don't know why I started hearing the Voices, or why they've stayed, or how I'm supposed to get rid of them. I'm just hoping that they'll go away one day and I'll finally get better.'

I understand. But… can we at least be friends until that happens?

I sighed and considered it. If he was my friend, then maybe he would be less likely to hurt me and maybe he could convince the Voices to be less harsh.

'Okay.'

I turned off my Orca then went over to my bed and sat down on the unmade sheets. I glanced at my Hourglass – 19:10. I sank back against the headboard, already a little fearful of the impending scenario.

How long have the Voices been playing these nightmare scenarios with you?

'They appeared during my A-Level exams, so… about four months.'

And you still get scared of them?

I shrank back even further; my hands were clammy. Eros would appear any moment now. 'Of course. I don't know what they'll make me do from one night to the next and I don't know how to make them stop. Why do you want to know?'

He didn't respond. Before I could say anything else, I whined in pain as the buzzing got worse and Eros cleared his throat inside my head. 'Scenario: follow the cockroaches into the basement. If you do not follow them into the basement, you lose. Do you accept the scenario?'

'Please Eros, not the basement. You know I'm not allowed in there.'

'Why do you think we're making you play it?' asked Terry. Even though I couldn't see him, I knew he was smirking.

'Do you accept the scenario?'

I sighed. I suppose it wasn't as scary as the other scenarios they had made me play so far. Bugs and insects didn't bother me. I got up from my bed and went over to my desk, then dug out two of Iliana's forgotten hairgrips from underneath my books and notepads.

'I accept.'

The two yellow buttons popped up in front of me and I selected the "Yes" button. A cockroach crawled from under my bed as soon as I selected the option. I followed it out of the room, watching as it squeezed under the basement door. Ten more cockroaches followed.

'Psyche?' I whispered, watching as her blue and white hologram flickered to life in front of me. She was much more beautiful than Eros and Terry. The Greek Goddess had long curly hair and a chiton fell over her body like water.

'Yes?'

'Watch out for Macy for me, please.'

Psyche nodded as she smiled at me, then floated around the corner of the hallway. I knelt down in front of the door, bent both of the hairgrips, then slotted one into the bottom of the lock. I put the other grip in the top and wiggled until they worked their way through the pins.

'What are you doing?' Terry asked. His loud voice made me jump.

'Picking the lock. My Dad taught me.'

'Then why have you waited until now to do it?' he asked as his hologram manifested next to me.

'I was never forced to before. Even though part of me wants to know what's in the basement because my Mum is so private about it, the other part of me never wants to find out. It could be something awful.' The first two pins in the lock moved up easily, but the third one was harder to release. I pushed it up and smiled when I heard the faint click.

'Have you done it?' Terry whispered.

'No. There are five pins. That was only the third. Why are you speaking so quietly? Macy can't hear you.'

'Just thought I should join in. I finished all my homework. Well, I don't actually do my homework voluntarily, but my Mum keeps going on at me because my GCSEs are coming up next year…'

I ignored Terry as he rambled on about his impending geography test and I moved forward with the hairgrip, pushed the fourth pin out of the way and then the fifth. The lock clicked again and I turned the hairgrip that had stayed in the lock at the bottom. The door clunked louder this time and opened. I made my way into the basement and switched on my Hourglass' torch.

'This place smells,' Terry said, hovering down the wooden steps in front of me.

The basement was quite small, and he was right, it did smell a little. It was probably just damp. Macy's recharging station was at the bottom of the stairs and a long switch cord dangled above it. In the light of my torch, I spotted the cockroaches crawling along the concrete floor and scuttling up the leg of a table. I moved my Hourglass so I could see the whole table. It was in the far corner of the room and the surface was covered with boxes filled with tiny vials. Each one contained a clear liquid.

'Congratulations. You won the scenario. You gained 13XP,' Eros said, confetti exploding in front of me.

I scowled, about to complain about the lack of XP, but decided against it. I had completed the scenario, but I still had to work out a way to lock the basement door. Not to mention survive the rest of the night with Eros and Terry. I didn't want to rile either of them and give them a reason to hurt me. On top of that, the relief that usually came with finishing a scenario never happened. I was usually happy to be done, but I wasn't today, not now that I had seen these vials. What was my Mum using them for? Terry moved closer to the table.

'What do you think is inside them?' he asked, trying to flick the vials with his fingers, but he frowned when his hand went straight through the container.

'I'm not sure.'

'Gracie!'

I turned around and saw my Mum at the top of the stairs, her face was dark and livid. 'Mum, I —'

'Which part of "never go down into the basement" do you not understand?!' She ran down the stairs, almost tripping in her heels and dragged me away from the table. 'I always knew you were stupid, but since when have you been unable to follow basic instructions?!'

'I just —'

'Don't try and justify your actions! The basement is off limits for a reason!'

I had never seen her so angry as she shoved me up the stairs and back to my bedroom. I couldn't say anything else to try and defend myself. Mum wouldn't give me a chance. She just slammed the door in my face.

'Macy!' she shouted from the other side. I could hear the android's joints creaking as she moved.

'Yes, Mrs Thrace?'

'Make sure that Gracie doesn't come out of her room until the morning.'

'Of course, Mrs Thrace.'

The door clicked and I knew Macy had locked it electronically, so there was no way I could bypass it from this side. I suppose I could activate the primary user switch with the password Dad gave me. But why bother? There was nowhere I wanted to go. I should wait until things got worse before I used the password.

Mum had yet to get totally unreasonable. I had broken into the basement after all. I could hear her walking away from the room before giving Macy another verbal volley. 'Oh and Macy, get rid of those spiders by any means necessary. Do you understand?!'

I sighed and went over to my bed, not waiting to hear Macy confirm she had understood. I reached for my pyjamas, but I flinched when Eros appeared in front of me.

'Has Gracie-wacy gotten into trouble?'

'If your wife had done as I asked, then I wouldn't be in this mess.'

Psyche floated through the door with a scowl on her face. 'You said to watch out for Macy. Unless I'm mistaken, your mother is not Macy.'

'Piss off Psyche, you're useless!'

She disappeared but Eros stayed. He rushed at me, his eyes full of hate. 'Don't ever talk to my wife like that again!' He spat every word in my face and then slapped me hard.

I fell onto the bed, cradling my cheek in my hand. After all of these months, I should have known better than to speak back to one of the Voices. The pain in my cheek made me want to cry. I buried my head into the duvet so Eros wouldn't see. 'I'm sorry,' I mumbled, 'it won't happen again.'

He hummed. 'You are currently at Level 52 with 37XP left to gain until Level 53. You have until the 31st December to reach Level 75.'

'That's not possible.'

Rule 9: The Voices can decide if the Player must get to a certain Level by a certain date.

'31st December. Or we'll have to find something *really* horrible for you to do.'

Rule 10: If the Player does not achieve the set Level by a set date, the Voices can hurt the Player or force the Player to hurt someone else.

He lifted my head off the bed by my hair and smirked when he saw the tears in my eyes. He slapped me again, this time a lot harder and I couldn't hold in the whimper that escaped. 'Maybe I'll hurt you again. Who knows? I might punch you this time. Break a few ribs.' Then he grinned. 'No, I know. I'll make you break your own ribs.'

'I'm sorry,' I whispered, letting my tears fall.

His grin got wider and he let go of my hair with force. 'Good night, Gracie Thrace'. Then he disappeared, his smug smile lingering in the air for a moment longer. The buzzing stopped and I sobbed properly this time. What was happening to me? I curled up on my bed and wrapped my arms around myself, hoping for someone, for anyone, to come and save me from my own mind – even if that person was Kai.

CHAPTER 7

Gracie!

'Mmmmm…'

Wake up, Gracie!

'What?' I mumbled, opening my eyes a tiny bit. Kai was hovering over me, wearing a white t-shirt and sweat pants, which I guessed were his pyjamas. His blue eyes were penetrating and alert. He was shaking me awake by my shoulder, all of the muscles in his arm tensed. 'Kai?'

You need to look at this.

I groaned and looked at my Hourglass. It was 05:30. 'No, I don't, Kai. Not at this time. Go back to sleep.' I rolled over in bed and lifted my duvet over my head, but Kai yanked it back down and thrust one of my notepads in my face.

Read it.

I glared at him but sat up, then activated the torch on my Hourglass so I could see what was on the paper in the dim morning light. It was the notepad I used for class and Kai had folded over a corner of one of the pages, indicating what he wanted me to read:

Too Much

Don't come near me.
Don't talk to me.
Don't even touch me.

I'll make your hands go numb.
I'll tear you apart.
You'll taste me like blood
in your mouth
for the rest of your life.

You want that?
You want your flesh
hacked from your body?
Your heart on the floor?
Make no mistake,
I'll smile as I rip the screams
from your throat
and laugh when you gaze at me,
eyes wide,
still expecting me to drop to my knees
asking for your forgiveness,
telling you that it was a joke.

Just a sick joke

as the needle punctures
your rotten flesh,

stitching you back up
like a useless ragdoll.

But I won't.
If you're lucky,
I'll roll your heart
in pools of melted glitter
before serving it up on a golden platter
for your father.

Like I said.
Stay away from me.
I'll rip you to pieces.

Eros

I stared at the page in my notepad for a little longer. It was in my handwriting. Eros had used my own hand to write this whilst I slept. I looked at Kai and he took the notepad from me, his face grim.

Enjoy that?

'No. It was… violent. Gruesome. Will you rip out that page, please?'

Kai nodded and placed the torn paper in the bin by the door.

Eros didn't write that.

'But he signed it, and he's the only one who's sick enough to write something like that. The other two couldn't have done it.'

It was Psyche, Gracie.

'Psyche would never do something like that.'

This wasn't the first time I'd defended Psyche, but as I said the words I could hear doubt in my voice. Terry had warned me a couple of times that Psyche wasn't to be trusted. But Terry could be quite manipulative. Then again, last week, when I was in the basement, Psyche hadn't told me about my Mum arriving. But I had only asked her to keep an eye out for Macy, so that could have been a misunderstanding. It was plausible that Eros could have written the note, considering what he'd said when he'd slapped me…

I looked up at Kai again. I trusted him a lot more than the Voices and there was something about him that I sort of liked. I'd been jealous when he told me he had given his second button to someone and relieved when I found out it was only offered to his Aunty. But why had I felt like that? The answer seemed obvious – I had *actual* feelings for him. But that wasn't possible. He wasn't real. He was just a voice inside my head.

Gracie, it was Psyche, trust me.

I nodded, still not sure. 'I'll ask her about it tonight, after the scenario, okay?'

He nodded and disappeared. My notepad fell to the floor with a soft thud and I crawled back under the duvet. I closed my eyes again but my Hourglass started vibrating almost immediately. Iliana's name lit the screen. I pressed accept, then buried my face into the pillow. 'Iliana, it's half five in the morning.'

'And you're awake, so that's great.'

'What do you want?'

'I've been messaging Chris all night. He's invited us to a party at his place on Saturday!' she squealed down the line and I pushed my head further into the pillow.

'That's great, but could it really not wait until class?'

'Err, no! I'm in love!'

'No, you're not. You've only just met him.'

'It was love at first sight,' she joked. 'Have you fixed up another time to meet Joe yet?'

'No.'

Iliana shrieked and I moved my wrist away from my head. 'Why not?!'

I thought about telling her I liked someone else, but then she would only pester me until I told her who that "someone else" was.

'Don't get me wrong, Joe's really nice. But I'm not interested.'

'That's why you should meet him, Gracie. So you can get to know him better.'

'Maybe I don't want him to get to know *me*.'

Iliana sighed. 'We'll talk about this before class, okay?'

'Whatever. See you.'

I hung up and rolled over in bed, rubbing my eyes. I was tired but I probably wouldn't be able to fall asleep again. Now what should I do? It was a shame Kai wasn't here to talk to. I was getting used to him being around, even though I knew almost nothing about him. It would be good to find out more. I loaded up my Orca and typed Kai's name into the search bar.

'Kai…' I hummed. He had never told me his last name. I clicked enter anyway and selected the first entry:

Kai, in Japanese, means ocean. Kai is also a Japanese name, short for Kaito. For Japanese children the honorific "-chan" is often added to the end of their name to express endearment.

I smiled, imagining calling him "Kai-chan". He would probably call me a racist if I did. I turned off my Orca and glanced at my Hourglass – 06:01. I huffed. I didn't want to get up yet. Sleep was the only solace I got from my worries and these stupid scenarios. The basement scenario last week had been a confusing one. I groaned as I remembered those vials and rolled over in bed. I wanted to know what the vials were for but things had been pretty frosty with Mum since then. I would just have to live with not knowing.

CHAPTER 8

Saturday 28th September 2047
Level 53: 483 XP
Time to sunset: 0 hours 5 minutes

The warm water quickly steamed up the cubicle. A hot shower was just what I needed before I had to attend this party. It had been a while since I'd been to one and I could only hope that Iliana wouldn't abandon me for Chris as soon as we arrived. I wasn't the best at socialising with strangers.

I haven't seen you shower before.

I turned around to see Kai on the other side of the misted glass, his full colour hologram completely naked except for a towel around his waist. His blue eyes were piercing.

'Kai!' I shrieked and turned back around, trying to cover my body with my hands.

Are you scared of water?

'I'm scared of you seeing me in the shower. Go away!'

You should get out of the shower. Water isn't good for you.

'What?' I stared at the shower wall. 'Are *you* scared of water?'

Yes.

'How come?'

I nearly drowned when I was little.

'Oh. I'm sorry. If it bothers you that much, leave. I'm not making you stay.'

He hummed. *No. What if you slip and hurt yourself? You could drown. I need to be here to make sure you're safe.*

'I think I'll be fine.'

I'd rather stay and put my mind at rest.

I sighed as I realised he wouldn't be leaving. 'Fine. You can stay. Just... promise me you won't tell the Voices about this?'

Considering I've yet to actually speak to them...

'Just promise me, Kai-chan.'

Please do not call me that, ever again.

I winked at him over my shoulder and carried on washing myself. 'Do you want to come with me to Chris' party?'

As a date?

'No. Just together.'

Alright. Will Joe be there?

'Probably.'

And what will you say if he asks you out again?

I laughed. 'No.'

Good. I don't want you to go out with him.

I looked over my shoulder at Kai. He was staring at the bathroom floor, but I could see that his cheeks were tinged pink. 'Why does it matter to you if I go on a date with him?'

It doesn't.

He didn't look up at me so I switched topics, sensing his sudden awkwardness. 'I researched your name.'

Yes, I guessed. Please don't call me "–chan" again. It's so stupid and childish.

'But I read that it's a term of endearment. It's cute.'

You find me endearing?

I blushed under the water spray. I suppose I did, but he was more handsome than he was cute. I ignored his question. 'If you're afraid of water, why do you appear a lot when it's around?'

I don't know. It's odd. I didn't appear the other day because of water, though. I came to warn you against Psyche.

I sighed, not wanting to think about it. Psyche was nice to me. With her around, coping with Terry and Eros was a bit easier.

She's dangerous.

'You've said. But if you've never spoken to the Voices, how do you know she's dangerous?'

I can hear them talking inside your head.

'Oh? What do they say?' I asked as I adjusted the temperature of the water. The dial slipped between my wet fingers and seemed stiff as I attempted to turn it.

How much they dislike you. Erm… Gracie…

'Hm?' I jumped as Kai manifested himself inside the cubicle. His hands reached out and grabbed my waist, but I batted them away. 'Don't touch me when I'm naked!'

Gracie –

'Is that a normal thing to do in Japan? To go around touching naked girls without their permission?'

Stop being racist for just a minute and look at the water!

I looked up at the showerhead, but nothing seemed out of place. I looked down, and that's when I felt it. The water in the shower had risen up to our ankles without me even noticing. Why wasn't it draining away? The buzzing started. Eros manifested in front of me under the flowing water.

'Are you ready?'

'What for? It's not sunset yet.'

He smirked and tapped his wrist where an Hourglass should have been. 'Au contraire, Miss Thrace.'

I lifted up my wrist, and sure enough, the time was 18:46. Sunset. My heart felt like it was in my throat and my hands started to quiver. 'No! Wait!'

Eros ignored me. 'Scenario: escape the shower cubicle without drowning. If you drown, you lose. Do you accept the scenario?'

I selected the "Yes" button without hesitation then turned around to face Kai. He was pressed against one of the glass panels and his mouth was open slightly, his eyes unfocused. He looked like he was struggling to breathe.

'Kai,' I said, placing my hands on his shoulders. 'Kai, can you hear me?'

He looked at me, petrified. *Gracie, I…*

'It's okay. I want you to go back into my head and stay there until the scenario is over.'

But you need help.

I shook my head and squeezed Kai's shoulders. His eyes were wide with terror. The rest of him looked so small and scared. I smiled despite my own fear. 'I'll be fine. Psyche can help me. Just go, okay? I can handle this.'

He nodded and disappeared.

'Psyche?' I called out, and she materialised beside me in the cubicle with a bright smile.

'Hi, Gracie. I'm so sorry about this scenario.'

'It's okay. Just stay with me, please?'

'Of course, Gracie. Let's keep you calm, yeah? You won't be able to do anything if you're not. Take a few deep breaths. Can you switch the shower off?'

I smiled at her, but it dropped from my face when I tried to stop the shower. I pressed the switches, but the "On/Off" button was jammed. I tried to prize it free but it wouldn't budge. The controls that regulated the water flow were not working either. I couldn't even change the temperature anymore. Damn. I tried the showerhead next, giving it a jiggle to try and vary the spray of the water manually. Nothing happened. I yanked it hard and the showerhead came completely loose from the hose, causing water to flow into the shower cubicle at an even faster rate. Eros manifested beside Psyche in the water with a grin plastered across his face.

'Now this is a pickle, isn't it, Miss Thrace?'

I ignored him and turned to the door. I tried to pull it open, but it wouldn't move. The latch was stiff at the best of times, but now the water, which had nearly reached my knees, was pressing against the door and stopping it from opening.

'That is a shame. The water is coming out awfully quickly.' Eros tutted. 'What are you going to do now?'

'Don't be so mean to her. She's trying her best,' said Psyche encouragingly.

'You know I'm at *my* best when I'm mean, darling.'

Psyche giggled.

'If you're not going to be helpful, then you can both just leave,' I said, trying the door again, even though I knew it wouldn't move.

'Why won't it open?' Psyche asked.

'Because the weight of the water pressing on the door is too heavy for me to move. Let's try the plug.'

I took a deep breath, then plunged my head underwater. The water level should have been going down by some degree even if the flow was cranked up to its highest setting, so Eros must have blocked it with something. Holding my breath, I reached for the plughole. There was no hologram covering it, but each of the tiny triangular holes had been filled with a hard substance that looked like cement. I tried to scrape it out with my fingernail, but it was completely solid.

I lifted my head back up above the water line and gulped in some air. 'Why the hell did Eros put cement in the plughole?!'

Psyche looked confused. 'What?! No, he can't have done that.'

'Just go,' I said.

The two holograms disappeared. With the water now at my waist, I grabbed my shampoo bottle and started bashing it against the glass door, but it wouldn't break. I shouted for Macy, but the glass was toughened to keep the water inside. There was no response as I waited in trepidation – she probably couldn't hear me all the way from the kitchen. I carried on banging on the door, but it was no use. I stood still in the centre of the cubicle for a moment. The water was making me tremble and I felt the beginnings of a panic attack building. But I couldn't let that happen. What would Dad do in this situation? I bit my lip. He fought terrorists with androids so he always had to think quick on his feet.

' Thinking of my Dad cleared my head and I snapped back into action. The water was nearly at my chin now and I grabbed the shower fixings to help me swim upwards. There was an air vent at the top of the shower, but it was just to let steam out. The water had no real way of escaping.

'Kai-chan?' I whispered. 'I don't know what to do.'

Neither do I.

He was safe inside my head but he sounded like he was on the verge of a panic attack too.

Just take a couple of seconds to get calm and think. Did you learn anything about water in school?

'Yes, but...' I sighed as I realised what I would have to do.

What's wrong?

'I think I know a way out of here. I just hope it works.'

Damn, I hated physics. I swam upwards, still holding onto the shower fixings for stability, and positioned my feet so they were against the door. I tilted my head, so my lips were nearly pressed against the ceiling and kept breathing. I wrinkled my nose as the water filled my ears, but instead of shaking my head to get rid of the unpleasant squelching sensation, I stayed still and took in one final deep breath before the water covered me completely. I squeezed my eyes shut and concentrated on the door, then I gave it a firm push with my feet. The hinges buckled under the pressure and gave way easily, causing the door to open in the wrong direction. All of the water rushed out, flooding the bathroom.

I barely registered Eros telling me that I had won the scenario. I let go of the shower fixings and dropped to the floor of the cubicle, shaking uncontrollably. I pulled my sodden towel to my cold body, taking in deep breaths. I didn't know how I was going to explain the mess, or even clean it up, but that was the least of my worries. Why was there cement in the plughole in the first place? Real cement. Who the hell would do that? Terry was malicious but he hadn't even shown up for this scenario. Psyche wouldn't have done it and I was sure it wasn't Kai. So it was Eros then? I thought the nightmare scenarios were just a weird twisted game. I didn't think any of the Voices could actually kill me.

Gracie?

Kai appeared in front of me looking concerned and sympathetic. I let him hug me even though I was soaking wet and shivering.

Are you okay?

'Not really,' I mumbled against his chest.

Kai squeezed me tight. He glanced down at the plughole and saw the cement.

Who did that?

'I…I think it was Eros.'

'It wasn't me.'

I peered over Kai's shoulder and saw Eros and Psyche standing at the other side of the bathroom, watching us. 'Then who was it?'

Psyche shrugged. 'I don't know.'

Kai scrutinised them with his sombre eyes. *I think they're telling the truth.*

I tightened my grip on Kai. 'Then who did it?'

I don't know.

Slowly, not wanting to slip on the wet tiled floor, I made my way over to the door and opened it a crack with trembling hands. 'Macy?'

She whirred around the corner from the kitchen a moment later with a fake smile on her leather face. 'Yes, Miss Thrace?'

'Can you get me another towel, please?'

'Of course, Miss Thrace.' She returned with a dry towel and I quickly wrapped it around myself before I opened the door fully.

'Erm, the bathroom needs cleaning. Well, more drying than cleaning. And the door has come off its hinges so that needs fixing. And there's cement stuck in the plughole, so it needs unblocking. And the shower needs turning off and repairing. And… do you mind if you don't mention any of this to my Mum?'

Macy's pretend smile widened. 'Certainly, Miss Thrace.'

'Thanks, Macy.' I gave her a smile, a real one, and went to my bedroom. I dried myself off and put my hair up in the towel, then I got changed into the yellow and white dress that Iliana had made me buy. Just as I fastened the leather belt around my waist, Kai wandered into the room in his pyjamas. 'You're wearing that to the party?'

No? Because we're surely not going after you just nearly drowned in the shower.

'I promised Iliana. If I don't go, she'll want to know why and I don't even know how to begin explaining this.'

Are you sure? You seem a little… traumatised.

I shrugged. 'It's fine.'

Kai came over and laid a hand on my shoulder. *You could have died, Gracie. You seem in denial.*

I smiled at him. 'I had it handled.'

Barely.

'I need to continue my life despite these nightmare scenarios. I'll be fine once I distract myself.'

You were shaking before.

Kai took my hands in his but I jerked them out of his warm grip. What was the point talking about the nightmare scenarios with him? He wasn't real. If I needed to talk to someone, it would be someone who could actually support me. But I didn't intend to talk to anyone about them. No one would believe me if I tried to explain what I was going through, so it didn't matter how I felt, traumatised or not. I had to carry on as if things were fine, even if I was feeling less relieved after every nightmare scenario ended. 'I'm okay, really. Come on, get changed.'

No one can see me, though.

'I can see you. Get changed.'

I sighed and sat down at my desk, then took my hair out of the towel. I gave it a quick blast with the hairdryer then tried to tame it a little with my hairbrush. I also applied some makeup. By the time I had finished, Kai had changed into a blue shirt and a pair of black jeans. 'No shoes?'

We're inside.

'Asian.'

Racist.

'Come on. Let's go.' I slipped on a pair of white pumps, but before we could leave the room, Eros manifested in front of my bedroom door.

'Going somewhere?'

I nodded and took a step away from him. 'Yes. To a friend's party.'

Eros hummed. 'I can't remember the last time you went to a party. Oh, wait. Yes, I do. It was the party with the android clown. Have you been too afraid to go to another party since then?'

'No…' I whispered, already knowing where this conversation was going.

'It's just that you had no friends to invite you.'

Gracie doesn't need plenty of friends. She has a few close ones. That's all she needs.

I shot Kai a pleading look. Although I appreciated him standing up for me, this would make things ten times worse. Eros transferred his gaze from me to Kai.

'I forgot to introduce myself to you in the shower. My name's Eros. You're the new one, aren't you?'

Yes.

'Then why aren't you helping us make Gracie play the scenarios?'

Because she doesn't deserve it.

Eros sneered and looked back at me. 'Did you tell him to say that?'

I shook my head and kept silent, not wanting to make this situation any worse. Eros hovered over to me and his lips brushed against my ear.

'We'll make you pay for your boyfriend's mistake.' Then he disappeared and, thankfully, the buzzing went with him.

'Now we really need to go or we'll be late.'

I'm sorry. I made things worse.

'It's okay. I'm used to it.' We left my room and I stopped by the bathroom. 'Macy, I'm going out.'

'Have a wonderful time, Miss Thrace!'

Kai followed me down the hallway and I waited by the front door, watching as he put his trainers on. 'Ready?' He nodded and we left the house, making our way to Tufnell Park Road where Iliana lived.

Are we not taking the Airground?

'No. Iliana only lives ten minutes away and I don't use the Airground unless I have to.'

You don't like it?

'No, not really. I don't really trust the quantum levitation system. Same thing with the Hourglass.'

I quite like the Hourglass.

I glanced down at Kai's Hourglass that was attached to his left wrist. The time showed 04:28.

'I just don't like the idea of everyone being made to wear one. You know, the other week, when we were shopping in the Underground, that little girl hiding behind the gate didn't have one.'

We arrived at Iliana's and I knocked on the door. Iliana opened it. She was wearing the purple dress she had bought the other week and her hair was tied up in a bun, but she hadn't finished doing her makeup. She was also holding a glass filled with amber liquid. 'Hey, girl! You look great! You want one?' she asked, her words slightly slurring together.

'No, I'm good.'

'Suit yourself. Just wait in the hall for a minute. I won't be long.'

I nodded as she went upstairs, knocking back the remainder of the amber liquid. I stepped inside but Kai lingered on the doorstep.

'What's wrong?'

I can smell a dog.

'You don't like dogs?'

He shook his head and then his blue eyes grew wide in alarm. I turned around and smiled when I saw Luna bounding towards me. She was a white husky with a black nose and light blue eyes that looked like the sky had been trapped inside them. She started licking my hands with her rough tongue, making me laugh – it was the first time I had laughed in a while.

'It's nice to see you, too, Luna.'

Kai stepped into the house and knelt down beside me, a frown on his face.

I don't like dogs.

'Is that a Japanese thing?'

No, you racist.

'You love me really, Kai-chan.'

'Who on earth are you talking to?'

We both turned and saw Iliana standing on the stairs, now ready. 'To Luna. She was messing up my dress, weren't you girl?' She barked, nuzzling one of my hands.

'Then who's Kai-chan?' Iliana asked, coming into the hallway and slipping a pair of black five-inch heels on her feet.

'I think you've drunk too much already!' I joked.

She stuck her tongue out at me and we left the house, heading to Landseer Road where Joe and Chris lived. 'Have you spoken to Chris today?' I asked.

Iliana nodded and a dopey smile crept onto her face. 'Yeah. We've got such a good connection.'

'Great.' I smiled at her, feigning enthusiasm.

'What's up with you? Is it because Joe's going to be there?

'No, it's just…' I glanced over at Kai, who was watching me closely. The corners of his lips revealed a hint of a smile and it made something inside my stomach flip. I felt a bit sick. 'I'm not bothered about Joe.'

Iliana sighed and linked her arm in mine. 'Alright. But, please tell me if you change your mind.'

'I will.'

'And by the way, why is your hair so frizzy?'

'Oh, I was in a rush and didn't have time to dry it properly.'

Iliana rolled her eyes.

We arrived on Landseer Road. It was obvious which house belonged to Chris and Joe. The front door was open and music was blaring out. Iliana dragged me towards the house and pushed past a few people who were vaping on the path outside. Iliana had been here a few times this week. She took us straight into the first room off the hallway, which must have been the dining room – a big table and chairs were pushed against the wall. The music was louder and it was already full of people. At the other side of the room, Chris was leaning against the wall with a beer in his hand, chatting with two mates. He smiled when he saw Iliana approach and wrapped his arm around her waist, pulling her close. I stood in the doorway for a moment, biting my lip. I wasn't the best in social situations where I didn't know anyone. Kai walked down the hallway and into the kitchen but quickly came out again.

They're playing "Ring of Fire". Let's go in the living room.

I followed him through another door next to the kitchen and was glad to find the room empty. It was pretty big for a student house, with two leather settees and a large Baiji television mounted above the fireplace.

How can two students afford to rent a house like this in London?
I shrugged. He did have a point. 'I don't know, Kai.'

'It's because you're too stupid,' Eros said from inside my head.

'Eros… Please, I've already played the scenario. Can't you leave me alone for just one night?' I asked quietly, swallowing the lump that had settled in my throat.

Terry snickered. 'No can do.'

The Voices started banging on my skull. It felt like they were trying to crack it open so they could escape. I groaned and held my head in my hands. I rubbed my temples, hoping that I could hold it together. I squeezed my eyes shut to stop myself from crying, but the hot tears slid down my face anyway. 'Please… stop… I'm sorry for what Kai said.'

Kai's hologram disappeared and after a moment, the banging stopped and my head no longer felt like it was going to split open. I looked up, and through my tears, I saw Kai again. He curled his sleeve around his palm and started to wipe away the stains on my cheeks.

'How did you do that?' I asked when the pain in my head had gone numb.

Do what?
'Get them to stop.'
I just asked them.

'But you didn't say anything. I didn't hear you.'

Kai smiled and pulled back from my face. *You can't always hear the Voices, you know. You never hear them when they're planning what scenarios to make you play. Not even I can hear them all the time. They decide what we can hear, not you.*

I nodded. 'I see.'

Do you want to go home?

'No. I'll stay. Iliana will hate it if I leave. We only got here five minutes ago.' I sniffed and wiped a hand over my clammy face.

But you don't even like parties. Why did we come?

'I never said I didn't like parties.'

You're not exactly acting like you're having fun.

'I haven't been to enough parties to know if I actually like them or not. I just wish Iliana hadn't gone off with Chris so soon. I could go and talk to Joe, but he might try and ask me out again...'

Please don't say "yes".

'I'm not going to.'

Kai smiled at me and the queasy feeling in my stomach returned, only this time, I actually felt like I was going to be sick. I clamped a hand over my mouth and ran out of the living room and up the stairs in search of the toilet. The bathroom was opposite the staircase. I pushed open the door, not checking to see if anyone else was in there, then knelt down and threw up in the toilet. I tried to move my hair out of my face, but hologram hands grabbed it for me and held it in a loose ponytail.

It's alright, I've got you.

When I finished, Kai flushed the chain for me as I cupped my hands under the tap, sipping the cold water. 'You've gotten better at holding things,' I said as I wiped my mouth with the back of my hand.

You've only just noticed?

I smiled at him just as the door was pushed fully open and I saw Joe in the landing.

'Gracie? I heard someone throwing up in here.'

'Yeah, it was me.'

'Are you okay?' he asked, stepping into the bathroom.

Kai walked towards him, inspecting Joe's face. *I don't like his nose.*

I glanced at Kai but didn't reply. 'I'm fine. I probably just ate something that didn't agree with me. I promise I'm not drunk already. I haven't even had a drink yet.'

Joe smiled and Kai retreated back to my side. 'Then let's get you a drink. Come on.'

'Actually, I was wondering if you knew where Iliana had gone.'

'Yeah, she's in Chris' room. Second door down.'

I smiled in thanks and exited the bathroom. There was an open door right next to the bathroom, which probably led to Joe's room and the second door was closed. I walked over to it and knocked, but there was no reply. 'Is she in there?'

'Probably. I wouldn't disturb them, though, if I were you.'

'What do you mean?'

He just laughed. 'Chris has been going on about her since they first met. They're pretty close already. Come on, you can chill in my room. I'm sure you don't want to play "Ring of Fire" in the kitchen.' He went into his bedroom and I moved to follow him, but Kai grabbed my wrist and pulled me back.

I don't trust him.

'I'll be fine,' I whispered.

Kai led the way in, doing a sweep of the area without touching anything. There was a bay window at the front of the room and Joe was already sitting on a double bed opposite. Covering the floor were various sports science books along with football almanacs and some coursework, which made a trail towards the desk against the wall. In the opposite corner was the wardrobe and a brand-new games console linked up to a huge Baiji.

'Your room is messier than mine.'

He laughed and patted the space on the bed beside him. 'I didn't expect you to be messy.'

I just shrugged. 'I don't like my family's android, Macy, going into my room to clean up.'

'You don't like androids?'

I shook my head and sat down next to him. I didn't want him to ask why I didn't like androids so I changed the subject. 'How come you're not downstairs with everyone else?'

He chuckled. 'I'm not bothered about parties – it was Chris' idea.' As he spoke, Joe's eyes raked up and down my body. 'You look gorgeous in this dress. Will you be wearing this on our date?' he asked, giving me a playful nudge. I recoiled slightly. Joe's forwardness made me feel a bit uncomfortable.

'Errrr… well… I've actually decided that I don't want to go on a date with you. It's nothing personal. You're really nice but I've just got a lot going on right now.'

Joe's eyes narrowed slightly. I guess he didn't get rejected very often. I opened my mouth to justify my decision further, but a cry from Iliana saved me. I ran out into the hall and watched as Iliana stumbled out of Chris' room, eyeliner and mascara smudged on her cheeks.

'Iliana?!'

CHAPTER 9

'Iliana?! What's wrong?'

My best friend ran towards me and I wrapped my arms around her. 'Take me home, Gracie,' she said, her words slurring together even more than before and her legs were shaking. My knees buckled slightly as she slumped against me.

'Yeah, of course.'

'Here, I'll help,' Joe said, coming out of his room. He wrapped Iliana's arm around his shoulder and guided her down the stairs, leaving me to follow.

'Where does she live?' he asked when we made it out onto the street.

'Oh, it's not far. I can take her from here.'

'It's fine,' he insisted. 'Where does she live?'

I hesitated. If Chris had done something to upset Iliana, I wasn't sure letting Joe help us was a good idea. But Joe was waiting for my answer. His expression firm and slightly irritated.

'Tufnell Park Road.' Joe nodded and started walking, Iliana crying quietly in his arms.

Come on, let's go back to yours.

Kai walked up beside me and grabbed my hand. 'I can't leave Iliana with him,' I whispered.

Why not? She'll be fine.

I ignored Kai and followed Joe down the street in silence. When we arrived at Iliana's house, I pressed her Hourglass against the front door and it unlocked with a click.

'Thank you for bringing Iliana home, but I can take it from here. I'll see you later.' I told Joe firmly.

He let go of Iliana and I led my best friend into her house, shutting the door behind me so Joe knew he wasn't welcome. 'Come on, Iliana. I'm taking you to your room.'

She allowed me to help her upstairs. Her bedroom was much cleaner than mine except for the hair products and makeup on her dressing table. I sat Iliana down on the bed and removed her heels for her, then grabbed her baby wipes from the nightstand. Still crying, she started removing her makeup whilst I drew the curtains.

'Is your Mum in?' I asked, getting Iliana her pyjamas from her wardrobe.

'Japan.'

I nodded and helped Iliana undress. She couldn't seem to do much in her state. Iliana's Mum was often away and it had been a few years since Iliana's Dad had been alive. Once Iliana finished changing into her pyjamas, I guided her to lie down and pulled the duvet over her.

'What happened with Chris?' She started to cry again and I hugged her. 'It's alright. We can talk about it later. Try not to think about it, okay? Goodnight.' I left her bedroom and leant against the closed door for a moment. Iliana was usually quite dramatic, but I hadn't seen her cry like this for a long time. Sighing, I went downstairs and saw Kai waiting by the front door.

Joe's still outside.

'Really? I thought he'd have got the message that the evening was over. I don't really want to see him again right now.'

Is there a back door?

'Yeah, but there's a large wall around the garden.' I walked over to Kai. 'I don't want him to know where I live, so we might be walking for a while.'

That's fine. Just say the word and I'll punch him.

I smiled at Kai and he opened the front door. Joe was standing on the pavement opposite the house, but I couldn't read his facial expression. He looked... focussed... but I wasn't sure if that was a good thing.

'You didn't have to wait for me. I can make it home on my own.'

'It's alright.' His voice not giving anything away either.

'Well, ummm, I'll see you in Engineering on Wednesday.' I started to walk off, planning to head onto Holloway Road, but Joe held my wrist.

'It's okay. I'll walk you home.'

'There's no need, really.'

'I insist.'

He let go and I tried to smile as I led the way.

Are you okay?

I managed to shrug my shoulders a little, just enough so Joe wouldn't notice. I turned onto Parkhurst Road, trying to slow my pace so Joe would get bored and leave. There was no one around. I went onto Hillmarton Road, which was only a street away from my house. The only other street I could go onto was Camden Road and by then Joe would start asking me why I had led him in a circle.

'Gracie?' Joe asked near the abandoned bus stop outside St. Luke's Church. I turned around, Kai standing in between Joe and me.

'Yes?'

'I'm sorry if I came on a bit strong back in my bedroom. It's just, you seem really nice and I'd like to get to know you a bit better. Could we meet for a coffee – just as friends?'

'I –'

Before I could say anything else or before Kai could step in, there was a groan from behind me. I turned around and saw an Irukian. His white clothes were ripped and he had wrapped some of the material around his bleeding wrist as a bandage but it was not stopping the flow of blood. His skin was pale, almost as white as his clothes and what was left of them hung off his emaciated frame. I stepped towards him, but Joe grabbed my wrist again.

'Don't go anywhere near that thing. Irukians are degenerates, the scum of society,' he hissed.

I stood in silence for a moment, shocked by what Joe had just said. Irukians scared me sometimes, but I didn't consider them to be less than human. 'Does it matter right now? He's losing a lot of blood. He needs our help.'

'He needs nothing from us.'

I tried to pull away but Joe wasn't letting up. 'Please, Joe, just let me help him.'

He shook his head. He was about to speak again but Kai punched him in the jaw. It came out of nowhere. Joe let go of my wrist and sat down on the pavement, a bit dazed, groaning and holding his hands to his mouth. Kai gently turned my wrist over in his warm hands.

It looks sore, but I think you'll be okay.

I nodded, not believing what had happened. I knew I found Kai's hologram to be a tangible object, but… punching someone? Causing them actual pain? How was that possible? And why did he even do that? There would have been an easier way to make Joe let go of me. 'Kai-chan…'

I'm sorry, but I didn't know what else to do. He was hurting you.

'I know… thank you…'

Joe groaned again and Kai pulled me away, towards St. Luke's. 'If you help that degenerate, you know I'll have to report it to the Police?'

I think it's time we leave, don't you?

I nodded and went to the Irukian, who was now slumped against the church doors. The dolphin symbol painted there a few weeks ago was now slightly faded. 'Sir?' I asked, kneeling down. 'Can we help you?'

The Irukian's eyes swivelled around to look at mine. He looked weak. 'Archway…' he whispered.

'The station?'

He managed to nod and I took the Irukian's arm that wasn't bleeding and hooked it over my shoulder, then Kai came over.

Where are we taking him? To hospital?

'We can't. He has no Hourglass. We need to get to the Archway Airground Station.'

'No…' The Irukian said. His voice was weak and cracking. 'Underground Station.'

Kai looked up at me, one black eyebrow raised.

CHAPTER 10

The Archway Airground Station, like all Airground Stations, was just a plastic and metal shelter.

'Over there…' the Irukian said, managing to point across the road. Nestled in between a row of shops was the entrance to Archway Underground Station. It was blocked by a metal gate that had been pulled across the tiled corridor and secured with a large padlock. A strip of faded Police tape was partly attached to the metal bars, one end fluttering on the ground in the slight breeze.

Kai and I walked towards it, and the Irukian produced a large key from his jacket pocket and handed it to me. It was rusty and the handle was worn from use. Slowly, I lifted the Irukian's arm from over my shoulder and stepped towards the padlock.

Wait.

I turned to Kai, the Irukian now slumped on the ground over his hologram body. 'What's the matter?'

It might be dangerous.

'I know, but we don't have time to do anything else. The Police will be here soon.'

I looked back at the padlock and turned the key, the rusty metal made a crunching sound in the lock. The padlock clicked and the round bar opened. I slipped it off, then pulled the metal gate to one side. In the entrance to the station was a teenage girl. Her hair, face and clothes were dirty. She looked me up and down, then took a step away when her eyes made contact with my Hourglass.

'What do you want?' she asked, her voice full of suspicion.

'This Irukian is hurt. He told me to bring him here.'

She nodded and went over to the Irukian, hooked his arm over her shoulder and helped him down the corridor. 'This way,' she said, her voice echoing off the walls.

I started to follow her, but a little boy darted across the corridor in front of me, sprinting over to the gate. He couldn't have been older than six or seven. His face and clothes were just as dirty as the girl's had been. He grabbed the padlock from the pavement then shut the gate, locking it from the inside. He caught me staring and glared at me, then spat on the floor. 'Hourglass girl,' he hissed, teeth bared.

Shocked, I turned around and followed the girl down the corridor. Kai stayed close to me. It was dark so I switched on the torch function on my Hourglass. The floor was dirty and a little wet. We passed several tents with people sleeping inside. Some people were just resting on the tiled floor, their clothes either too big or too small for them. They all looked filthy. We passed through the deactivated ticket barriers and down the disused escalators. Dust and rubble had gathered in the ridges of each step. On the walls, placed next to semi-destroyed white tiling, were posters for West End shows that had stopped running years ago.

At the bottom of the escalators, there were two entrances to the platforms. One, which had been the Southbound platform had planks of wood nailed to it and rubble was cascading onto the floor through the gaps. We followed the girl and the Irukian to the Northbound side. On the platform and tracks were more tents. Some people were curled up and sleeping on metal benches. There were scorch marks on the walls and advertisements were still stuck to the tiled tunnel.

The girl let go of the Irukian as she jumped off the platform and onto the tracks, then helped him down. Kai and I did the same, then followed her down the tunnel. The dark shaft was lit with dozens of tea lights and more tents were pitched under the curved roof. The light from my Hourglass caused several people to poke their heads out of their tents. First, they glared at me, then they retreated back into their tents with anxious eyes.

I stepped closer to Kai and poked his arm. 'Why is everyone so afraid of me?' I whispered.

I think it might have something to do with your Hourglass. Is that girl wearing one?

I glanced at the girl. Both of her wrists were dirty, but neither had an Hourglass. She was an Irukian. More and more people came out of their tents, all disturbed by my torch light, none of them wearing an Hourglass.

125

Halfway down the tunnel was an Underground train. Its walls were a dirty white and its doors were faded red. A set of doors to the second carriage were open and the lights were on, showing three men chatting on the blue fabric seats. They weren't as dirty as the other Irukians we'd seen, but their faces and hands were still grimy. When the bleeding Irukian came into their line of vision, two of the men jumped out of the carriage.

'David?!' one of them shouted. The Irukian, or David, mumbled something and the two men took him further down the tunnel.

The girl walked off and the other man came to the doorway of the carriage. He was wearing a long purple coat, shirt, and waistcoat with a thin chain on the front of it. 'You brought David here?' he asked.

'Yes. He was like that when we found him.'

The man nodded. 'Come in.' He went back into the carriage and I glanced at Kai.

He seems okay. I'll punch him if he's not.

'Punching people is not the answer to everything,' I whispered.

I climbed into the carriage and Kai got in after me. It was identical to an Airground carriage – blue fabric seats and blue poles to match. Part of the carriage had been turned into a bedroom-come-office; a pillow and duvet on one row of seats and a desk in front which was filled with papers, a ring of rusty keys and a few small jars of clear gel. The man sat behind his desk and I sat opposite him on the makeshift bed. Kai stood guard between us.

'Thank you for helping David. He's a new recruit.'

'What was wrong with him? He was losing a lot of blood.'

'He's been having some trouble with his wound since his Hourglass was removed. This can happen in the early weeks. The body is used to pumping blood harder to power the Hourglass. When it's removed, the blood pressure can force the wound to re-open. If he keeps inactive, it should heal quicker. We'll monitor him closely from now on.'

I nodded, a little disgusted that Irukians were getting people to cut off their Hourglasses. I didn't like my Hourglass, but it was too dangerous to cut it off. If you didn't have an Hourglass, then you weren't allowed treatment at a hospital.

'Okay, I need to go. I was with a guy earlier and he said he was going to call the Police when I found the Irukian, you called "David". We – I mean – I managed to stall him for a bit, but they'll be on their way soon...'

'Don't worry about it. You won't get arrested.' He grabbed one of the jars on his desk and passed it to me. 'Smear some around your Hourglass. No one will be able to find you then.'

'I'm not sure I should do that.'

'It just shuts down your Hourglass' tracking software. It'll come back on when you remove the gel.'

I opened the jar and spread the sticky clear substance around my Hourglass. The screen faded and the red tracking dot in the top right-hand corner disappeared for the first time in my life. I felt free in a strange sort of way. 'Thank you.'

'No problem. You can keep it. I'm sure there are plenty of times when you might need to disappear above ground for a few hours. Consider it a thank you gift for helping David. Would you like a cup of tea before you go? It must have been a struggle carrying David here.'

'How do you plan on making it?'

He smiled. 'We have a kettle in the next carriage. It doesn't work brilliantly, but we make do. Milk and sugar?'

'Milk, no sugar.'

He stood up with a smile. 'Don't go anywhere. It takes a while to boil.'

He went into the next carriage and I watched him through the small window as he poured water out of a jug and into the worn spout. The red light that signalled it was boiling kept flickering on and off. It was going to take a while. Maybe I should have told him I didn't actually like tea.

Do you think we should go?

I shrugged. 'He seems harmless. Why? Do you think we should?'

I don't have a particularly bad feeling about this place, which is odd, considering we're underground in structurally unstable tunnels. I just want you to feel safe, though.

I smiled at him. 'I don't feel safe, but I don't feel like he's going to murder me. We can stay for a bit.'

The kettle finally boiled and the Irukian poured two cups of tea, then added some powdered milk. He gave each cup a vigorous stir, then carried them through to where Kai and I were waiting.

'Thanks,' I said as I took it from him. I subtly inspected the pale grey liquid swirling in my cup and tried to ignore the coagulated powder floating around the rim.

'I hope it tastes alright.'

'I'm sure it's fine,' I told him with a smile, then took a sip. It wasn't fine. It was the worst thing I had ever tasted, but I continued to drink. He'd gone to so much effort. His tea went untouched as he watched me swallow the lumpy liquid.

'Is it good?'

'Yeah. Great stuff.'

'I'm Hayden Dobson, by the way. I run the Northern Line of the Underground.'

'You run it?' I asked, confused.

'Ever since the law forcing people to wear an Hourglass was passed, Irukians have been living down here, on each of the lines. I'm in charge of the Northern Line.'

'There's more of you?'

Hayden nodded, shrugging off his purple coat. 'If you don't have an Hourglass, you're not considered a citizen in this country. No Hourglass means no healthcare, no education, no job, no house, no money, nothing. No one ever bothered to repair the places that VIRENT bombed, so that's why we live here.'

'You hate wearing the Hourglass that much?'

'We hate IrukaTech more. They run our country. They control our Government and they continue to bribe

Catherine Bell and her Cabinet. That's why everyone has to wear the Hourglass. Not because of some rubbish excuse to lower crime rates. It's to control us all. Yet people think Irukians are the mad ones for not wanting a watch surgically attached to our wrists.'

I shuffled my feet on the linoleum floor. 'I think most people have got the impression you're 100% anti-technology.'

Hayden's eyes hardened. 'We're not. Just anti-Hourglass. And anti-Izumi.'

'What's he got to do with this?'

'He *owns* IrukaTech. He's behind all of this.'

I nodded but didn't agree with him. It seemed unlikely. Izumi may be a little strange, but he was a kind man. There was no way he would want to do the things Hayden described. But even if it was true, it would be incredibly hard to pull off. And what would their motivation be for tracking everyone if it wasn't to lower crime rates? Hayden was wrong. I decided not to tell Hayden who I was, in case he had heard of my connection to IrukaTech. Why was he telling me all this anyway? He'd only just met me. Was he trying to recruit me, to get me to cut off my Hourglass as well?

'I need to be getting home.' I stood up, still holding the jar and went to the entrance of the carriage.

'Yeah, it's pretty late. I'll walk you to the gate.'

As we jumped down from the carriage there was a shout in the tunnel. 'Daddy!' I turned and saw two young boys and a little girl running towards Hayden, and the little girl leapt into her father's arms.

'Shouldn't you three be in bed?'

The oldest boy shrugged. 'We don't know what time it is.'

Hayden sighed and manoeuvred his daughter around so he could reach the chain that was tucked into his waistcoat pocket. He brought out a round silver box, like a locket pendant but larger and clicked it open. 'It's two minutes until midnight. Go back to bed.'

'How do you know what time it is?' I asked, stepping towards Hayden.

With a smile, he showed me the silver box. Inside, protected by a sheet of glass, was a tiny clock face. I had seen analogue clocks before, but only ones like Big Ben or the ones kept in the British Museum. This was *so* tiny. 'How can anyone fit something so complex inside something so small?' I asked, confused.

The younger of the two boys sniggered. 'Is she stupid, Daddy?'

'She has an Hourglass, Callum.' The little boys both looked at my wrist then ran off, back towards the tents on the platform.

'Sorry about them,' Hayden said, 'they've only seen a couple of Hourglasses before.'

'It's fine.'

The little girl in Hayden's arms smiled at me, adjusting her arms around her Dad's neck. The skin on her wrists was pale and clean. She had probably never even been above ground, judging by her age. The Underground was bombed in 2025 and the Hourglass was released in 2023.

She was more than likely born in these train tunnels. If she had never been on the surface, did that mean she had never been to school? I hadn't seen any form of rudimentary classrooms so far.

'Can any of the children down here read and write?' I asked.

Hayden shrugged. 'Not really. They all know a little, but what's the point in teaching them? We don't have any books for them to read.'

The blonde girl in Hayden's arms pouted. 'I want to learn, Daddy.'

'You don't need to learn, sweetheart.'

'I still want to!' She turned her head to look at me, her blue eyes sparkling and inquisitive. 'Will you teach me?'

'Ermmm…'

'You can't ask her something like that,' Hayden said.

'But I really want to learn!'

I smiled. 'No, it's okay. I don't mind. I want to do it. I can come by early in the morning.'

'Yay! My name is Daisy by the way!'

'I'm Iliana,' I told her.

Hayden sighed. 'Fine, you can teach her. Come by early tomorrow morning. You can see David, too. I'm sure he'll want to thank you himself. I'm sure he's very grateful you brought him back here.'

'Do you mean come on Sunday morning?'

Hayden smiled and shook his head. 'It's already Sunday morning. I meant come by on Monday morning. Honestly,

132

you have a watch surgically attached to your wrist and you don't know what the time is.' He handed me a rusty key from his ring. 'Use this and come to this carriage. If anyone tries to stop you, just wave your Hourglass in their face and they'll back off. But do *not*, under any circumstances, lose this key.'

'I won't.'

'Are you okay to leave on your own? I need to get Daisy back to bed.'

'Yeah, that's fine.' I nodded and thanked him, then Kai and I began our walk back to the surface. Kai stayed silent until I had put the padlock back on the gate outside. The little boy who had spat at me earlier glared at me through the metal bars. As soon as the padlock clicked shut, Kai grabbed my hand and pulled me onto the street.

Why is your name Iliana all of a sudden?

'If I told him my real name, he might know my connections to Izumi. If they did something to me down there, no one would ever know because of this gel thing.'

Oh. Okay. Can we go back to yours now?

I nodded and we made our way down Junction Road. Just as we neared the crossroads it formed with Bickerton Road, two Police cars sped past me and Kai, heading up Junction Road in the direction of the Airground Station.

'Do you think they're for me?'

If they are, they'll probably be going to the last recorded location logged on your Hourglass.

We turned on to Hungerford Road. Even from the other end of the road I could see that the light was still on in the kitchen. Either Mum was home and she had decided to make something, or she hadn't come home yet, so Macy was still working. We went into the house and I locked the front door, then waited for Kai to take off his shoes. In the kitchen, Macy was still up, her eyes closed in rest mode. As I entered, there was a whirring sound as she rebooted.

'Miss Thrace. Good morning. What would you like for breakfast?'

'Errrr... it's a bit too early for breakfast, Macy.'

'It is quarter to one on Sunday morning. This is the optimum time for breakfast. Can I interest you in a banana milkshake?'

'No, just put yourself back to standby.'

She did as I asked. I sighed, then went over to Macy. I had grown used to her over the years despite my fear of androids. She was in desperate need of repair and we really should have sent her back to Jangmi, but she had so much wrong with her that they would most likely just give us a completely different android. I could probably fix her myself, but I was too scared of making her go rogue. Then she would have to be destroyed.

Should I put her to bed in the basement? I dismissed the thought quickly. I couldn't, even if I wanted to. The day after the basement scenario, my Mum fixed the door with an electronic lock, so there was no way I could get in.

I left the kitchen and went to my bedroom, where Kai was already slouched on the bed.

You okay? You took a while in the kitchen.

I nodded and placed the gel jar and rusty key under my bed so no one would find them. 'I was just thinking about Macy. She needs repairs, but if we get her fixed, there's a chance she won't come back the same, or come back at all.'

Kai cocked his head to one side. *She's just an android. It's not like she has a real personality. It's just programming, and Jangmi won't change that part of her during repairs. She'll be fine. You could do with a new android anyway. Macy's obsolete.*

I nodded. He was probably right. I wiped the gel from my Hourglass. Kai walked over to me and took my hands in his.

How is your wrist?

'It's still a little sore, but I'll live. Thank you for helping me.'

It's alright.

We both got changed into our pyjamas, no longer caring about what the other looked like naked, and I climbed into bed. Kai sat on the floor at my bedside and created a hologram pillow and duvet with his hands.

'You could share my bed if you like.'

He glanced up at me. *Are you sure?*

'You're not real. It's not like you can do anything. Besides, it'll be more comfortable than sleeping on the floor.'

Kai went over to the other side of the bed and slipped under the duvet. We had our backs to each other and it was creating a cold channel down the middle of the bed. I wasn't about to suggest that we move closer together. But if Kai suggested it... maybe I would do it. 'Night, Kai-chan.'

Good night, Gracie.

I settled further into the mattress and brought the duvet up to my nose, feeling sleep quickly creep up on me. This evening had been so strange, and I had to go back to the Underground on Monday morning... and Macy needed repairing... and why wasn't Mum home yet... and was Iliana okay... and –

You looked beautiful in your dress.

REPORT ON PARTICIPANT 1 OUT OF 4: Miss Gracie Thrace

28/09/2047   Observed talking to herself at a residence on Landseer Road in the living room. She leaves gaps in the conversation as if someone else is talking to her. Later that evening, a bleeding Irukian appears and Miss Thrace helps him. Miss Thrace says the word "Kai", so it seems she has acquired a new voice by the said name.

POLICE REPORT:

Miss Gracie Thrace's Hourglass tracker was traced to the Archway Airgound Station at 22:34. The signal was lost and did not reappear until 00:55 at Hungerford Road in her residence.

Investigation ongoing.

CHAPTER 11

My Hourglass' alarm went off at 05:00. Kai's back was pressed against mine and I felt his spine jolt at the noise. He sat up slowly and rubbed his eyes.

Why is it set for that time?

'We're going back to the Underground, remember? We have to be early or someone will see us.' He nodded and left the room whilst I got dressed and got my things for university ready. I placed the rusty key and jar of gel at the bottom of my bag, then sat on my bed and waited for Kai. The other night Kai had told me that I was beautiful. At least, I thought that was what he said. I was tired and I'd had a long day. Had I imagined it?

As we walked up to Archway Underground Station, the streets were almost deserted. Only a few black cabs crawled past us.

How come your Mum wasn't home the other night?

'She was probably working overtime. She does that quite a lot.'

Do you think she's having an affair with Izumi?

I laughed. 'I doubt it. Besides, it's common knowledge he's not over the death of his wife yet.'

He had a wife?

'Yeah, back when he used to live in Japan. She was Ichigo's mother and she did have another child, a boy, I think, but they both died in childbirth.'

Kai nodded. *When did this happen?*

'Errmm... well, I never met his wife, since she died before I was born, but Ichigo has told me that the boy should have been a couple of years older than me. So, about twenty years ago? Give or take.'

We arrived at Archway Underground Station and I glanced around, making sure no one was in the area before we approached the entrance. The Airground didn't start running until half past six, and no one seemed to be around yet. I took the gel out of my bag and smeared it around the Hourglass, then I got out the rusty key. I unlocked the padlock and only opened the gate enough so Kai and I could just slip through. I fastened the padlock onto the inside of the gate and switched my Hourglass' torch on. It looked much the same as Saturday night – people sleeping in tents, some sleeping on the floor, dust and rubble still collecting in the ridges of the escalator steps. When I reached the platform and tunnel, a few people were awake, but as soon as they saw my Hourglass, they retreated back into their tents.

Kai and I made our way down the tunnel to the Northern Line Underground carriage where the second set of doors were still open. I climbed into the carriage and found Hayden asleep on his bed, wearing the same waistcoat and shirt as the other night. The hem of his shirt was riding up his body, and I saw that he had a tattoo on his hip. It was a circle, with a rose in the centre, exactly the same as the Jangmi logo. Why did Hayden have the Jangmi logo tattooed onto his body? Hayden woke with a start and sat up, brown hair a mess from sleeping on the seats.

'It's a bit early, isn't it?'

'I said I would be here early.'

Hayden got up and grabbed his purple coat from behind his desk. He seemed surprisingly spritely considering he'd only just woken up. 'Let's go to the hospital first. I'm sure Daisy will be up by the time we're done.'

Hayden jumped out of the carriage and Kai and I followed him down the tunnel. Just a few metres away were a dozen beds and there appeared to be a doctor and two nurses moving back and forth between each one. 'This is the Northern Ward,' explained Hayden.

David was in the last bed on the left side, set against the curved wall of the tunnel. He was awake and still emaciated, but he was less pale. His white clothes were gone and he was now wearing faded jeans and a red shirt. He sat up when he saw me coming and gave me a small smile.

'Thank you.'

'It's okay. How's your wrist?' I asked, looking down at his arm. It was bandaged up and there was no blood leaking through it.

'It still hurts, but I should be fine. I would have died if you hadn't found me.'

I smiled. 'I was just on the street at the same time as you were. Anybody could have found you.'

'Thank you anyway.'

'Daddy! Iliana!'

I smiled when I heard Daisy's voice and turned towards the sound. She was running down the tracks as fast as her little legs could carry her. 'Hi, Daisy,' I said, and she give me a toothy grin. 'Are you ready for your first lesson?'

She nodded eagerly and Hayden rolled his eyes. 'She's all yours. I'll be in the carriage if you need anything.'

The little girl jumped up and grabbed my hand, pulling me down to her level. 'Can we go to my tent?'

'Of course.' She dragged me further down the tunnel, Kai following with a smirk on his face.

This will be interesting. I don't imagine you're a very patient teacher.

I glared at him and he laughed. Unfortunately, the sick feeling in my stomach returned. I tried to ignore it as we came to a small pink tent with a little sign on the outside that said "Diays".

'Your tent looks lovely,' I told her.

'It's better inside.'

She pulled me through a small gap in the tarpaulin. The roof was only just high enough to allow me to sit without craning my neck. There was a sleeping bag rolled out against the far side next to a tiny table with two teddy bears sat around a cracked tea set. I took a notepad out of my bag and set it on the table, moving the teddies and tea pot carefully to one side. I turned to the back where the pages were blank.

'What's that?' Daisy asked.

'It's called a notebook. It's what you write in.' I got a pen out of my bag and wrote down the letter "a", then took Daisy through the whole alphabet and taught her the "abc" song.

'You have a pretty voice,' she told me when I finished singing.

'Thank you. Do you want to have a go?'

She nodded and sang it back to me. I was impressed by how quickly she picked up the tune. Her voice had a sweet, lyrical tone, which was lovely to listen to. When she finished, she looked at me eagerly. 'Did I get it right?'

'Yeah, you did really well.'

Next, I wrote Daisy's name on a page of my notepad for her to copy. Her writing was weak and wobbly but after a few attempts she was able to write the letters with more confidence and the word "D-a-i-s-y" was surprisingly legible. I ripped out a few pages of my notepad and handed Daisy my pen. 'Have these so you can practise your writing.'

'Thank you!' Daisy looked delighted. I suppose she probably didn't get many gifts living in the Underground. She wrapped her arms around my neck and gave me a gentle kiss on my cheek. Then she held up one of her teddy bears and lightly touched its nose to my cheek. 'Mortimer says thank you, too.'

I just smiled at her and put my things back into my bag. 'You're welcome. I need to go now, though. Will you take me back to the entrance?'

Daisy bit her lip with her only middle tooth. 'Only if you promise to come back.'

'I pinky promise,' I said, holding out my little finger. She stared at it, confused. 'A pinky promise is when you hook your little finger together with someone else's. It means you can't break the promise. If you do, the other person is allowed to break your fingers.'

'Okay!' She hooked her little finger around mine, shaking them a little, then stood up. Her head didn't even reach the top of the tent. She kept hold of my hand and clutched Mortimer with her other. 'Let's go!'

Kai followed Daisy and me back to the entrance, running to catch up with us.

You're a good teacher.

'I shot him a look to check if he was joking. He just smiled, his blue eyes glimmering in the candlelight. The sick feeling returned, except this time it made my heartbeat speed up. My vision blurred a little and I had to pull on Daisy's hand to make her stop for a second.

'Are you okay?' she asked, face almost as concerned as Kai's.

'Yeah, I just feel… a bit weird.'

Kai held my arm rigid at my side. *What's wrong?*

His hand on my skin made my heartbeat speed up even more. I thought about how Kai had seemed jealous whenever the subject of Joe came up, and what he may or may not have said on Sunday morning, just as we were falling asleep. This wasn't happening. This wasn't real. I couldn't fall for a voice inside my head. Even if I did have feelings for Kai, I shouldn't be reacting like this.

'I'm fine. Let's go.' Kai let go of my arm. Daisy pulled me through the tunnel and only let go when we reached the gate. I got the rusty key out of my bag and undid the padlock. I slid open the metal gate just a fraction.

I looked at my Hourglass. The screen was dim because of the gel, but I could just make out the numbers. It was 07:30. I'd been in the Underground tunnels for longer than I thought. On ground level, there were people going to work and cars were filling up the roads. There was no way I was going to get out of here without being seen. I fastened the padlock back onto the gate and dropped the key into my bag.

'Daisy, is there another way out of here? One where no one will see me?'

Daisy nodded. 'Yes. But it's a long way.'

'Is there anywhere closer?'

'Not that I know.'

I sighed. I was going to be late for class either way. 'I guess we'll have to go that way then.'

'Just don't tell Daddy,' she whispered.

'I won't. I pinky promise.'

***

We eventually reached Euston's Underground platform, which had been mostly destroyed by VIRENT's bombs. No one was living here, unlike every other station we had been through.

'How do you know your way around?' I asked Daisy as we walked through the tunnels.

'My brothers and me like to go exploring. Daddy is super busy so we have to look after ourselves. As long as we stay out of trouble, he doesn't mind what we do. Well, he'd probably mind us doing this, but he doesn't know about it.'

Daisy skipped along the tracks for a while, pigtails flying out behind her. She finally stopped when she came to a low pile of rubble with a metal gate in front of it. In the bottom corner, there was a small hole that had not been blocked up. On the other side of the metal gate was the row of shops where I had bought my dress with Iliana.

'You were here, weren't you? With your brothers? Do you remember me? I saw you all run off.'

She smiled. 'I remember. You were funny. You were talking to yourself. Daddy said only crazy people do that.'

Kai laughed and I subtly pinched his arm. 'Yeah, well, sometimes I find it helpful to talk out loud.' I crawled through the small gap. Kai quickly followed me. 'I'll see you soon,' I whispered to Daisy and she grinned. I watched her skip off down the tunnel and disappear into the darkness.

I found Iliana in the library at a table near the welcome desk, a few sheets of paper in her hands.

'I am so sorry I'm late. Something happened.'

'Is that "something" the reason why you have dust in your hair?'

'What? Oh.' I reached up, brushing away the dirt with Kai's help. 'It was Macy. She punched the wall and I had to repair her. Crazy android.' I just shrugged, pretending like it didn't matter. It was getting so easy to lie with practise, even to my best friend.

'It's fine. Here.' Iliana handed me the papers she was holding. 'Miss Dyna let class out a little early so I got my notes photocopied for you. The homework is on the last page.'

'Thanks.' I put the notes away in my bag and hesitated. I knew the subject needed broaching sooner or later. 'Are you ready to talk about Chris and what happened on Saturday night?' I asked.

Iliana sighed and shuffled her chair closer to mine. 'I like him, I really do...'

'But?'

'But... well, we were kissing in his room and it was great and everything, then we started chatting and... he told me that he interns at IrukaTech.'

'Ah.' So Iliana's reaction was all because of her hate towards the tech giant. Everyone had to wear the Hourglass, so using their technology wasn't a deal breaker for her but working there was, it seemed, too much. She hated IrukaTech, their tracking software and almost everyone associated with the company after what had happened to her Dad. To be honest, she was only a few more drunken nights away from becoming an Irukian.

'Iliana, I know you'd rather not be associated with the company in any way, but you got over my Mum working for them, as well as Izumi being my godfather. If it's just an internship, he'll get some experience and then leave. IrukaTech – as much as you hate it – is a world leading company. A reference from them could set up Chris' career. I'm sure if you just explain to him about your Dad, he'll completely understand why you feel the way you do about IrukaTech.'

'It's just… as soon as he told me, it brought back so many bad memories.'

'I'm sure it would have. But you really like Chris, and you shouldn't give up on a relationship with him because of an internship.'

Iliana nodded, allowing a small smile to grace her face. 'Yeah. I suppose you're right. It's just an internship. He won't be there forever.'

'Exactly.'

'Do you mind if I go and see him right now? Just to explain the way I reacted?'

'Take all the time you need.'

Iliana smiled and scooted out of the library. Kai came to sit in Iliana's chair, his small smile sending my heart racing again.

Brunch?

'Brunch? As in a date?'

If you like.

CHAPTER 12

It was Friday afternoon by the time Joe finally caught up with me. He'd been stalking me all week, waiting for me outside class, following me onto the Airground. I thought I'd managed to evade him. Apparently not. The lunch rush at the café had just finished. I leant against the front counter, exhausted.

I could have helped you serve customers.

'Yeah. Because floating cups of coffee is *so* normal.'

Normal doesn't sound much fun.

I just laughed, but the sound turned into a sigh. I knew Kai wasn't real, but he felt like he was. He washed, he ate, he slept, he changed his clothes and he was mostly tangible. On that first day he appeared he couldn't hold a glass of water, but he had learnt how to clasp things quickly. People often walked through him, but I could feel him. He was real to me.

The café door opened and the smile dropped from my face when I saw Joe in the doorway, with a fading purple bruise on his jaw. Kai started to walk towards him, but I grabbed his hand and pulled him back as subtly as I could.

'Leave it,' I whispered. 'We're in a public place. He can't do much here.' Kai just nodded, not saying a word. His bright blue eyes blazing as Joe reached the counter.

'What do you want?'

'An apology for this bruise for starters.'

'You deserved that.'

'Oh, come on, that's a bit harsh.'

'I don't think so.' I was determined to stand my ground. Two more people entered the café and started to queue behind Joe.

'Oi, are you going to order something or not?' We both turned and saw Miss Leyshon by the door that led up to her flat.

'He's just a classmate, Miss Leyshon. He needed some help. I'm sorry. He's leaving now.'

She nodded, her expression grim, then turned to Joe. 'Get lost then.'

Joe scowled at her. He turned back in my direction and looked like he was going to say something else but then he changed his mind and made his way out of the café. Miss Leyshon slinked after him but stopped short of the door and scooped up some dirty dishes from a table. She dumped them on the counter and I placed them in the sink as Miss Leyshon took the next customer's order. Kai and I stood at the sink together – me washing, him drying.

That was a close one. I should have done something as soon as he walked in.

'Kai, it's fine. I don't want you punching anyone when there are people around to see.'

When I left the café at the end of my shift, Joe was waiting for me outside the corner shop next door. He smiled when he saw me and sauntered over. The look on his face was the same as when I'd first met him – sweet and charming, just wanting to help me find a classroom. But now I knew he had an unkind side too and it scared me a bit.

'I want to apologise,' he said.

'W-what?'

'I want to apologise for my behaviour. The way I acted towards that Irukian was unacceptable. You have a soft heart, Gracie. I obviously came across harshly. I've given you a bad impression and I really want to apologise to you.'

I just nodded.

'Can I see you tomorrow? We can spend some time together and I'll buy you lunch to make it up to you – no strings attached, I promise.'

Both Kai and I sighed. He was so persistent. 'Joe –'

'A couple of hours. That's all I'm asking. I think you'd really like me if you gave me a chance.'

I looked over at Kai who was standing behind Joe. The hologram was shaking his head at me. He already knew what I was going to say.

'If, and that's a big if, I spend some time with you, will you leave me alone if I ask you to?'

'Sure,' he said, his smile reassuring me.

'Okay, then.'

He grinned. 'Perfect. Meet me at the Embankment Airground tomorrow at eleven?'

I nodded and he walked off, a slight spring in his step. How could he turn from cruel to charming just like that? I started to walk home. Kai had simply disappeared without saying a word.

'I don't actually want to date Joe, but if he's going to leave me alone afterwards, then I don't mind that much. I mean, it's not ideal but... anyway, what do you think?'

There was no response.

'Kai? Kai-chan?'

No reply.

'It doesn't mean anything. I swear it doesn't. It's just to get him to leave me alone.'

Still nothing.

'When we get home, we can watch some anime together?' I offered, smiling at the air in front of me, waiting for him to manifest.

He didn't.

'I'm sorry, Kai. I really am. But if this gets Joe to back off, it'll be worth it.'

Kai didn't reply again and I walked home after my shift, alone, for the first time in ages. It felt odd not to have Kai by my side. He wasn't permanently around, he came and went during the day. But he was with me more often than he wasn't and he always appeared when I called for him.

Why was he acting like this? I knew he didn't like Joe, but this reaction seemed a little bit extreme for Kai. He was usually calm and passive. Was he... jealous? I shook that thought from my head as soon as it entered. Kai couldn't be jealous. He wasn't capable of it. Well, he was probably capable of faking it, the same way he did with everything else, like when he ate and slept. But whatever he felt wasn't real.

I unlocked the front door with my Hourglass but jumped back slightly at the sight of Macy waiting in the hallway, her head tilted as she smiled at me.

'Welcome home, Miss Thrace.'

'Er, thanks, Macy. Why are you standing by the door?'

'I have been here since you left for the café this morning. I wanted to welcome you home.'

'Right, could you, maybe, not do that in the future? It's a little creepy to be honest.'

'Of course, Miss Thrace.' Her head whirred as she took in the new information, then she stepped to one side so I could get passed. 'Will you be joining your mother for dinner? Mrs Thrace informed me that she will be home for 19:00.'

I huffed. I didn't enjoy eating with my Mum, all her complaints gave me indigestion. But it would be nice to have some company after playing a nightmare scenario if Kai wasn't going to show up. 'Yeah, alright. Shout for me when it's ready.'

'Yes, Miss Thrace.'

I walked along the hallway towards my bedroom and checked my Hourglass. Almost scenario time. I groaned as I flopped down onto my bed. Kai wasn't always around for the scenarios either, but he was usually there to comfort me afterwards. I could only hope that tonight's scenario would be easy. But whenever I wished that, it never happened. I closed my eyes and took a few deep breaths. I could do this tonight, whatever it turned out to be. Right?

Eros manifested above me, clinging to the ceiling like a spider as he smirked. 'Scenario: the android clown's body is in the shed and you need to give him a proper burial. If you don't bury him, you lose. Do you accept the scenario?'

My body instantly went cold and my heart began to pound. 'What...?' I whispered. 'You can't be serious...' My hands prickled as I dug my fingernails hard into my palms. I felt clammy and weak as the words "clown" and "burial" bashed against my ear drums. I definitely *could not* do this.

Terry appeared beside Eros. 'We're very serious. Remember when we asked what had happened to the android's body? Well, we found it. It was in your Dad's shed all along.'

I sat up, now feeling sick. They had to be lying. They had to be. I never went in there. I had no reason to. So how could they have found the clown in Dad's shed? He tinkered with Macy in there at the weekends, experimenting on her and attempting to improve her. There was no way he had found and kept the android clown. Why would he? I had to check before I accepted the scenario. I staggered from the room, then went into the kitchen where Macy was cooking.

'Macy, I need to go out in the garden for a little bit. Don't, under any circumstances, follow me.'

'Of course, Miss Thrace. I'll stay right here.'

I went outside and jogged across the cold paving stones leading to the shed at the far end of our garden. It was more like a mini hut and from the outside it only looked large enough to fit two people. How could my Dad have been hiding the android clown in there? He had told me I could come and hide in his shed if things with my Mum got too much. Why would he say that if he knew the android clown's body was in there?

I hesitated in front of the door. The garden was silent but I could hear children's screams in my head. The memories were real and still raw. I opened the door a crack and peaked into the gloom. It took a few moments for my eyes to adjust to the dim light. What I saw made me recoil and I clamped a hand over my mouth to stop the shriek that wanted to escape.

On the floor, eyes up, was the android clown. Its rainbow suit was ripped and stained with dried blood and its manic grin was still plastered across its horrible face. Its head was snapped to one side from where I had hit the blue wire at the back of its neck. There was still enough light outside to discern every little feature on the clown's body, and the more I stared at it, I realised that the body didn't flicker. This wasn't a hologram. This was real.

'I… I don't understand,' I whispered. This was the second scenario that had been real. First there was the cement in the shower cubicle, and now this. The rest of the scenarios had been entirely made up, using holograms to bring everything to life. How could the Voices do this? They had threatened to find the android clown's body before, but I thought it was just that – a threat. I didn't expect them to follow through with it or believe they *could* follow through with it.

'Psyche?'

She manifested beside me and instantly wrapped an arm around my shoulders. 'It looks horrific. It must have been scary for you at that party when that clown started attacking everyone.'

'Yeah, but… how did it get here?'

'Like Terry said. It was in here all along.'

'That can't be true… why would it be in here?'

Psyche shrugged. 'I don't know. You should ask your Dad.'

I shook my head. Terry had to be lying. The corpse of the android clown might be real, but they certainly didn't find it here. I didn't know how or where they had located it, but it hadn't been in my Dad's shed all this time.

'You need to accept or decline the scenario, Gracie,' Psyche said gently.

The yellow "Yes" and "No" buttons popped up in front of me. I hesitated as I stared at them. There was no way I would be able to start the scenario now. Mum would be home soon and Macy was still active. My neighbours would be around, too. But there was nothing in the rules to say that I couldn't accept the scenario now and not play it straight away. Terry had read the rules enough times for me to be sure. As long as I finished the scenario by sunrise, I would still win. Depending on whether or not I could actually do it. My hands were shaking so much I could hardly move them to choose the buttons. I eventually selected "Yes", then I secured the shed door and headed back to the house.

'What are you doing?' Psyche asked. 'Why aren't you digging?'

'Because I don't want anyone to see me. As long as I'm finished before the sun rises I'll win, right?'

Rule 4: The scenario can only be played between sunset and sunrise in accordance with the time displayed on the Hourglass.

Psyche gave me a wide smile. 'Yes! I knew you'd work around the rules somehow! With some scenarios it isn't possible, but I knew you'd figure it out eventually!'

I gave her a small smile. 'Thanks, Psyche. Your support means a lot.'

'But you'd rather have Kai here, right? Don't worry, I'm not offended. If I was going through all of this, I'd want Eros supporting me.'

'Eros doesn't really seem like a supportive kind of guy. But, anyway, I don't have feelings for Kai. He's not real. I just like him being here.'

The smile returned to Psyche's face. 'Whatever you say. But, real or not, Kai seems nice from what I've seen of him.'

'Why the hell are you talking to yourself outside?'

I looked up and saw Mum standing by the French doors, glaring at me in her white lab coat.

'I was just… you know… erm…'

'Get inside, you idiot. It's freezing.'

I followed her back into the kitchen where Macy was serving food. We both grabbed a plate and sat together at the small table.

'How was work today?' I asked after eating a mouthful of food. I didn't feel like eating. It didn't taste great and I didn't want anything in my stomach during the scenario. My constitution had never been the strongest. However, I also didn't want to look odd. Well, any odder than I already did after standing in the garden talking to myself.

'Fine.'

I didn't really care how her day was, but I didn't want to sit in awkward silence either. Why couldn't she put any effort in? I really needed the distraction. 'Class was good yesterday. I didn't get a chance to tell you since you were working late, but we've just started looking at screenwriting. It's really interesting and –'

'Gracie,' she said, looking at me with sharp eyes. 'I've had a rough day. We were really busy at work and I'm coming down with a cold. I really don't care how your class was. Can we have a bit of quiet, or you can take your food to your room.'

I stood up from the table but didn't grab my plate. 'That's fine with me. I wasn't hungry anyway. Why can't you even talk to me for ten minutes?'

Instead of backtracking and apologising like I hoped she would, she just stared at me indignantly. 'Stop whining, Gracie.'

Without another word, I left the kitchen and went to my bedroom. I shut the door and leant against it, then called out for Kai, but he didn't appear. I sunk down to the floor. I really needed him right now. He didn't need to appear, he could just stay in my head and reassure me that way. But I would have preferred him to manifest, so he could hug me, like he'd done after the shower cubicle scenario. Or hold my hand like he did when I felt down.

I sat against the door and listened to Mum moving around the house. Hours later, she finally unlocked the basement door and guided Macy inside. The electronic lock clicked as she shut it and I heard her footsteps on the stairs. She was finally going to bed. I put the book I'd been trying to read to one side then groaned as I stretched. I was dreading this scenario. This was so much worse than the shower cubicle scenario. I wasn't scared of water like Kai and whilst it had been slightly traumatising to fully submerge myself, the android clown was personal and would affect me more. I really needed Kai.

'Kai?' I asked again, but there was nothing. The air around me stayed silent and still. 'Psyche?'

She appeared in front of me with a smile. 'Are you ready to start?'

'Do you mean mentally or physically?'

'Why not both?'

'Physically, yes, we just need to wait for my Mum to fall asleep. Mentally, no.'

Psyche frowned in concern and knelt in front of me. 'You've got this, Gracie. I'll even help you dig if you like.'

Rule 6: The Voices can help the Player during the scenario.

'Thanks. Can you even do that? I thought you couldn't touch objects.'

Psyche smiled. 'I've been practising.' She picked up the book I had been reading to demonstrate and flicked through the pages. 'Cool, isn't it?'

I managed to smile at her. 'Come on.'

I crept out of my room and down the hallway. I could go straight into the kitchen and outside, but what if my Mum was still awake? I glanced up the stairs and tiptoed halfway up until I heard her loud muffled snores. That was quick. I didn't even know Mum snored. She really must be getting a cold.

I padded back downstairs into the kitchen, and quietly opened one of the kitchen cupboards. I took out two saucepans and held them both in one hand. I seriously doubted there would be a spade in my Dad's shed. I went over to the French doors and tried the handles, but they were locked. Thanks, Macy. Were these doors added to my Hourglass as ones I could unlock? Oh, god, I couldn't remember. If I tried and they weren't, then I could set the burglar alarm off. But I couldn't think of a reason why they wouldn't have been added. I pressed my Hourglass to the lock and the door clicked open.

'Are you having trouble, Gracie?'

'Can you keep your voice down?!' I whispered. She just smiled.

'Sorry, I'm just excited! I really like sneaking around. Eros and I used to do it all the time.' Psyche was absolutely smitten with Eros. I don't know how he did it. Looking at the two of them he was punching far above his weight.

Psyche followed me outside and we went back to the shed. My Hourglass showed 22:01. It was a lot darker now and the shadows from the moonlight crept across the small garden and along the shed door. I switched on my Hourglass' torch and took a deep breath. My hands were trembling. I willed Kai to appear but nothing happened.

I slowly turned the door handle and looked inside. The android clown was still on the floor. I ignored him and swept my torch along everything else inside the shed. There was a workbench attached to the left wall, with cables, wire cutters and pliers sat on top – but no tools to dig a hole. An old box of grass seed was on the floor in the far corner.

I shone my torch back on the android clown. Its head was lolling to one side and its eyes were exactly the same as they had been in the scenario I'd played the day before I'd started university – one glass lens smashed and the other with the fake ball loose inside the socket. I forced myself to look away from its face and at the rest of its body. I was about the same size as the clown now, give or take a few inches, so the grave would have to be about as long as me. Surely it wouldn't have to be that deep, though? Two feet, at most. It's not like any animals were going to dig up the corpse of an android. I shivered at the thought of calling it a "corpse". The android was real, but it had never been a person. The word "corpse" felt wrong and too gruesome. I shut the shed again, then turned and handed Psyche one of the saucepans. 'We're digging with these.'

She took it from me and frowned. 'It might take a while…'

'We don't really have a choice. Come on, let's dig behind the shed, so we won't have to carry the android far and Mum won't see.'

Psyche watched as I marked out an area of grass that was roughly the same length as my body, then we both started to dig. Luckily the ground was soft and the soil moved easily but it was slow going and my hand started to hurt after only five minutes. I threw the saucepan in frustration and started to pull at the soil with my hands. I kept glancing up at the neighbours' windows to check no one was watching.

After three hours, we were done, and I sat back with my hands on my knees, exhausted. I had dirt on my face, in my hair, up my fingernails and all over my clothes. Psyche still looked immaculate. Her chiton was squeaky clean and none of her curls were out of place. I smiled as I thought of what Kai would have looked like if he had helped me. He would have been smeared with mud and probably would have thrown some at me.

'Gracie? Are you ready to put the android in?'

I nodded. 'Yeah, just give me a minute to catch my breath.'

I listened as Psyche's chiton rustled behind me and then she stopped. When she didn't move again, I turned around and saw she was right behind me, her hands outstretched, as if ready to push me into the grave.

'Er, Psyche? What are you doing?'

'Oh! I was just going to give you a massage. Your shoulders must hurt after all that digging,' she said with a smile.

'I'll be fine. Come on, let's get the android.'

I got up and went over to the shed, shining my torch back on the android. The metal was rusty and flaking away. It looked like rotting human flesh, but at least it didn't smell, despite the dried blood on the rainbow suit. The clown still made bile rise up in my throat. I didn't want to touch it.

I knelt down and slowly brushed my hand against the android's arm. It felt no different to Macy – perhaps a little colder, but it was the same. Except that Macy hadn't tried to kill me. My hands started to shake again but I ignored them and hooked one of the android's arms over my shoulder. Its head lolled against my neck and I squeaked a little as I dropped it. The body clanged as it hit the shed floor and I immediately looked over at my neighbour's house. A light flicked on at a first-floor window. I held my breath and I waited until the light went off a few moments later.

I picked up the android again, ignoring how the fake hair scratched my neck, then whispered for Psyche to come over. She put the other arm over her shoulder and together we dragged the metal body across to the shallow grave. I carefully unwrapped the arm from around my shoulder, but Psyche let the arm just drop from her and the android jangled as it fell into the grave.

'Psyche!' I whispered, but it was too late. The light at the neighbours' first-floor window turned on and the curtains moved as someone tried to peep out. I felt Psyche's hands on my back.

'Quick! There's no time!'

She pushed me into the grave and I fell down hard onto the clown's metal chest. I wanted to scramble up and get out, but I forced myself to stay completely still as I stared into the eyes of the horrible android. It was still holding the same frenzied look as all those years ago at the birthday party. Its metal teeth glinted in the moonlight and reflected my petrified face. Its sharp fingers dug into my hips. Androids these days had fake flesh and nails covering their hands to make them appear more human, but the first models didn't. Their fingers stuck out, sharp and shiny as quicksilver, capable of drawing blood. Capable of slitting the throats of children. I shut my eyes as I felt myself start to shake again. I didn't want to remember, but the memories I'd tried so hard to hide came rushing back and all I could hear were screams as the clown ran around Anna's back garden, killing all of my friends.

'Gracie?' I sat up, panting, and saw Psyche knelt beside the grave. Her eyes flickered with concern as she stared at me. 'Gracie... you're crying. And there's blood on your waist... oh, god, you're bleeding.'

I shook my head with a sniff. 'It's fine. Have they gone back to bed?'

Psyche nodded, a lot less chipper than she usually was. 'I think so. The light's gone off. I'm sorry about pushing you in, I didn't know what else to do. There was no time to hide anywhere else.'

'It's fine. I'm fine. Could you just go and get the grass seed from the shed?'

'Of course.'

She got up, and when her hologram went inside the shed, I keeled over in the grave and threw up on the android clown. When I had finished retching, I climbed out with shaking legs and sat down on the cold grass. I wanted nothing more than to run inside and go to sleep, but I still wasn't finished. Together, Psyche and I pushed the soil back into the grave and then I sprinkled the grass seed. Mum and Macy would definitely notice the massive patch of soil if they came out in the garden, but it was done. Hopefully the shed would hide most of it. The fake confetti was thrown at me and Psyche smiled as she spoke.

'Congratulations. You won the scenario. You gained 340XP. You are now Level 57. You have until the 31st December to reach Level 75.'

There was no feeling of relief, like there used to be when a scenario finished. I was too tired and scared. 'Doesn't Eros usually do that?' I asked weakly. Psyche's smile widened.

'Yes, but I told him I would do it tonight. You looked like you could do without him harassing you.'

'Thanks. And thank you for helping me. I really needed it.'

'It's no problem. Just call me when you need me. Goodnight, Gracie.'

I watched her disappear, then hobbled back to the house with the two dirty saucepans. My whole body ached. I was exhausted. I locked the French doors behind me, dumped the saucepans in the sink after giving them a quick rinse, then limped back to my bedroom and collapsed onto the bed. I should have showered, or at least changed my clothes, but I didn't want to. I half expected Kai to be waiting in my bedroom to greet me. He could have made that scenario so much easier just by being there with me. Now I didn't even know if I would see him again.

I squeezed my eyes shut as I felt them fill with tears. I just needed someone to hold me, whether it was Kai, Iliana, or my Dad. Hell, I'd even settle for Macy. Just someone who would tell me it was alright and the nightmare scenarios would go away one day and that I wouldn't always feel this alone and isolated.

No one came.

CHAPTER 13

The next morning, I didn't get up until half past ten. My eyes were tired and crusty, and when I finally forced myself to look in the mirror, there was dirt all over my face and arms. I wiped myself down with a flannel instead of showering, then got dressed. I found my oldest pair of jeans and a plain, creased t-shirt. I stared at myself as I threw my hair into a ponytail. I looked an absolute mess, even without the dirt on me. My face was puffy from crying last night and the bags under my eyes looked worse than ever. I just wanted to stay at home and feel sorry for myself, but I couldn't. All I had to do was spend an hour or so with Joe and then he would leave me alone for good. I just had to get through today. I could do this. Even if I was still thoroughly shaken.

I left my room and went into the kitchen. I needed a glass of water – my breath stank from throwing up last night. Mum was at the kitchen table sipping a cup of tea. She heard me come in and I stood frozen in the doorway.

'Where on earth are you going?' she asked.

'Out with a friend.'

'Could you at least put some clean clothes on?'

'Nope.'

Mum sighed. 'Well, when you get back, will you give them to Macy to wash?'

'Why do you care?'

'I don't really, but you look a state. If anyone we know sees you wandering around London like that, what would they think of you? Or me?'

'I don't know. Why does it matter?'

My Mum glared at me but didn't reply. Instead, she stared out of the French doors, looking toward the grave-sized patch of soil behind the shed, but she didn't say anything. With a shrug, I grabbed a glass and filled it up with water.

'Where's Macy?'

'Cleaning the bathroom. Since you never do it.'

'You don't do it either and bathroom cleaning is in Macy's job description.'

She glared at me again. 'Have a nice time, Gracie,' she said dismissively.

I put the glass back in the sink, then went out into the hall and grabbed one of Dad's old army jackets from the coat rack. I slammed the front door behind me and began walking to Caledonian Road Airground Station. 'Kai?' I asked hopefully when I was halfway there. Nope, still nothing.

'Sorry, I'm late,' I said as I walked over to Joe. He was leaning against the Airground shelter, arms folded across his chest and a grumpy pout on his face as he checked his Hourglass.

Joe managed to smile. 'It's fine. You're here now and that's what matters.' His brown eyes looked me up and down. 'Come on, I thought we could go to the National Gallery before lunch.'

We walked up the cramped Villiers Street, a place that I always loved coming to with my Dad. Shops and cafés were stuffed into every available space. When I was younger, there had been a lady at the top of the street who sold flowers and when she saw Dad and I walk by she would always give me a snapdragon, since she knew they were my favourite.

We went across Trafalgar Square, which was as busy as always, and Joe rambled away to himself as I stared at Nelson's Column. Security androids were on duty next to the lions, making sure no one climbed on them. There were a few kids playing by the fountains, splashing their parents. Leaving Joe to walk up to the gallery on his own, I went over to the fountains and put my hands in the water. Kai had to come now. He couldn't stay away. He had to come back.

'Gracie?' I turned around and saw Joe waiting for me with both eyebrows raised.

'Sorry… my hands felt sticky. I think I might have touched some chewing gum on the Airground.'

He nodded and I pulled my hands out of the water. 'Right. Let's go then.'

We climbed up the concrete steps to the National Gallery, letting the security androids search us before they let us in – VIRENT were larger than ever. Joe walked into the first room, smiling as he looked at each of the paintings. He seemed very relaxed in this environment. 'Let's go to Room 34. There's something really cool in there.'

I nodded, following him. It was disturbing how he could switch between happy and creepy so quickly. And he liked paintings? For someone who was into Electronic Engineering and Sports Science, he didn't strike me as the kind of person who enjoyed coming to an art gallery. We entered Room 34 with its high ceilings and intricate arches, the paintings on the wall from the 18th and 19th Centuries. In the centre of the room was a set of leather settees and Joe bounced down onto one. I sat on the same settee but a good few inches away.

'Do you recognise these settees?' he asked with a grin.

'Should I?'

'They were in *Crimson Bird*! Have you seen it?'

'The James Bond film? No. It's so old. Didn't it come out in 2030 or something?'

'2032, actually. Have you seen any of the more recent ones?'

'Ermmm…' I bit my lip as I thought. 'My Dad made me watch *Execution* with him last year.'

'What did you think?' Joe asked, grinning like a little boy – his mood swings really were freaky.

'The storyline was terrible. The action was good but there was hardly any plot to it. Although, I suppose that's what it's all about. A load of action scenes strung together with a tenuous plot.'

Joe's grin disappeared and a disappointed look flashed across his face. He stood up abruptly and went to look at the paintings. I stayed on the *Crimson Bird* settee and played games on my Hourglass until Joe had finished. He was smiling again when he came back and tried to take hold of my hand as we left the gallery. I stuffed it into my pocket, not wanting him to get any ideas.

'Fancy some lunch?' he asked.

I shrugged. I wasn't all that hungry. But it was probably a good idea I ate something considering what had happened last night, even if that meant I had to eat with Joe. 'I don't want much.'

His smile dropped. 'I was thinking we could go to a restaurant.'

I shot him a hard look. 'Let's just get a sandwich,' I said firmly.

Joe sighed but agreed and we bought two sandwiches from the nearest shop before making our way back down Villiers Street. His left hand swung in between our bodies and I watched out of the corner of my eye. Every so often it twitched, as if he was stopping himself from grabbing hold of me in some way. I stuffed my hands in my pockets again and stepped to the side slightly to increase the space between us. My whole body was tense.

Joe turned to look at me, but instead of frowning and asking why I was clearly so edgy, he surprised me with another smile. 'We should go on the London Eye.'

'Can I go home after that?'

He nodded. There was a hint of a glower in his eyes, but he said nothing.

We walked past Big Ben and over Westminster Bridge, then continued along the riverfront together. Both human and android street performers were entertaining people, but instead of watching them, I stared into the murky water. Kai had first appeared as a hologram when I had travelled across the Thames. Where had he gone now? Joe and I got in line for the London Eye and when it was our turn to climb into a levitating pod, Joe held out a hand to help me up. I swatted it away and jumped into the pod by myself.

'I'm not six,' I told him with a glare.

He just smirked. 'I like women who are feisty.'

I ignored the sexist comment and walked over to the windows. I had seen this view of London many times – I didn't mind it all that much, but I just wished Kai was with me, not Joe. I wished it was Kai who had picked me up, taken me out, or just tried to make me smile in some way. I scrunched up my eyes, refusing to cry whilst Joe was in the vicinity.

I walked around the pod, still as amazed as I had been when I was a little girl at how the pods would levitate and rotate in a perfect circle. As much as I hated what technology had done to society, I would always stare in wonder at the floating London Eye.

As I walked around some more, I saw that in the pod below me was Maida from my Creative Writing course. Her hair, face and body looked immaculate as she stared out of the window, her eyes not moving and her body not reacting to any of the children around her who wanted to see the view from her position in the pod. She should have noticed those children behind her and she should have seen me looking at her. Why wasn't her third eye working? Well, if she actually was an android and had a third eye. I was still unsure.

Joe came over to me and I crossed my arms over my chest so he couldn't attempt to hold my hand. But he persisted, slowly following me around the pod for the full revolution. After half an hour, we finally got off the London Eye, then headed back to Waterloo and got on the Airground.

'Is this charade finally over?' I asked him as we floated through the air towards Leicester Square Airground Station.

His lips curled into a smug grin. 'Almost. We'll get off at Caledonian Road and then I'll walk you home.'

I grimaced. I didn't want him to know where I lived, but I realised that I had no choice now. I couldn't lead him in a massive circle around Holloway like I tried to last time. We changed onto the Piccadilly Line at Leicester Square, then got off at Caledonian Road. As we walked to Hungerford Road, I kept my hands as far away from Joe as possible and nodded along as he jabbered about classic action films and how he wanted to recreate some of the gadgets in Electronic Engineering class.

'Is this it?' Joe asked when we came to a stop outside my house after what seemed the longest walk in my life.

'Yep. Bye.' I walked towards the front door but Joe grabbed my arm.

'At the end of a date, you're supposed to kiss.' He leant in to kiss my cheek but I stepped away from him and held out my hand. With a sigh, he kissed my knuckles instead then smiled at me. 'Until our next date, Gracie.'

'I wouldn't count on it.'

He just laughed as he walked away and I pressed my Hourglass against the front door, electronically locking it behind me when I was safely inside. Once I was sure the lock had clicked into place, I sat down in the hall and leant my head against the wall. Could things get any worse?

CHAPTER 14

I went into the kitchen. Macy had her hands in the sink, but she wasn't washing anything – just staring out of the window in front of her. She turned around and smiled when her third eye saw me.

'Welcome back, Miss Thrace. How was your day?'

'Bloody awful. And I'm starving. Could you make me a bowl of noodles, please?'

'Certainly. Would you care for a banana milkshake to go with it?'

'A glass of normal plain milk is just fine.'

Macy lifted her metal hands out of the sink and went over to the cooker.

'Macy, dry your hands first.'

'Well done, Miss Thrace! Kitchen safety must always come first.'

I groaned – I hated it when she used that phrase. 'Could you bring it to my room when it's ready, please?' She nodded and her neck crackled with static.

In my bedroom, I slipped off my shoes and let my Dad's army jacket drop to the floor, then I collapsed onto my bed and closed my eyes. The last 24 hours had been so horrible. I just wanted Kai back.

How was your date?

I sat up and saw Kai by the side of my bed, arms crossed and not looking impressed. 'Kai-chan!' I jumped up and tackled him to the ground in a hug, the Japanese hologram coughing beneath me.

Jesus Christ! Get off me!

I sat up, unable to stop smiling. 'I didn't think you had Jesus in Japan.'

Racist.

I carried on hugging him and felt his arms wrap around me. I tucked my head into his neck and hummed, glad that he was back. 'Why did you leave?' I mumbled. 'I needed you. I really needed you. Last night… I had to bury the android clown… and you weren't there.' I looked up at him through my tears. 'Why did you leave?'

Kai cupped my cheek with one of his hands. *I'm sorry. I was jealous.*

I leant back then, letting his fingers slip away from my face. 'You were jealous?'

He nodded. *I always get jealous when I see you with Joe.*

He reached to caress my cheek but I pulled away at the last second. 'You shouldn't be getting jealous, Kai.'

Why shouldn't I? I like you and I don't want you going on dates with other people.

I shook my head and moved towards the window. It was beginning to rain. 'You can't like me.'

I know that Eros and the others have made your self-esteem low, but —

'It's not about that… you're not real…' I whispered. 'Your feelings… aren't real. All day, I haven't been able to stop thinking about you, but what's the point? You're not real…' My tears began to fall and I leant against the window ledge as I cried. Kai wrapped his arms around me from behind, but I pushed them away. 'Don't, Kai. There's no point. You won't ever be real.'

Kai placed his hands on my shoulders and turned me around to face him. His brow was furrowed and his lips were pursed. He would have looked angry if it weren't for the tears in his beautiful blue eyes.

Why does it matter so much?

'Because we can't be together if you're not real! I don't plan on being like this my whole life, whatever *this* actually is. As soon as I'm better…when I stop hearing voices, you'll be gone.' It was useless. I didn't even know what I was saying. I couldn't tell anyone what was wrong with me and not even the internet could give enough answers to diagnose me. How was I supposed to get better when I didn't even know what I was curing?

Then stay like this!

I shook my head, my tears falling faster now. 'I can't… my head… it hurts so much…' As I spoke, the buzzing seemed to get louder and I sunk to the floor, crying harder. Kai sat next to me, his expression a lot softer.

I'm sorry. I shouldn't have said that. I don't understand how much it hurts you, but I see how scared you are every time you play a scenario. I want you to get better, I really do, but I want to be with you as well.

He lifted up one of my hands and held it to his chest, where his heart should have been, but I felt no beat beneath my fingers. His chest didn't even rise and fall from breathing.

I know I don't seem real but everything I've ever told you has been real. About my Aunty and my housekeeper and my feelings for you. I'm not making it up and I'm not just saying this to convince you to be with me. My feelings are real and I like you, Gracie.

My lips trembled as I wiped away my tears. 'I like you too, but… what happens if I do get better? I'll never see you again.' The thought brought on a bought of fresh tears but Kai hugged me before they could fall.

I'm not going to pretend that everything will be okay because I have no idea if it will be. But we'll find a way to be together, even when you're better.

'Kai… that won't be possible…'

He pulled out of the hug and looked at me, his falling tears making his bright blue eyes shimmer like sunlight bouncing off a lake of sapphires.

Yes, it will be. My memories of my Aunty and my housekeeper can't come from nothing. I must have had a past, a life. Even if I don't look like this, parts of me have to be real.

I nodded. 'I suppose… yeah. It's plausible.'

A look of relief came over Kai's face.

Does that mean we can try and be together?

I nodded and he smiled. He looked happier than I had ever seen him before. 'But we take it slow, okay? Because you're not real… or might not be real… I think it'll be for the best if we don't rush into anything.'

Kai beamed. He looked relieved. *That's more than I can ask of you.*

I sniffed and wiped away my tears, then reached out to Kai and touched his cheek with my fingers, my hands shaking as I felt the moisture on my skin. Kai was right. The memories he had must have come from somewhere. Even though he didn't have a heartbeat, his body warmed up mine whenever he held me and he could cry real tears. That had to mean something. We both stood up just as Macy entered the room.

'Here is your milk, Miss Thrace. Your noodles shall be ready shortly.' The android glanced at me, her purple eyes looked confused and quizzical. 'Have you been crying, Miss Thrace? Would you like me to call Mrs Thrace for you?'

I shook my head. 'I'm fine. I'm just… happy,' I said with a sniff.

'Would you like me to tell you a joke? It will make you cry with laughter once again.'

'No.'

'What time did the man go to the dentist? Tooth hurt-y.'

'Please leave, Macy.'

'Yes, Miss Thrace.'

She retreated from the room, not bothering to shut the door behind her. Kai and I sat down on the bed together, but I kept my eyes on the duvet, not wanting to look at him in case I got embarrassed. What were we now?

Gracie?

I nodded and sniffed again. 'Sorry. I just feel a little… awkward.'

Don't be. It's just the same as before. How was the date?

'Awful. I wish you had been there today. And last night.'

Me, too. I'm sorry.

'It's fine,' I told him with a shrug. He was here now and that's what mattered.

I wanted to take you on your first date.

I smiled. 'You did. We went to that party together.'

That was an awful first date. Eros and Terry upset you, Iliana was in a state, then Joe hurt you and we had to take that Irukian to the Underground.

'Well, I enjoyed it because you were with me.'

You're so cheesy.

Macy entered the room carrying a steaming bowl along with a pair of chopsticks and placed them next to the glass of milk. 'Your noodles are ready, Miss Thrace. Is there anything else I can get for you?'

'Yes, actually,' I said, glancing at Kai, 'could you bring another pair of chopsticks? I want to see if I can eat noodles with two sets of chopsticks in the same hand.'

Macy left the room again and Kai started chuckling.

'What's so funny?'

I understand that those chopsticks are for me, but now you've said it, you have to try and eat the noodles in the way you told Macy you would.

I grabbed my pillow and hit him hard, causing feathers to fly as his hologram fell to the floor.

Are you going to apologise for that?

'Nope.'

Kai grabbed my legs and pulled me down next to him, then brought me into his arms.

I've missed you, he whispered.

'I missed you, too.'

REPORT ON PARTICIPANT 1 OUT OF 4: Miss Gracie Thrace

04/10/2047	After a week of avoiding advances, Miss Thrace agrees to go on a date.
05/10/2047	The date with Miss Thrace is unsuccessful. She didn't seem to enjoy it, nor has she disclosed any information about the voices she hears.
	She is unreceptive to romantic advances – perhaps Kai's placement has worked. More data is required to draw this conclusion.

CHAPTER 15

'You did what?!'

'I went out for lunch with Joe, and no, I don't want to talk about it.' Iliana, Kai and I were in a café on New Oxford Street, sipping hot chocolates and catching up for the first time in ages.

'You can't go on your first ever date and then not tell me about it!'

It wasn't her first date, Kai said, glaring at my best friend. Obviously, Iliana didn't hear him.

'There isn't much to tell. He dragged me around London and wasn't particularly interested in anything other than James Bond. I said I didn't want another date with him after he walked me home. I had a terrible time and I don't want to talk about it.'

Iliana sighed and leant back in her chair. 'Alright. But he'll probably tell Chris what happened and Chris is going to tell me if I ask him. He's been on a secondment and got back late last night.' On cue, Iliana's Hourglass beeped and she accepted the call on speakerphone. 'Hi, Chris!'

'Hey babe. I was wondering if you want to come round for a bit. I've finished work for the day, so I'm free. But only if you're free! Don't feel like you have to come over, I don't mind.'

'Don't worry, I'll be there soon.' She ended the call and glanced at me. 'Sorry. I need to go.'

'Yeah, I guessed that.'

Iliana just smiled and stood up, then walked around to my side of the table to hug me. 'I'll see you before class tomorrow. Meet at your house?'

'Sure. Have a nice time with Chris.'

She bounded out of the café and Kai slid into her seat. Ever since our argument about whether he was real and could actually have proper feelings, Kai had been around more or less all of the time – joining me for showers and sharing my bed. He was completely making up for my ruined Saturday with Joe and the scenario he had missed.

Gracie? It's sunset in a minute.

'What?!' I shouted, then smiled awkwardly as a couple at the next table turned to look at me. I glanced at my Hourglass – 18:07. Sunset was at eight minutes past. 'Let's go,' I whispered.

I grabbed my jacket and left my unfinished hot chocolate on the table. We'd only got two steps out the door when the buzzing started and Eros spoke.

'Scenario: the video game character, Il-gob, is in London. In order to win the scenario, you must collect all seven sins. If you let Il-gob catch you, or if you don't collect the sins by sunrise, you will lose. Do you accept the scenario?'

I glared at the hovering "Yes" and "No" buttons. Who the hell was Il-gob? I tentatively selected "Yes" even though I had no idea what I was agreeing to. The buttons vanished and I turned to Kai.

'Who's Il-gob?' I asked, ignoring all of the New Oxford Street shoppers who were staring at me.

He's the antagonist of a Korean video game.

'Have you played it?'

Yes.

'But you're Japanese.'

And you're a racist. He sighed. *Look, you really shouldn't have accepted the scenario. Il-gob is… not very nice, to say the least.*

'I don't particularly have a choice. I have to play it eventually.'

Rule 5: If the player continues to refuse the scenario, they will be forced to play it half an hour before sunrise.

I grabbed Kai's hand and pulled him down an alleyway, away from the shopper's puzzled looks. 'Tell me about Il-gob.'

He's a Korean angel of death. Well, I guess devil would be more appropriate. He comes for people who commit any of the seven deadly sins. The game makes you commit each of the sins so, as the plot progresses, you have to continually avoid him.

'And if he catches you?'

He helps you to kill yourself. I think the game was made to try and combat suicide in South Korea, to show how the people you leave behind feel.

'It doesn't sound like a very good game.' Given recent scenarios, he might actually make me kill myself.

Gracie, look at me.

I did as Kai asked. There was no point in hiding the tears in my eyes from him. He could hear them trapped in my voice. 'I'm scared.'

I… I don't think Eros and Terry will be able to make you kill yourself.

But Kai clearly wasn't convinced. He took my hand in his and gave it a gentle squeeze.

We're going to be fine. I'll help you.

I nodded and blinked away my tears. 'What do we need to do to win?'

The sins are diary entries from the Hwaseong serial killer. He was never caught, and the diary entries are fake, but they each detail how the murderer engaged with the seven deadly sins when he was active. In the game, you play as a detective and you gradually collect each of the diary entries as you commit the sin, trying to find out what happened to women the killer murdered. Then Il-gob comes for you. The game takes ages to complete, probably about three days if you don't get stuck, eat, or sleep whilst playing, but it seems like we need to get all of the diary entries at once for this scenario. We need to start moving, though. Il-gob can teleport, so we need to be looking in all directions at all times.

I nodded and followed Kai's instructions. 'Say if you see anything,' I said.

Okay. Which way are we going first?

'Well, the Voices like everyone to hear me talking to myself, so not in Holloway or anywhere else that's quiet. It has to be Central London.'

Eros manifested then, clapping his hands. 'Well done. You're starting to get the hang of this.'

'Even so, do you really expect me to find all the sins? Central London doesn't mean two streets. It's huge,' I said, 'it'll take me forever.' I was astounded how the Voices had managed to set this up. Hiding holograms around my house was one thing but hiding them all over London was another. How was it possible?

Eros grunted and something manifested in his hands. 'Here's a map. The locations of the sins are all marked on there. But there are no street names, just landmarks. I'm not going to make it too easy for you, am I?'

I took the hologram from him. 'Thank you.'

Psyche appeared beside her husband and smiled at me sweetly. 'Would you like my assistance, Gracie?'

'No offence, Psyche, but you weren't brilliant last time when I asked you to look out for someone. And I don't fancy being pushed over if you panic. I think I'll just stick with Kai.'

The smile melted from her face and she disappeared. Eros immediately floated closer to me. 'Didn't you listen to me before? I told you not to upset my wife again.' I closed my eyes, preparing for him to hit me, but nothing happened.

Leave her, Eros. She can't help it if your wife is incompetent.

Eros slapped Kai instead of me, then he disappeared into my head.

'Are you okay?' I whispered, turning to look at Kai.

Yeah. It didn't hurt that much. Rather me than you.

I smiled, but it turned into a frown when Terry appeared in front of me with his teeth gritted. 'I told you that Psyche wasn't to be trusted.'

I told her too.

'She only glared at me. That doesn't mean she's going to murder me in my sleep.'

'I wouldn't count on that,' Terry warned, before vanishing back into my head.

Where to first?

Kai peered at the map and I took a closer look. It was the size of an Orca but as thin as tracing paper, covered with bright lines and dots. I could see my hands underneath. Monuments were marked, including – the London Eye, Tower 142, Nelson's Column, Marble Arch, the British Museum and St. Paul's. There was a star on the map, which I presumed to be my current location, and there were seven dots. Two were clustered together and another four were more spread out and almost on the edge of the small map. The last one was moving.

'Ermmm… well, there seems to be two around here, but the map is so small that I'm not sure where. So, let's just head this way.' I pointed to where New Oxford Street and Tottenham Court Road met. We made our way along the bustling street, keeping close together and looking every which way.

'Any sign of Il-gob yet?' I asked.

Nope.

'You don't sound very scared. Weren't you scared of him when you played the game?'

Well, yes, but he's not real. Why would I be scared of him?

I sighed as we continued to walk. 'I know you're just pretending to be brave so I'll feel better.'

Kai paused. *And what if I am?*

'Then I'll say "thank you".'

Gracie! Look!

I swivelled around, eyes scanning the entire street, unsure what I was looking for. 'What is it?'

Outside the theatre.

I turned to look at the Dominion. The off-white coloured building was already lit up, its name outlined in a brilliant silvery glow and its bedazzled display shimmering alongside the flickering lampposts.

'I still don't see it.'

On the theatre doors.

I crossed the road and saw an orange hologram stuck to the doorframe. I ripped it off to get a closer look. The hologram seemed to be stuck to an actual piece of paper, but it was too bright for me to see the original. The hologram showed some Korean characters.

'Do you know what it says?'

Yes. Something in Korean.

'Oh, wow. Thanks, Kai.'

No problem.

I looked at the two dots that had been clustered close together on the map. One had now disappeared. I could see that the other sin seemed to be roughly back in the direction we had come from.

'We've missed one.'

Kai glanced at the map but frowned a moment later. *I don't know why I'm bothering to look. I don't know anywhere in London.*

I couldn't help smiling as I scanned the map again. The next nearest sin seemed to be near Marble Arch. 'Let's get that one later.'

We carried on down Oxford Street, bustling in and out between the shoppers until we got to Marble Arch. There were some school kids messing around on the edge of Hyde Park amongst the android dog walkers, but there didn't seem to be anyone who looked like they should have been in a video game. I squinted as I glanced towards the Park and smiled when I saw an orange hologram curled around a wooden bench slat. I led Kai towards the bench and detached the page.

What's underneath the hologram?

'I don't know. You can read them later when the scenario's over and the holograms disappear.' I folded up the paper and put it in my pocket. My jeans started to glow slightly orange.

Where next? Kai asked as he gently took my hand in his.

I brought the map up closer to my face, but it didn't become any clearer. There was another sin a short walk from where we were. 'I think we should head into Marylebone.'

Is Baker Street in Marylebone?

I nodded, realising that was probably where the sin was. Eros had purposefully picked busy places, and Baker Street would be one of them. 'Yeah. You like Sherlock Holmes?'

Of course. Who doesn't?

'My Mum.'

Kai sniggered. *I should have guessed.*

We walked the rest of the way in silence but I kept checking the map and scanning the crowds for Il-gob. Not that I knew what I was looking for. We turned onto the infamous road and I tugged on Kai's hand.

'We're here.' He didn't reply. 'Kai-chan? What's wrong?'

Gracie… He's here, too.

I glanced over Kai's shoulder and saw a man at the other end of Baker Street. He was about my height and dressed in weird robe-like clothing with an oddly shaped hat, all completely black. His face was pure white, like porcelain, and riddled with cracks – as if his head had been dropped and the shattered pieces crudely glued back together. Water fell from his fingers and the dripping sound resonated on the busy pavement. His hologram flickered, so I knew he wasn't real, but I still felt my heart leap into my throat and my adrenaline start to flow. I turned back around and took a deep breath, trying to calm myself down a little.

'That's not good.'

No, it's good. If he's here, it means we're near a sin.

As Kai finished speaking, I spotted an orange hologram stuck to a lamppost right outside the Sherlock Holmes Museum. I let go of Kai's hand and ran towards the sin, ripping it off the lamppost. Tourists were outside the museum waiting for their twilight pre-Halloween tour to start. They stared at me curiously, but I had no other choice. I stuffed the hologram into my pocket and stayed still. Kai bumped into my back a few seconds later.

Did you get the sin?

'Yeah. Where's Il-gob?'

About ten metres away.

I found one of Kai's hands and took it in mine, holding it tight even though we were both shaking.

I'm not trying to rush you or anything, but Il-gob is literally a few metres away from my face.

I started running – pulling Kai behind me – down Baker Street and cutting on to Melcombe Street towards the train station. I ignored all of the businessmen and women who stared at me as I barged past. Out of breath, I dragged Kai into Marylebone Station and sat down on the nearest available bench.

'Can you see him anywhere?' I asked as I gulped in air.

No. I think we lost him. Are you okay? Still scared?

I nodded. 'Not as much as I thought I would be, but yes.'

You're doing fine. Don't worry. I'll be here the whole time.

Then he leaned in and kissed me on the cheek. I stared at him and when he registered the surprise on my face, he furrowed his brow.

Sorry. Bad timing.

'It's okay,' I said with a smile. I could handle a kiss on the cheek. I looked back at the map. The star had moved close to another dot, so we were near another sin. It was probably in the train station somewhere. I glanced around the waiting area. I had seen pictures of what Marylebone Station had been like before the bombings. There had been shops lining the edges of each wall and people running to catch their trains. Pigeons flew around and the escalators that led to the Underground had been busy. I had never seen it like that. Now, only half the shops remained and a brown slab of concrete across the floor indicated where the escalators were once in use. Some of the ground was patterned with scorch marks from the VIRENT bomb in 2025. The station was still busy. Trains left and arrived every other minute, but no one hung around for long.

What are those? Kai asked as he pointed to the wall next to the ticket office.

'Train timetables. To tell you where and when the trains are going.'

One of them is glowing orange.

I looked a little closer and shook my head. 'You're imagining things.'

Kai tutted as he walked off and I watched as he sorted through a stack of timetables from London Marylebone to Oxford. He pulled out an orange paper from the back and turned around with a grin.

Told you.

'Shut up.' I took the crumpled poster from him. It was bigger than a train timetable and I still couldn't read what it said beneath the Korean writing. I put it in my pocket with the others. 'We've almost got half. It's been a little too easy so far.'

And now you've jinxed it. Where to next?

I glanced at the map. Four dots had vanished and the remaining ones were around Trafalgar Square and Tower Hill. The last dot was still moving, this time on the other side of the Thames. 'The one in the Trafalgar Square area seems the closest.'

We left the station and got on the Marylebone Airground, where we took the Bakerloo Line down to Charing Cross. When we got off, instead of heading towards Trafalgar Square, Kai darted into Charing Cross Station and I followed him inside. Charing Cross still had all its shops open since it hadn't been bombed. Kai was at the ticket office, rifling through the train timetable stacks. By the time I reached him, he had gone through them all apart from the pile labelled Charing Cross to Hastings. 'Do you really think that'll work again?'

It's worth a try.

I stood next to him, pretending to look at the Gillingham stack that he had already been through, then smiled when he didn't pull out a diary entry. 'Told you. Nice try, genius.'

Shut up.

'Come on. Trafalgar Square. That seems like the most obvious place.' He nodded and we made our way down the Strand and across to Trafalgar Square.

He brought you here, didn't he?

'If you're talking about Joe, then yes. I don't particularly want to talk about it.'

I want to bring you here on a date, so you'll forget about that day and only have good memories of this place.

Kai squeezed my hand and I smiled. Going on a proper date with Kai would be amazing. It would be even better if he could be really there with me, in the flesh. My happy thoughts ceased when Il-gob appeared in front of us. He was a good distance away, but I could hear the water dripping from his fingers. Even though I couldn't see his eyes beneath the hat he was wearing, I knew he was staring straight at me. My grip on Kai's hand tightened and he squeezed my fingers slightly.

What's wrong?

I tried to reply, but I couldn't get any words out. My mouth felt like it was filled with cotton wool. Kai turned and his blue eyes widened when he saw Il-gob. Without having to say a word to each other, we ran all the way up Charing Cross Road until we had reached Leicester Square. As we moved further away from Il-gob, the cotton wool feeling faded. When it had disappeared completely, I pulled on Kai's hand and we came to a stop.

Are you okay? Kai asked when he got his breath back.

'I'll be fine.'

We'll need to go back to Trafalgar Square later, right?

I looked down at my map and the star seemed to be dancing right on the edge of wherever the sin was located. 'Maybe. Let's look around here first, though. It's still pretty busy.'

Despite the crowds, Leicester Square was always a place I found pretty. It had tall buildings, all off-white in colour and mostly modern in design. It also had a statue in the centre surrounded by little fountains that had been turned off for the night. We looked around, checking each of the trees to see if they had a sin pinned to them, but we found nothing. 'Let's move on.'

Kai nodded in agreement and we re-joined hands. We continued on towards Covent Garden. When we arrived, it wasn't as busy as it usually was during the day, but there were still people milling around the menu boards outside restaurants, deciding where to go for dinner.

It doesn't seem that busy. The Voices wouldn't have put a sin here.

I referred to the map and smiled when I saw the star and dot were aligned now. It had to be around here somewhere. 'Then let's find where it is busy.' There was a burst of string music from the market hall so I took Kai inside. The entire Northern Hall was packed with people watching a string quartet and opera singer perform. 'This is exactly where they would hide it.'

Kai let go of my hands and stood next to me, both of us scanning the area. After a moment, Kai pointed next to the band where a young man in his early 20s was handing out a stack of leaflets. One of them, towards the bottom of the pile, was glowing orange.

You go up and talk to him about the band and I'll try and slip that page out of his hands without him noticing.

'Or we could just wait until he gets down to that one and make sure he hands it to me.'

We'll be here all night if we do that.

Kai took off, weaving through the crowd towards the young man. I followed him, knowing I wouldn't have been able to convince him otherwise. I smiled as the young man approached me and handed me a leaflet.

'Oh, thank you! The band's great! Are you part of it?'

'Nah, I just help out, but my brother plays.'

He pointed towards the cellist and I nodded, trying to make sure that my smile didn't look false. Out of the corner of my eye, I could see Kai inching towards the leaflets.

'So, how long have they been together?' I asked.

'Only a couple of months. Woah!'

The leaflets fluttered to the floor and I helped the man gather them up. Kai grabbed the orange hologram and took off through the crowd. When I couldn't see him anymore, I stopped helping and followed. The man shouted for me to come back, but I ignored him. I found Kai leant against the market hall wall, holding out the page to me with a smirk on his face.

I told you my plan was better.

I took the page off him and put it in my pocket. 'You just started your plan without letting me agree to it. That doesn't mean it's better.'

Same thing. Where to next?

I consulted the map. There were two sins left and the moving one had travelled to the Victoria Borough of London. The other one, although at Tower Hill, would be easier to find. 'Tower of London.'

Shall we get the Airground? It looks like a bit of a walk.

'I think we should keep out in the open in case we need to run.'

I led Kai down to the waterfront and we walked along the length of the Thames, hand in hand. We might have actually looked like a real couple if anyone had been able to see Kai beside me. It was cold near the water and it was dark. I couldn't stop myself from shivering. Kai wrapped an arm around my shoulders and pulled me closer to his body. He was always so warm and I curled up into his side.

'Thank you. You've made this scenario a lot less scary than it probably should have been.'

It's alright. What's the Tower of London by the way?

'It's a sort of castle and was a prison at one point. Now, it's just open for tourists.'

Let's go together one day.

'You sure? It's a bit morbid.'

I don't mind as long as I'm with you.

I felt myself blushing and I turned away from Kai. We walked onto Lower Thames Street, still on the waterfront, and the Tower of London came into view. It was lit up beautifully. 'Let's take a look around then. Watch out for Il-gob.'

Kai nodded and we joined hands again. We wandered around the Tower of London perimeter until I saw an orange hologram stuck to a lamppost. I took off the sin and put it in my pocket. 'That was easy. Just one more to find and then we can go home.'

Before I could check the map for the moving sin, I spotted Il-gob on the Tower battlements. His pale, cracked face shone in the spotlights. He was staring straight at me and I could hear the water dripping from his fingers on to the pavement below. The cotton wool filled my mouth again and I felt myself wretch slightly. I squeezed my eyes shut, hoping that would make him go away, but when I reopened them, he had appeared a few metres in front of me with his arms outstretched. I let out a whimper.

Run Gracie. NOW.

Kai grabbed my hand and started pulling me behind him. I struggled to keep up but I had to – I couldn't lose this scenario. I had never lost one before. I followed Kai towards St Paul's Cathedral. I risked a glance over my shoulder. Il-gob was running after us. His jaw was clenched and the broken pieces of his face seemed to move as he ran. I tried to speed up, but with every step we took, Il-gob gained on us.

I can see the last sin!

The orange hologram was illuminated on the back of a bus waiting at a stop. The red paint of its exterior was shining in the lights of St. Paul's Cathedral. The bus set off and I groaned, trying to run faster. That's why it had been moving all evening. 'There's no way we can get that!'

Yes, you can!

Kai propelled me forwards and I leapt onto the back of the bus. I ripped off the sin, then jumped onto the pavement before the bus could gain too much speed. I ran over to Kai and hugged him, both of us grinning and neither of us caring about the strange looks I was getting. I laughed and kissed him on the cheek.

'You find this funny, do you?' I let go of Kai and saw that Psyche had manifested next to me. I had never seen her look so angry.

'Psyche? What's wrong? We won!'

She ignored my question and glowered at me. Her eyes were fiery and wild. 'No, you didn't. You still have to get home without letting Il-gob catch you.'

'You didn't say that before.'

Then everything froze and went red. I was still on the street outside St. Paul's, but I couldn't move, and neither could the people or cars around me. Terry and Eros flickered into view beside Psyche.

'Ermmm... darling, that's not allowed.'

'Shut up!' she screeched. 'I'm in charge of the nightmare scenarios, not you!'

'But you still can't change the original scenario,' Eros told his wife. 'It's against the rules to change it.'

Rule 2: The scenario cannot be changed once accepted.

Rule 7: Details of how to win the scenario must be given truthfully by the Voices.

Psyche screamed. It was so manic and piercing, I would have put my hands over my ears if I had been able to raise them. She ran at me, grabbing handfuls of my hair, dragging me down to the pavement. I willed my arms to move, to fight back, to stop her. I couldn't even shout. I gave in and waited for the sickening crack that was bound to come when my head connected with the pavement.

Get off her!

Kai yanked Psyche from my hair. I wanted to cry, but tears wouldn't fall. Psyche disappeared and so did the redness. The usual confetti was thrown in front of me.

'Congratulations, Gracie. You have won the scenario. You have gained 51XP. You are now Level 59. You have until the 31st December to reach Level 75.'

I just nodded. I felt too drained after the scenario to comment. Terry and Eros disappeared and Kai took my hand.

Are you okay?

'Yeah…' I wasn't really. My head hurt from where Psyche had pulled my hair, my legs hurt from running so much, and I felt betrayed.

***

'Where to?' the android cab driver asked.

I leant my head against the window, expecting Kai to speak, but I sat up when he poked me in the ribs.

He can't hear me.

'Right, sorry. Hungerford Road, Holloway, please.'

''course, luv.'

I tried not to groan as I registered the android's pre-programmed cockney accent.

Can we have a look at those sins now?

I nodded. I didn't want to speak in front of the android in case he struck up a conversation with me. I didn't really feel like talking. I got the sins out of my pocket and showed them to Kai. The orange holograms had disappeared and we could see all the pages were the same underneath – dark blue, slightly crumpled, with bright white text on the front that said "Irukians Rising". There was a rose stamp in the bottom right-hand corner – the same rose logo used for the Jangmi androids. Why had the Voices make me collect propaganda posters? What did Jangmi have to do with the Irukians?

I sighed and looked out of the window. We passed a black brick building with the sign "Revs" in green lights above the entrance. A long queue of students were waiting outside. I had never gone to a nightclub because of the nightmare scenarios. Clubbing had never looked enjoyable, but it would be nice to have the option to go.

When we arrived home I paid the android with my Hourglass, then used it to open the front door. It was now

22:30. Mum was waiting in the hall when I entered, not looking impressed. 'Where the hell have you been?'

'Everywhere,' I told her. Which wasn't a complete lie. I walked past her and went to my bedroom without another word. I flopped onto my bed with my jacket and shoes still on. My scalp still hurt from where Psyche had grabbed it and the buzzing was still persisting. My head really ached. Kai stepped into the room a moment later, his shoes off, and he gave me a soft smile.

I'll look after your scalp. You can go to sleep.

'You need to sleep, too.'

He came over to the bed and kissed me tenderly on the forehead.

I can survive without it for a few hours. Goodnight, Gracie.

CHAPTER 16

Over the next week, I didn't see Psyche – not even once. Every time I played a scenario, I asked Eros and Terry where she was and how she was doing but Eros just ignored me. Terry would grin and flick my forehead, then say things like "she's not to be trusted", "I did try to tell you", "she'll probably try to kill you in your sleep". When I flicked him back, he would disappear. I still found it hard to believe that Psyche was the one in charge of the scenarios. I had thought she was so sweet and kind. She must really hate me to have devised all the horrible things she had made me do.

I couldn't get Psyche off my mind in class yesterday either, since Miss Dyna had decided to run a lesson on how myths and legends impact writing, which included talking about Eros and Psyche. I perked up then. I had taken the time to research Kai, but never Eros and Psyche. Miss Dyna described how Psyche overcame many trials, set by Aphrodite, Eros' mother, before Aphrodite would approve her son's relationship with a mortal being. I slumped back in my seat. Psyche told me just before we buried the clown that if she had to complete that scenario, she would have wanted Eros by her side. Was that why she was making me play the nightmare scenarios? Because she wanted someone else to understand how she felt having to prove herself to a goddess? But what was my prize? At the end of her trials, she got to be with Eros for eternity in Olympus. What would I get? The scenarios happened every night with no end in sight, just a goal of reaching a certain Level by a certain date or I would be punished. It was pointless. So why was she doing this to me?

At the end of class, I took my time packing away my things, my mind still preoccupied with Psyche. Even in the myth, she was kind. So, why was she mean to me? The Psyche I knew was just a hallucination, but why was her personality not like the legend?

'You okay?' Iliana and Maida were waiting for me.

'Yeah, sorry, I've just got a lot on my mind.'

'It's alright. I'll see you at the café after Electronic Engineering?'

I nodded and went over to the lecture theatre door. Iliana and Maida followed, the latter with a pout on her face. 'It is so sad. I wanted to spend extra time with you both. I wanted to have a banana milkshake with you.'

I turned around to face Maida. 'A banana milkshake?'

She nodded, her movements becoming less fluid. 'Can I interest you in a banana milkshake, Miss Thrace?'

'Bloody hell.' I quickly glanced around the lecture theatre. Everyone else had left.

'Why are you calling Gracie "Miss Thrace"?' Iliana asked, looking confused.

'Come on, Maida, we're going to the Tech Centre. They have loads of banana milkshake there.'

'Do not worry, Miss Thrace. I can make a banana milkshake right here.' The fingers on Maida's right hand turned into blender blades and Iliana screamed. I grabbed the blades before they could start moving and wrapped my hand around them tightly, trying not to wince as they dug into my skin.

'Yes, but the bananas and other ingredients we need are in the Tech Centre. So, let's go.' Maida nodded and let me lead her out of the room. Iliana followed, looking pale.

'What's going on?' she whispered as she helped me walk Maida out of the Grad Hub.

'I told you on the first day of university. Maida is an android but she doesn't know. Something must have made her malfunction. We need to get her to one of the Electronic Engineering classrooms in the Tech Centre.'

'Can you fix her?' Iliana asked as she took Maida's other hand.

'I don't know. I've never had to fix an android that's broken before without my Dad.' I had repaired Macy a handful of times but it was only minor tweaks, like when one of her eyeballs fell out. 'Maybe Professor Long will be able to help. Come on, we need to get to the Tech Centre before the rest of my Electronic Engineering class does.'

Maida babbled about bananas and milkshakes for the entire walk, which gained us some funny glances, but the looks would have been stranger if Maida's blender hand had escaped my grip. We found Professor Long alone in his lab, reading *The Hitchhiker's Guide to the Galaxy*. He looked up when we entered and gave me a small smile.

'You're a bit early, Gracie.'

'Yeah, sorry. Could you put a sign on the door telling people that the class is cancelled and then lock it?'

'Why?'

I let go of Maida's hand and the blades started spinning. 'She thinks she's human.'

The Professor put down his book and strode over to the door. He was completely unphased, as if this wasn't the strangest thing he had seen all day. Iliana let go of Maida's other hand. 'What are we supposed to do now?' she asked, watching Maida wander around the room with her blender hand spinning.

'Just distract her for a minute.' I dumped my bag next to a computer as I started it up. I got out my tool kit, ignoring the bleeding cuts on my hand.

'Errmm, Gracie, she's kind of getting closer to me with those things.'

I ran over to Maida who was backing Iliana into the windows. I punched the android in the back of the neck where I knew the bright blue wire that powered her would be. Immediately, the spinning stopped and Maida fell over. Iliana screamed again. 'What was that for?!'

'She could have killed you with her hand if she had gotten any closer. That might have erased all of her memories, but if we're quick, we might be able to save her.'

Professor Long helped me drag Maida towards the computer. I sat on the floor next to Maida and my hands went to the hem of her jumper. I was about to lift it up when Iliana shrieked. 'What are you doing?!'

'I need to look at her circuits.'

'But. That's, you know… her chest! We could get in trouble for sexual assault or something.'

'Iliana, her fingers just turned into blenders. I don't think accusations of sexual assault are the issue here. Androids are shaped to look like us, but they don't look like us underneath.' I rolled up Maida's jumper and Iliana gasped. The artificial skin on her chest was made out of dusky pink leather and her breasts were just two lumps of material, like a doll. She had no nipples, no ridges, and no curves where ribs or muscles should have been. Just a flat expanse of leather with the Jangmi rose logo stamped across Maida's belly button area. Running down the centre of her chest, right in between the two breast lumps, was a seam where all of her circuits could be accessed. It had been recently resealed as there was an extra line of black thread lying over the original pink stitches. I grabbed a scalpel from my toolkit and sliced open the seam. Iliana shrieked again as the leather chest fell away and revealed a sheet of metal, the I/O shield, which protected the wiring inside. I unsnapped the sides and handed it to Professor Long, then Iliana knelt down beside me to inspect all the wires and circuits, even though she had no idea what she was looking at.

'What's that?' she asked, pointing at a small white square that was held down with a latch.

I slapped her hand away. 'The processor. Don't touch it.'

'Why not?'

'That's the android's brain.' I slid out a black tray connected to Maida's chest and unscrewed it, then handed it to the Professor. 'Please could you see if you can find anything on this?'

'Was that the hard drive?' Iliana asked.

'Yeah. It stores all her data and it's her long-term memory. It might have malfunctioned.'

'But, how did you know that something was wrong with her?'

'She asked me if I wanted a banana milkshake. Macy does that all the time. I think it's a bug or something.' I moved some of Maida's wires out of the way and found two slits in the side of her case that had been sealed shut with silver thermal paste. The openings were exactly the same size as Macy's slits, where she inserted bread to make me toast. Maida was meant to have been a housemaid model.

'Gracie, I found something,' Professor Long said.

I went over to the computer and was immediately presented with lines upon lines of code. I had no idea what any of it meant. 'You're going to have to help me here.'

'According to the data, early this morning, someone got that android, cut her open and changed her security settings to get her under their control.'

'Can you change them back?'

The Professor started adding to the end of the coding lines, but he shook his head. 'Not from this screen. I need the BIOS setup screen.' He started rummaging through his desk 'Damn where did I put that standard format cable?'

'I have one in my toolkit, Professor,' I said as I grabbed it from my bag.

'Good. Plug her into this end and I'll plug her into my computer.'

I took the cable over to Maida and turned her over, finding a tiny hole in her hip where the cable could be inserted. I connected the cable to Maida's port and the BIOS setup screen began to load on the computer. Professor Long scrolled through each of the tabs, finally coming to the security settings. He clicked on recent changes and groaned when a box appeared on the screen. 'It wants a password,' said the Professor. 'Do either of you know what it is?'

Iliana looked straight at me. 'Any ideas?'

'No. Why would I?'

'Well… you knew she was an android! And you took her apart! Shouldn't you know?'

I shook my head and the Professor smiled after registering the blank looks on our faces. 'Okay, don't worry. Since neither of you know the password, I have invented a little programme of my own which might just assist. But if anyone asks, including the Police, you know nothing about it. Understand?'

Iliana nodded. 'It's fine. Just do it.'

'Here we go then, fingers crossed.' In a matter of seconds, the Professor's computer made a sharp *ping* sound. 'Password is Da15y. Hm, like Daisy. I'll just reverse the changes then reinstall everything. She should be fine after that. Unless you hit her too hard. How did you know to do that, anyway?' the Professor asked as he typed away.

I just shrugged. I was not going to tell them about that now. I stood motionless, taking stock of the situation. Maida was now flat out and incapacitated. She looked rather peaceful. I took a deep breath, appreciating for the first time the stress we had been under.

'Is it okay if we leave Maida with you, Professor? We have to get to work.'

'Sure. I'll replace her hard drive and reboot her.' The Professor handed back my cable. Iliana was staring blankly at Maida, still in shock if her facial expression was anything to go by.

'Are you okay?' I asked Iliana once we left the Tech Centre. 'I know you don't like androids and frankly, seeing your friend's fingers turn to blender blades is enough to mess anyone up.'

She just shrugged. 'I don't know. It was weird to see you just open her up like that. Maybe you should have done Electronic Engineering instead. You would have been brilliant at it.'

I smiled. 'It's not like I did much. I only took out the hard drive. You could have done that if you knew what it was.'

'Yeah, I suppose. *You* seem to have gotten over your fear of androids, though.'

'Maybe,' I replied.

'What do you mean "maybe"? I've never seen you act so calm and collected before. You've got your Dad's knack for mechanics. Don't avoid doing something you're good at just to spite your Mum, no matter how horrible she is to you.' Iliana paused to let her advice sink in. She looked tired and overwhelmed. 'Do you mind if I catch you up? I just want to clear my head.'

'Sure. I'll see you at the café.' She smiled in thanks and walked off.

She's right, you know

Kai appeared next to me. 'And where have you been all day?'

In bed. I was tired.

I smiled and carried on walking. 'What is Iliana right about then?'

Everything she just said. You're not as scared of androids as you think you are, and you shouldn't study Creative Writing just to annoy your Mum.

'I don't *enjoy* Electronic Engineering. Yeah, I'm good at it. I know that. I'm good at writing too and I *enjoy* it. Surely that matters more?'

But won't Electronic Engineering pay better than writing?

'I think me being happy is most important.'

I suppose. Kai wrapped an arm around my waist and pulled me close. *To the café?*

'Yep. We've got a shift to do.'

I don't work there.

'Then you shouldn't have decided to hang around my brain, should you?'

We walked in silence towards the café as I contemplated what had just happened with Maida. The whole situation was strange. How did Maida not know she was an android? Even if she was consciously pretending to be human, she would still know she was an android when she changed her clothes. Maida would have seen her fake skin and the stitching that held it all together. But she truly didn't seem to know she was an android. Did someone power her down at the end of each day? Someone had obviously tampered with her, so that meant someone knew what she was. But *who* was doing this? *Why* were they doing this? *What* was the point? I had no idea.

REPORT ON PARTICIPANT 1 OUT OF 4: Miss Gracie Thrace

15/10/2047   Miss Thrace spends the evening in Central London – noted as odd behaviour considering she usually plays the nightmare scenarios at home or in quiet places.

She starts at New Oxford Street, then walks to Tottenham Court Road, Marble Arch, Baker Street, and then runs to Marylebone Train Station. She gets the Airground to Charing Cross, then she walks to Trafalgar Square. From there, she runs to Leicester Square, then walks to Covent Garden. She then walks along the Thames to Tower Hill, then runs back towards St. Paul's Cathedral, before finally getting a taxi home.

She is seen ripping Irukian Rising leaflets off buildings which is presumably part of a scenario.

Multiple times during the evening, she talks aloud to herself. She is most likely talking to Kai or one of the other voices. She does not seem to care about people hearing her any longer – her perception of what is real and what is not seems to be blurring. More investigation is required.

CHAPTER 17

When Dad was in Egypt, we sent letters to each other. It was old fashioned and they always took forever to arrive, but we had no choice. Everyone fighting VIRENT had to have their Hourglasses deactivated just in case VIRENT got hold of the Hourglass trackers. When I arrived home, Dad's first letter was on the doormat. My name and address were scrawled across the envelope in small, familiar handwriting.

Gray,

I know this letter will have taken a while to arrive. It always does. I hope you're okay. I hope you and Mum are getting along alright. I know Mum can be difficult sometimes. She is proud of you, I promise you she is. Remember she does love you.

How was your first day at university? I remember my first day. I fell down a flight of stairs in front of the whole lecture hall and I was so embarrassed, but no one mentioned it. I hope your first day went better. How is your course going? Are you enjoying it? You've probably found a lot of androids working at the university. I know you don't like them but I'm sure you've got used to them by now.

Is your job at the café going okay? Is Miss Leyshon still ruling her premises with an iron fist?

I hope Iliana's well. She seemed okay on the day I left. Has she set you up with any university lads yet? A word of warning, if you do have a boyfriend by the time I come home, let him know that I'll be checking his Hourglass tracker records.

I'm afraid I have some bad news, Gray. Unfortunately, I won't be back for Christmas like I thought. VIRENT have got more rogue androids and we're working around the clock to keep them under control. You know that I'd rather be at home with you. I think about you all the time.

Look after yourself and keep strong. I'll be home soon, I promise.
Love,
Dad x

I folded the letter up and put it into the envelope, tracing the Egyptian postmark and android oil stains with my finger. Was it weird that I would rather be in Egypt with him, than here, relatively safe in London with Mum?

Is that a letter from your Dad? Kai asked, manifesting beside me on the bed.

'Yeah. He won't be back for Christmas,' I shrugged, then picked up a pen ready to write my own letter. I searched through the mess to find a clean piece of paper and came across Izumi's party tickets.

Have you decided who you're going with yet?

I shook my head and put the tickets to one side.

I'll go with you.

'I think Izumi wants me to bring a date who is visible, no offence.'

Then take Iliana.

I smiled at Kai and shook my head. 'Iliana hates IrukaTech. I'll just get one of the lads who works at the café to go with me. They won't mind.'

Kai came up behind where I was sat and wrapped his arms around my shoulders, his chin resting on top of my head.

Just don't let them think it's a date.

Professor Long emailed to tell me that Maida was up to talking. We had fixed her a week ago, but I hadn't seen her since. I went down to the Tech Centre and found Maida in Professor Long's lab, sitting on one of the benches. She looked up when I entered and smiled at me, her neck crackling with more static than usual. I sat down opposite and registered her appearance. She was wearing men's clothes that were a little too big and her curly hair wasn't as perfect as usual.

'How are you feeling?' I asked.

'I am not sure. Professor Long is letting me stay with him for the time being. He says I should not be on my own right now. I am so confused, but how can I even feel confused? I am just an android.'

The way she spoke now sounded less robotic and more natural. The only thing that made her android-like was her movements which weren't as fluid.

'You sound better. More human.'

'Yes. Professor Long added more lines of code to my hard drive and processor. It makes me talk more informally.' She paused. 'When did you first know I was an android?'

'When you turned around in class on the first day. I could hear the static. Then, when you learnt my name, I could hear your head whirring as it took in the new information. And the way you spoke. No one speaks like that.'

She nodded. 'Thank you for helping to fix me.'

'It's alright,' I said. 'Your security password was Da15y – Daisy. Know anything about that?'

'I had a little sister called Daisy. I think. Can androids have relatives?' Maida sighed and rubbed her head. 'It is in my memories that I had a little sister called Daisy. We were homeless. Our parents had died.'

I nodded, thinking of Daisy from the Underground. I dismissed the thought as soon as it arrived. It was just a coincidence. 'Is Professor Long treating you okay?'

'Yes. He is a bit cautious around me. I suppose he probably thinks that I am going to attack him at any given moment, but he is nice enough. I am not sure what I am going to do now.'

'You just need to take your time to figure things out.'

'Yes. I am going to go back to Professor Long's home for now. Thanks again, for fixing me.'

I smiled and she left the room, leaving me alone in the engineering lab. Kai manifested beside me and I leant my head on his shoulder. 'I should have asked Maida about her third eye. It doesn't work.'

What do you mean?

'When I was on my date with Joe, we went on the London Eye. Maida was in the pod below us, but she didn't look up at me when I was staring at her. Also, on the first day of university, she didn't notice me staring at the back of her head. All androids know exactly what's going on around them. That's how Macy knows when I go in the kitchen. She could have her back to me and she would still say "Good morning, Miss Thrace".'

Oh. That makes a lot more sense now. Why don't you take Macy to Izumi's party?

I laughed and hugged Kai. 'I want to go with you.'

You said I can't.

'I know.'

Can I at least dance with you?

'I don't think that'll be possible at the party. There'll be a lot of important people there and my Mum will murder me if I dance with an invisible person.'

I didn't mean at the party. I meant now, as practise.

I smiled and slid off the bench. 'You can dance?'

If I couldn't dance, do you think I would be offering?

'No, I suppose not.' I went over to him and he wrapped an arm around my waist, holding his other hand up in the air.

Have you ever done this before?

'Yes. I've been to IrukaTech's parties with my parents every year since I was a child.'

And you've danced every year?

'Yes. But… only with my Dad. He used to let me stand on his feet so he could move both of us.'

Cute. One hand on my shoulder, hold my hand with the other.

I did as he said and Kai held my waist tighter, bringing me closer to his body. I tensed as I was only used to my Dad holding me like this. What was I doing? Kai smiled and kissed me on the cheek.

Relax, Gracie. I'm not some stranger. I'm your boyfriend.

We'd never put a label on what we were before and it worried me to think that a hologram, who may or may not be real, was my boyfriend.

Kai registered the look on my face and frowned. *Too fast?*

'A little. Sorry. I know I asked to take this slow, but I didn't take into consideration what *you* wanted.' I looked at the floor, but Kai curled a finger under my chin and made me look up at him.

Don't be sorry. We'll go as fast or as slow as you like. As long as you're comfortable.

I smiled and pressed my body closer to Kai's. 'Okay. Let's start.'

We're going to do a simple box step. I'll lead, alright?

I nodded and looked back down, but this time it was to watch my feet to make sure I took the right steps. Kai sighed.

Your Mum isn't going to be happy if you look down at your feet all night. Let's try again, okay? I'll lead you in a dance and you follow. Just don't look down at your feet.

I forgot about the box step and Kai led me around the room, turning this way and that, keeping eye contact with me. As I got used to the rhythm, he sped up, making me move faster. We danced around the room together, in and out between the benches and stools. I laughed as Kai danced quicker and squealed when he spun me around. I fell into his chest and he held me close, his lips resting on the top of my head and his arms around me.

I looked up at Kai, and part of me wanted to kiss him on the lips, but I decided against it and kissed his cheek instead. As much as I liked him, a big part of me was scared that this small relationship we had built up together would just vanish one day without giving either of us time to say goodbye. What would happen when I was better?

'Gracie? Were you dancing?'

I looked towards the door and saw Joe leant against the frame with a smirk on his face. 'Yes, I was practising,' I said, trying not to frown when Kai let go of me.

'What for?'

'A party. Why are you here?'

He ignored my question and came into the room. 'I can dance. Do you want me to help you?'

'No.'

He ignored me again and grabbed my waist. He led me around the room, jerking my body when I didn't go the way he wanted. I glanced over at Kai who was now sat on a stool, glaring at Joe. Maybe Kai would punch him again?

'Do you need a date for this party?'

'No.'

'Where is it?'

'Tower 142.'

'The IrukaTech birthday party? Don't worry, I'm already going. Chris hooked me up with a ticket. It'll be a great chance to chat to IrukaTech employees and get on the company's graduate placement scheme. So, I'll see you there anyway.'

He smirked again then waltzed out of the room, as if our awful date a few weeks ago had never happened. I turned around, expecting to see Kai sat on a stool, but he had gone. Again.

CHAPTER 18

Three weeks. Three weeks and not a sound from Kai. He hadn't helped me with the scenarios and he hadn't been around when I went near any water. I was willing to do anything to get him back and hear the buzzing sound that accompanied him. Even jumping in the Thames seemed like a great idea. No one held me in bed anymore or called me a racist or wrapped their arms around my waist or kissed me on the cheek when I was least expecting it. I hadn't felt this alone since Dad went on his first tour to Egypt. Now Dad and Kai were both gone, and I was left with a best friend who was obsessed with her boyfriend, a mother who hated me, an android who needed fixing and the three horrible Voices.

On the night of the IrukaTech party, I lay on my bed, picking at one of the threads on my dressing gown. The scenario had already been played and the buzzing, thankfully, had stopped. But I had a feeling I was going to enjoy the party less than a scenario. Mum barged into my room, Macy on her heels, and tutted.

'Sit up! Come on, we need to get you ready.' Mum was wearing a full-length green dress with rhinestones scattered around the bodice and her auburn hair was styled into a French twist. 'Macy, you do her hair and makeup.'

'Yes, Mrs Thrace.'

When Macy was finished, I stood gazing at myself in the mirror. My hair fell in sleek auburn curls down my bare shoulders. My dress was strapless and cerulean in colour with silver leaves wrapped around my waist. The skirt finished just above my knees and flared out like a tutu revealing my long, pale legs. I felt uncomfortable, standing in a strapless dress and wearing silver heels that I could barely walk in, but I did look kind of nice. I took a picture of myself with my Hourglass, then sent it to Iliana.

To: Iliana Lopez 17:38
[Picture attached]
Ready for Izumi's party.

From: Iliana Lopez 17:40
AHHHHHHHHHHHHHHHHHHHHHHHHHHHHHHHHHHH OMG OMG OMG OMG OMG YOU LOOK AMAZING :*

To: Iliana Lopez 17:41
Thanks :*

I stayed in front of the mirror for a few more moments, savouring the feeling. For the first time in a long time, I felt really good about how I looked. But then the buzzing returned and Eros manifested beside me.

'Wow, you look ugly.'

I turned away for him. 'Thanks,' I whispered. There was no use arguing. Kai wasn't here to get Eros to leave me alone.

'I don't understand why you're even going. No one will want to dance with you and Kai's left you, so you can't even dance with him.'

Psyche appeared on the bed and snarled at me. 'I'm not surprised. He probably only pretended to be your boyfriend out of pity.'

Before I could reply, Mum came back into my room. She was carrying a small, metal rectangle with tiny silver leaves decorating it, just like the ones on my dress. 'Hold out your Hourglass.' I did as she said and she unclipped the metal case from around my Hourglass, revealing the scarring on my wrist. She clipped the new case onto my Hourglass and adjusted it slightly. 'There. I had the design department make this for you to go with your dress.'

'Oh. Thank you,' I said, a little wary. She hardly ever did anything nice for me.

'Don't thank me. It was your father's idea. He wrote and asked me to arrange it. He feels guilty about missing Christmas.'

There it was. Of course this wasn't her idea. 'I'll tell him thank you when I see him.' Whenever that may be.

There was a knock on the front door and Mum left the room to answer it, her green dress flowing behind her. I stayed in front of the mirror and wrapped my arms around my waist, closed my eyes, and wished that Kai was holding me. Eros slapped my hand away. 'Kai's not here. You only have us. Remember that,' he hissed.

'Gracie! The car is here,' my Mum shouted to me.

'I'll be there in a second!'

Eros and Psyche disappeared back into my head and I looked in the mirror once more as the buzzing stopped. 'Kai? Kai-chan?' I asked.

There was no reply. With a sigh, I left the room and went into the hallway where my Mum was standing with Macy and Geoff.

'Please have a good time tonight, Mrs Thrace and Miss Thrace.' Then Macy's left shoulder opened, revealing a small compartment packed with tiny pink tubes. 'Would you like a complimentary breath mint?'

Mum groaned and closed the compartment. 'No, we wouldn't. Go and clean the kitchen, Macy.'

'Yes, Mrs Thrace.' Macy went down the hall and walked headfirst into the bathroom door before righting herself.

'How have you been, Miss Thrace?' Geoff asked with a smile.

I shrugged. 'I would be better if I didn't have to go to this party.'

He chuckled. 'I'm sure you'll have a good time. And, if I may say, you look very beautiful tonight, Miss Thrace.'

I smiled at him. 'Thank you.'

Mum huffed and double-checked her clutch bag to see if the tickets were inside – she didn't trust me to look after them. We made it onto the street and I groaned when I saw the car Izumi had organised.

'There's only two of us. Why is there a limo?' I asked as we climbed inside. There were seats lining each wall and the ceiling was covered in tiny LEDs. I guess they were supposed to mimic stars.

Mum tutted. 'Because, Gracie, we are special guests of Mr Izumi. We can't just get a taxi there.'

I rolled my eyes and slouched down in the leather seat. Mum slapped my bare arm and I sat back up. 'What was that for?!'

'You'll crease your dress.'

I sighed and stared out of the window. I really hoped tonight could just be a normal evening. It was barely six o'clock but it was already dark. The Voices had left me alone – for now.

The limo came to a stop outside Tower 142, which was illuminated in white and blue light. It was always the brightest building on the London skyline on the 22nd November. Through the tinted windows of the limo, I could see photographers and journalists on the street, ready to interview the celebrities and public figures. The door was opened from the outside and Mum climbed out first. Some of the press knew who she was. She had been on the news as an IrukaTech spokesperson many times and whenever Izumi announced a new product, she was always close by his side during the press conference. I got out and joined Mum on the pavement. She waved to the cameras and answered a few questions as I stood awkwardly beside her. It was always like this. Mum would smile, wave and pretend that she was a nice person while showing me off as some sort of engineering prodigy, then shun me when the interest moved to someone else. Dad usually came to these parties, but this year was the first time he had been away in Egypt.

When Mum finished talking to the pack of journalists, she pulled me in for a couple of photos. I knew to smile as if we had the best mother-daughter relationship in the world, then she ushered me inside, flashing our tickets to the security androids. A handful of guests were in the foyer who must have been employees since they were greeting Mum as "Mrs Thrace" instead of "Sharon". IrukaTech had traditional values when it came to addressing senior members of staff. We took the lift to the 138th floor where the lift doors opened, revealing the party.

The 138th floor was one of the only floors in the building not used for work and the only floor not decorated with glass and chrome. The room was adorned with marble pillars, expensive wallpaper and the ceiling was painted to give the illusion that it was domed when it was actually flat. Around the edges of the room, guests were chatting and android waiters were serving drinks. An orchestra was playing songs for the few couples dancing in the centre.

Mum pulled me over to Izumi, who was not far from the orchestra and an ice sculpture of a dolphin. Small groups of guests – most looked like graduates or students – hovered around the IrukaTech owner, shooting intermittent looks in his direction, waiting for the chance to get his attention. Joe was among them. I had expected Chris to be here. Iliana hadn't mentioned he would be attending, but he was an intern at IrukaTech, plus he'd got a ticket for Joe. He must have been around somewhere.

'Good evening, Andy.'

'Sharon!' Izumi kissed Mum on the cheek, then hugged me.

'Gracie, you look absolutely stunning. Didn't I say you had grown into a beautiful woman?'

'I never disagreed with you,' I told him with a fake smile, trying to appear confident to not show up Mum. Joe came over, looking sharp in his black tuxedo, but I ignored him and carried on talking to my godfather.

'And thank you for designing the Hourglass case. It's lovely.'

'It's my pleasure, Gracie. Is this your boyfriend?' he asked, gesturing to Joe who was lingering uncomfortably close to my side.

'No,' I said firmly.

'My name's Joe. I'm a friend of Gracie's, sir,' Joe explained.

Mum laughed. 'I didn't think you knew any boys?'

Joe just smiled and shook hands with my Mum, who returned the look. Izumi was uncharacteristically solemn.

'You'd better look after Gracie. She means a lot to me.'

'I will, sir.'

I held back my laughter, thinking of everything Joe had done so far. Maybe I should tell Izumi? He would definitely get Joe to stop harassing me. Or maybe he wouldn't believe me...

'Why don't you two go and have a dance, hm?' Mum suggested. A smirk crept onto her face.

I didn't want to make a scene in front of Izumi so I let Joe lead me out into the middle of the room. I braced myself, preparing for Joe to crush my waist with his grip, but he was a lot softer than he had been in the engineering lab.

'I didn't realise you and Izumi were close,' he told me halfway through the first song. He shot the occasional nervous glance towards Izumi and my Mum, who had also been joined by the Prime Minister, Catherine Bell.

'He's my Mum's friend as well as employer. My Mum's worked here and known Izumi for ages. I was born when she first started working here. Izumi's known me my entire life. He's my godfather.'

Joe nodded, having gone a little pale. 'I see.'

'By the way, we're only having this one dance. One date was our deal and you still haven't left me alone. Don't come near me again tonight.'

'Whatever,' he said. His tone was dismissive and indignant.

'By the way, where's Chris? Is he around somewhere?'

Joe shrugged. 'I don't know.'

'What do you mean you don't know? You live together, he works here, and he got you the ticket for this party in the first place. How can you not know?'

'I'm not his keeper. He's more than likely here, I just don't know where. Why are you bothered? Afraid he'll cheat on Iliana?'

I wanted to say Chris wasn't like that, but in truth, I barely knew him. I had only gleaned snippets of information from Iliana and hadn't given any thought to Chris cheating on her. It just seemed a little odd that he wasn't here. We carried on dancing until the song ended and then went to the drinks table.

'Well, if it isn't Gracie Thrace.'

I recognised the scornful voice before I even turned around. Ichigo Izumi was a bully and had been nasty to me when we were children. It had been name calling mostly – but she had been quite spiteful after the android clown tried to kill me, which had been hard to handle. She had black hair, like her Dad. I had seen pictures of her mother in Izumi's office. She had been a beautiful Japanese lady with brown eyes like Ichigo – except in photos, her mother's eyes were kind and sparkling. Ichigo's eyes were beady like a tarantula's.

Ichigo looked me up and down, her eyebrows raised. 'Is this your boyfriend?' she asked after she glanced at Joe.

'He wishes. Who are you with?'

'Like I need to bring anyone. I'm working on that guy over there.' She stepped closer to me and pointed a manicured finger across to the lift where a lanky man was leaning against the wall, his dark brown fringe dangling in front of his eyes.

'Am I supposed to know who that is?'

Ichigo groaned. 'It's Freddie Tilson. You know, the singer?'

I glanced at the man again. 'He looks a lot older than you.'

Ichigo grinned. 'I don't know exactly. He's in his thirties, though.'

'Ichigo, you're only 23.'

She stuck out her bottom lip. 'Aww, little Gracie Thracie is all concerned for my safety. Chill, I can handle myself.'

I picked up a drink just as a middle-aged man came over to the three of us. He was almost bald and had big bags under his eyes. I didn't recognise him at first, but Ichigo apparently did.

'Defence Secretary, sir. How are you this evening?'

He smiled at the three of us. 'I'm well. And yourself?'

'I'm fine, as always, but you already know that about me,' Ichigo said with a satisfied smirk on her face.

He grimaced. 'I was actually inquiring about Miss Thrace.'

'Oh,' I said, surprised. I'd never met the Defence Secretary, so why did he know my name? 'I'm good. Thank you for asking, Defence Secretary, sir.'

'Please, just call me Jack. I was wondering if Miss Thrace would allow me the honour of dancing with her,' he said, holding out his hand. 'That's if her date doesn't mind.'

Joe nodded, looking a little overwhelmed by the situation. Jack took me onto the floor. He danced a lot slower than Kai or Joe, but at least he didn't stare at me. His eyes remained fixed on a spot over my shoulder.

'I didn't realise that you knew who I was,' I said after a moment.

'Well, Andy does a lot of work with the government and Sharon is practically his right-hand woman, so I've got to know your mother quite well. She's a very bright lady.'

I nodded, searching the room for my Mum and Izumi. They were in the far corner, by the door that led out to the emergency stairs.

'But it wasn't your mother I wanted to talk about,' Jack continued.

'It wasn't?' I tried to sound interested but I was still watching my Mum and Izumi. They were close together, deep in conversation.

'I wanted to talk to you about your father.'

'My Dad?' I turned back to the Defence Secretary, my tone guarded. 'How do you know my Dad?'

'I know him very well. Tell him that I was very impressed with that stunt you and he pulled at your university last month.'

'What? I'm sorry, sir, but my Dad is in Egypt fighting. I haven't seen him since September.'

Jack just smiled, then left the dance floor, leaving me surrounded by happy couples. My Dad was in Egypt, wasn't he? Where else would he be? And that stunt? What was the

Defence Secretary talking about? The drinks were flowing so perhaps he'd had a few too many. But he did know who I was. I looked for Mum. I wanted to ask if she could shed some light on what the Defence Secretary had said, but she had disappeared. As had Izumi and the door to the emergency stairs was propped open. What were they up to?

I brushed passed the dancing couples and made my way to the door. I decided to try my luck by going up the stairs since there were fewer floors to check. My feet were beginning to hurt, so I took off my heels and left them by the emergency entrance. My bare feet felt cold on the concrete steps. I climbed upwards and the orchestra's music drifted up the stairwell. The doors leading to the other floors were all locked until I reached the 141st floor, the penultimate floor. There were two doors here. The first I knew led to Izumi's office and penthouse on the 142nd floor. It was locked. I peered through the small rectangular window in the door. Beyond were more stairs leading to another door, light streaming out from under it. Maybe Izumi and Mum had gone up there? I turned to the other door, where a sign read "Floor One Hundred And Forty One – Development Laboratory". This was where Mum worked. I pushed on the door and it opened.

I switched on my Hourglass' torch, sweeping it across the large room. It looked like a typical office, not a lab. Desks and chairs were set out with charging stations for Orcas and there was a service user android charging in the corner. There were a few unkept plants dotted about and at the far end of the room was my Mum's office, separated by a white wall and tinted windows.

I started to walk over to it, but something shiny caught my eye in the torchlight. On top of one of the desks was a silver photo frame. Nothing important. I looked at the desk and, among other things, there was a file marked "Hourglass Tracker" with the London Metropolitan Police crest stamped on the front. I reached down to open it but paused before turning the first page. Was I allowed to see this? I glanced back at the cover. There was no note to say it was confidential. If it was, whoever worked at this desk shouldn't have left it lying around. I opened the file to reveal a set of blueprints that showed how to build the Hourglass trackers the Police used. It was a fairly simple design, just a mini-computer really, but there were instructions written beside it.

Using IrukaTech's online database – enter the person's name to retrieve their unique Hourglass code. Input the code into the tracker and the signal should appear to indicate the required person's location. Please contact IrukaTech if further assistance is required.

I left the blueprints and carried on exploring. The rest of the desks were fairly tidy. There were some personal effects, but I found nothing of interest. I eventually turned my attention to Mum's office, but I paused before I opened the door. I had been to Tower 142 loads of times, but I had never visited the floor she worked on, let alone her office. Mum would be angry if she knew I had visited her private workspace. I grabbed the handle and yanked open the door anyway.

I didn't know what I was expecting. There was a desk in the centre with an Orca on top, which was surrounded by massive stacks of papers and files. It was just as messy as mine at home. What a hypocrite. I was about to take a closer look when I saw another door to the left. This one had a porthole window, unlike the rest of the doors. I went over to it and tried the handle but it wouldn't open. I hesitated, taking a few moments to stare at the shiny metal lock. What could be in there? A stationary cupboard? It seemed bit of a weird thing to have adjoined to a private office. I went back over to the doorway that led out to the rest of the 141st Floor and peered around the corner. The wall extended pretty far – a lot further than the size needed for my Mum's office. If it was a stationary cupboard, it was a pretty big one.

I re-entered the office and finally went over to my Mum's desk. I switched off the torch on my Hourglass and put on Mum's desk lamp, then sat down in her chair. I gave it a few curious spins, eyeing all of her paperwork. This is what she did all day? It seemed pretty boring. I rested my elbows on the desk, then peered over the stack of papers. Her colleagues had family photos on display. My Mum had nothing apart from a picture of her with Izumi when they were a lot younger. I was disappointed but not surprised. Her job was the most important thing in her life, and by extension, that included Izumi too. But I had hoped there would be a photo of me or my Dad somewhere.

I shoved the photo frame to one side and started searching through the first stack of papers. As much as my Mum did love her job, she had never really explained what she actually did at IrukaTech. Whilst I was here I might as well try and find out more. There was nothing interesting in the first pile, but I found something in the second. It was a brown file with the word 'confidential' stamped in red ink across the front cover. Should I look at it? Would I get in trouble? Clearly I would. I glanced at the open office door. Everyone was at the party and I couldn't hear the orchestra music from Mum's office. It would be fine. How could I get caught? I opened the folder and my eyes widened when I saw that it was a C.I.A. file.

MKUltra… Illegal experiments on humans to develop drugs in order to weaken individuals and control them through the mind… citizens as unwilling test subjects… manipulation of brain functions through hypnosis, sensory deprivation, isolation, humiliation, verbal abuse…

I read the first few pages and the content was shocking. Project MKUltra appeared to be some sort of mind control programme that the C.I.A. had run in the 1950s. But why on earth was my Mum reading it? Why did she have the actual physical file from the C.I.A.? What on Earth was she doing at IrukaTech? I put it to one side and then hesitated. Should I carry on looking? I shouldn't. I definitely shouldn't. But my perception of my Mum had been warped since a young age. I needed to know what she was doing here. Maybe she was reading a file on mind control just for research. Maybe her work at IrukaTech was honest and decent. I carried on rifling through the papers on her desk, but there was nothing else of interest until I came across a single sheet of paper.

Participant 4: Miss Elena Cassidy
Age: 23
Birthday: 28 July 2024
Address: 278 Merton High Street, Wimbledon, London, SW19 1DF
Date first dosage of Hydrobliss administered: 20/11/2047

Participants? Hydrobliss? I started moving through the papers quicker now, looking for files on other participants. There was nothing on participants two or three, but right at the bottom of the pile was a thick file with "Participant 1" written on the front in my Mum's handwriting. I opened it, but I wasn't ready for what was inside.

Participant 1: Miss Gracie Thrace
Age: 18
Birthday: 5 May 2029
Address: 345 Hungerford Road, Holloway, London, N7 9LP
Date first dosage of Hydrobliss administered: 20/05/2047

I flipped through the file – there were photos of me, my medical records, my birth certificate. Towards the back of the file was a stack of reports, the last one dated a few weeks ago.

31/10/2047   *Miss Thrace observed dancing in the engineering lab as if she was being led around by another person, probably Kai...*

After Maida left, the only people in that room to see me dancing would have been Kai and... Joe. I skimmed through the rest of the reports and I started to panic. Everything that had been recorded took place on occasions when either anyone could have seen or when I was alone with Joe. He had written these and they had been addressed to my Mum. This meant that Joe must have been hired to spy on me, and he had been doing it before I even met him.

I put the file down and rested my head on the desk. This was too much to take in. I thumped my head down on the wood, trying to make sense of it all, and something chimed as it rattled. I sat back up and opened the first drawer in the desk. Inside were hundreds of tiny vials, each filled with a clear liquid, just like the ones I found in our basement.

Was this Hydrobliss? What did Hydrobliss do? And I was taking it? I glanced back at my file. I'd been taking this since May. But how? I never knowingly ingested it... Had my Mum been spiking my food with it? She had to have been. I was never usually in the kitchen when Macy was making meals, but my Mum would be, more often than not. And when I ate out... I held a hand to my head as I remembered the day we'd had lunch together in the cafeteria downstairs. I'd complained that the water had tasted funny and she'd told me it was filtered, then made me drink it. But maybe it tasted funny because she had spiked it. My hands shook as I picked up a vial and switched off the desk lamp. I could take it to one of the chemistry labs in the Tech Centre to get it tested. But what did all of this mean? What had Mum been doing to me? I had so many questions and I didn't want to stay in the Development Lab any longer.

My whole body was trembling as I left the lab and stepped into the stairwell. I wasn't prepared for what I saw next. In front of me, behind the locked door that led up to the top floor, were Mum and Izumi. They were kissing. I dropped the vial.

CHAPTER 19

Friday 22nd November 2047
Level 64: 444 XP
Time to sunset: 19 hours 32 minutes

When the glass smashed on the concrete floor, Mum and Izumi broke apart and looked at me through the window in the door. Izumi unlocked the door and ran out, grabbing me by the shoulders.

'Gracie, this isn't what it looks like.'

'Get away from me!'

My eyes blurred with tears. I pushed his hands off me and stepped backwards until I came into contact with the other door. My Mum rushed onto the stairwell, looking nervous.

'Gracie –'

'No! You get away from me, too! You're such a hypocrite! Always telling me that I'm the family disappointment! But what about you?! You're the bloody disappointment!'

'Gracie, do not speak to your mother like that!'

'I'll do whatever the hell I want!' I shouted, turning back to Izumi. I was still shaking but for a completely different reason now, all other concerns forgotten in my bout of rage. My Dad and Izumi had known each other for years and they trusted each other. But that had clearly meant nothing to Izumi.

'Gracie,' my Mum said, stepping towards me, 'I only say that because I want you to try and better yourself.'

'Better myself?! Just like you've done, getting your all-consuming all-powerful job? You probably only got this job because you slept with him!'

'Gracie!' My Mum's voice was cold and firm. She stepped towards me and seized my arm, gripping me tight. 'That is enough. You are going home, right now.'

'Sharon, just let her calm down first –'

My Mum didn't let Izumi finish. She dragged me down the stairs to the 138th floor and pushed me into the function room despite me fighting all the way. She shoved me over to the drinks table where Joe was standing alone watching the dancing. 'Joe!' she screeched over the music. 'Take Gracie home right now!'

'Yes, Mrs Thrace.'

'Gracie?'

I turned around and saw Izumi holding out my silver heels, which he had obviously found in the stairwell. I snatched them from him and stormed towards the lift without Joe's assistance, trying to keep any shred of dignity I had left.

As we waited for the lift doors to slide closed, some of the party guests stared at me, including Ichigo, who was smirking with her head leant on Freddie Tilson's shoulder. I glowered at my Mum and Izumi until the lift doors closed. As we descended, Joe cleared his throat. 'What was that about?'

I ignored him. When we got out at the ground floor, I headed straight for the exit. There were no photographers or journalists around, just the security androids. They held open the doors for us and Joe tried to grab my arm as I walked on ahead of him.

'I don't need you to take me home.'

'But your Mum –'

I spun round and glared at Joe. 'I know you've been working for her. I found the reports you wrote about me. How long have you been stalking me?'

'What are you talking about?'

I couldn't listen to anymore lies. I turned and ran towards Liverpool Street Airground Station, but I could hear Joe's footsteps pounding on the pavement behind me, and he grasped my arm again once he caught up.

'I've never stalked you, Gracie.'

'Drop the act, Joe. I found the reports. I know it was you. My Mum has been feeding me Hydrobliss, whatever that is, and you've been following me, trying to find out what effect it's been having on me.' I ripped my arm from Joe's grip and carried on walking, but he persisted.

'Gracie, I don't know what happened in the Tower with your Mum and Mr. Izumi, but it has obviously made you upset. You need to calm down.'

'Don't lecture me. I know what I saw.'

'You're being irrational.'

The word "irrational" reverberated in my ears and I finally snapped. I kneed Joe between the legs and left him groaning on the pavement as I ran for the nearest taxi rank. He had that coming for a long time.

***

'Good evening, Miss Thrace. How was the party?' Macy asked from the kitchen doorway.

I ignored her and went straight to my room, then locked myself in with my Hourglass. I kicked my shoes off and they smacked against the wall. I sank to the floor and burst into tears. Everyone had joked about Izumi and Mum. I never really thought she would do anything, though. Our family wasn't perfect, far from it, but I thought Mum and Dad loved each other. Then there were the documents I had found – MKUltra, that other participant, the reports on me… I knew Joe was involved. But did that mean that Chris knew too? Chris was an intern at IrukaTech. Maybe he had introduced Joe to my Mum. Should I tell Iliana? God, I needed to talk to someone about all of this. What was my Mum doing to me?

Gracie?

I looked up and saw Kai stood in front of me, his face showing concern even though he hadn't been around for three weeks.

Come here. He lifted me into his arms and carried me over to the bed. *What's wrong?*

I burst into tears again and he hugged me, letting me cry into his chest. 'Don't you dare leave me again, you idiot,' I whispered.

I won't. I'm sorry. I promise, I won't. Not ever again.

I carried on crying and Kai wiped away my tears. He got the baby wipes from my desk and removed my makeup for me, smiling once the cloth was in the bin.

You look even more beautiful without makeup.

'Thank you. No one else seems to think that I do.'

No one else matters except me. Tell me what happened.

I told Kai everything – Mum and Izumi's affair, the file, Hydrobliss, Joe's reports. 'No one is going to believe me. They'll think I'm making it up.'

I believe you. He looked nervous for the first time since I had met him. *Actually, I need to tell you something.*

'This sounds serious.'

It is. He shuffled away from me, stopping just outside my arm length.

'Is this about our relationship?' Just saying it made tears well up in my eyes and Kai moved to sit next to me again and took my hand in his.

Yes. But just listen, okay? When I first appeared, I told you that I hadn't met the Voices, but that's not completely true. We'd met once. They wanted me to manipulate you by being kind and flirting with you, to see if they could control you without having to use fear. I agreed.

'Kai...' I pulled my hand out of his and backed away from him.

But once I met you properly... He shook his head and sighed. *You're so wonderful. I... I started to fall for you and I really do like you, Gracie. So, I used my deal with them to your advantage. When we were at the party and Eros and Terry were hurting you, I made them stop, because they knew if I was the one to make them back off, then you would like me. I'd already fallen for you by then and I didn't want you to get injured.* He looked down at the duvet and shook his head. *I should have told you all this sooner.*

'Then why didn't you?'

I was scared of you hating me. I couldn't stand it if you hated me. But seeing how upset you were after finding out all the things your Mum has been doing to you…I know it would have hurt you more the longer I waited.

I stared at him for a moment. I could easily turn this into argument and ask him why he hadn't told me when he had first appeared, or when we had become friends, or when I told him I had feelings for him. But I really needed him tonight. I crawled over so I was sat beside him. 'You've told me now and you did the right thing. That's what matters.'

I gently took hold of his hand and Kai looked at me with those beautiful eyes that I loved so much. The ocean wasn't blue anymore, but I had seen photos and drawings of what it used to look like and none of them compared to all of the colours shining and shifting in Kai's eyes. I kissed him on the cheek and he grinned as a blush rose to his face.

You're so embarrassing.

I laughed and wrapped my arms around him. After everything that had happened tonight, having Kai back was exactly what I needed. We got changed into our pyjamas and climbed under the covers together. I laid my head against his chest and frowned when I couldn't feel his heartbeat. I tried not to think about it.

'Oyasumi, Kai-chan.'

Goodnight, Gracie

'Are you impressed with my Japanese?'

You always impress me.

REPORT ON PARTICIPANT NUMBER 1 OUT OF 4:
Miss Gracie Thrace

22/11/2047   SHE KNOWS. IMPLEMENT EXPOSURE
             PROTOCOL.

CHAPTER 20

Saturday 23rd November 2047
Level 64: 444 XP
Time to sunset: 0 hours 4 minutes

'So, are you going to tell your Dad?'

Iliana's voice was full of concern during our Hourglass call. I'd told her about Mum and Izumi but decided to skip over everything else. I had expected her to say, "I told you so", since she had already guessed they were together, but she didn't.

'I don't know. I want to tell him, but part of me thinks I should wait until he gets home and speak to him then, face-to-face.'

'He might not be home for months, Gracie. What about your Mum? Do you think she'll tell him?'

'I doubt it. But I haven't spoken to her about it properly yet. Not that I want to.'

I sighed and laid down on my bed. I already had enough to think about before I found Mum and Izumi kissing. It was all too much to take in. Kai came into the room, drying his hair with one of my towels.

Gracie, it's almost time.

I glanced at my Hourglass and almost swore. 16:01. Sunset was at 16:02 today. 'Sorry, Iliana, but my Mum's just come home. I have to go.'

'Screw your Mum! Who cares if she hears us talking about her?! She's the one having an affair!'

'Iliana, I don't want to make things any worse. I'll talk to you tomorrow, yeah?'

I ended the call just as Eros manifested in front of me, looking smug as usual.

'Scenario: you must help your Dad fight VIRENT in Egypt. If he dies, you lose. Do you accept the scenario?'

I sat up, my eyes wide in fright. The scenario was worse than burying the killer clown. How did they know?

Rule 11: The Voices are allowed to access the player's fears.

Kai walked over and sat down next to me. *It'll be okay. I'll help you.*

'But… my Dad…' I whispered, tears already welling up in my eyes.

I know you're scared, but I'll be with you the entire time, okay?

I pressed a kiss to his cheek in thanks.

'Please confirm your choice.'

The buttons popped up in front of me and I selected the "Yes" option. They disappeared and Kai pushed me onto the floor, holding my body low as a bullet flew passed my ear. Once he let go of me, I sat up a little, but kept my head down, and saw that the room had been transformed into an Egyptian wasteland. The laminate floor was now made of rubble so fine that it felt like sand and my bed had turned into a burnt-out car. The landscape extended for miles outside my bedroom walls, and in the distance, near where the front door would have been, was a semi-destroyed apartment block. I could still see the walls that had once separated the rooms inside, but now they just looked like prison cells without bars.

'What is this?' I asked Kai. 'I've never seen anything like this before.'

What do you mean?

'The hologram is huge. Eros and Psyche have never done this before. I didn't know they *could* do this.'

They're just trying to throw you off. You're still in your house. You can see the walls and doors. You just need to integrate them with the hologram when you move.

I nodded, still feeling a little dazed, but Kai was right. The Voices were trying to disorientate me. They had probably realised that it was getting harder for me to differentiate between scenarios and reality. So, why not just lay a hologram over my whole house? That would make it worse, guaranteed.

Sorry if I hurt you when I pushed you down, Kai said as he took my hand in his.

'It's alright. You were just trying to protect me.'

'I could protect you.' I looked up and saw Psyche sitting on top of the car, the hem of her chiton and her feet invisible.

'No, thanks.'

'Why not?' she asked, frowning as she slid off the car and sat on the other side of me.

I tried to move away from her. If I was rude, she would only make the scenario worse. I bumped into Kai's chest.

He wrapped an arm around me and poked his head over my shoulder so he was glaring at Psyche.

You're the one who's been making her play these scenarios all along. You said so yourself. Why would Gracie want you to help her? Just go. It's a wonder that you even have a husband. I have no idea how he puts up with you.

Psyche lunged at Kai, but he was stronger and managed to push her away. She hissed at him and then disappeared, giving the inside of my head a good flick as she went.

'I don't think you should have done that.'

I'll handle Psyche. You concentrate on your Dad.

I nodded and peered around the side of the car. A couple of feet away, where a pile of my dirty clothes had been, was a mound of rubble and a gun on the ground next to it. After taking a quick look around, I crawled over to the rubble and looked at the gun. Kai followed me.

What's that?

'An AK47. My Dad's regiment organises army fun days for soldiers' families. They sometimes teach us how to shoot guns at targets.'

I wiped the rubble dust off it. The hand guard, grip, and butt were all made out of wood, or something that resembled wood, but the rest of the gun was made out of black metal. There was congealed blood on the trigger.

'Should I take it?'

Kai stared at it. *Do you know how to use it?*

'No.'

I think you should leave it then.

There was an explosion not far off, about two houses away where the back garden should have been.

'The fighting is happening over there. That's where my Dad will be. Let's go.'

We moved forwards, keeping our bodies as low as possible. We crouched behind what was left of a wall. I scanned the area once again and felt a lump form in my throat. This was how my Dad spent most of his time, helping to evacuate refugees and disarm rogue androids. I didn't know how he could do it, how he could survive in this wasteland. I wouldn't last ten seconds if this was real. I felt proud of my Dad for giving his life to help fight VIRENT.

'I hate this scenario.'

It's okay. I'm here.

Kai gave one of my hands an encouraging squeeze and Psyche groaned inside my head.

Shut up, Psyche.

'You'll shut up if you know what's good for you.' Just as she spoke, a bullet pinged off the wall that we were using for cover.

'That was you, wasn't it?' I asked Psyche.

'Well, there are no VIRENT androids around here to do it for me.'

She didn't say anything more, so I poked my head around the wall and checked the area. There was no one around, but I stood up with caution, just in case any soldiers were hiding. When I deemed the area safe, I turned to Kai. 'The area's clear. Let's go.' We left my bedroom and moved down the hallway together, entering one of the partially destroyed rooms of the building when we got near the front door.

Where are your Mum and Macy? Kai asked as he crouched down next to me.

'Mum will have taken her out to help with the shopping. Or not help, since Macy keeps on breaking down whenever she's away from her power charger for too long.' There was another explosion, a lot closer this time, and the building shook. Dust landed on our heads. 'It's not safe in here.'

Agreed. Through here.

Kai started to wiggle his body through a gap at the bottom of the wall in front of us and I crawled after him. As soon as I stood up, I had a gun pointed at my head and I held up my hands in surrender. I could feel my blood rushing through my body, but after a few deep breaths and assurances in my own head that this wasn't real, I realised that Kai and I were surrounded by British soldiers, not a group of VIRENT terrorists. They were all glaring at me. The person holding the gun prodded my temple with the barrel and I risked glancing to the side to get a closer look at them. The bright Egyptian sunlight was blocking my view. I was only able to see the light glinting off the gun they held. As our eyes met, the weapon was lowered and the gunman took a step back. Out of the sunlight, I recognised him as Private Anderson, one of the newer soldiers in my Dad's regiment. 'Captain Thrace!'

The other soldiers parted and I saw my Dad. He was wearing his uniform along with heavy-duty boots and a helmet, a gun in his hands and a rucksack slung over his back. He turned around, face stern, but it melted away when he saw me. 'Gracie?' He stepped towards me, his gun now pointed to the floor.

Psyche appeared behind him, holding the AK47 and pointed it at his head. 'Time to say bye-bye to your Daddy, Gracie Thracie.'

'No!' I ran forwards, wanting to push my Dad out of the way, but Psyche pulled the trigger and shot him. Dad's hologram shattered into pieces along with the rest of the Egyptian landscape.

'You have failed the scenario. You gain nothing. You have until the 31st December to reach Level 75.'

'That's not fair!' I shouted, tears in my eyes as I glared at Psyche. 'You killed him! You can't do that!'

'It doesn't say that in the nightmare scenario rules. Right, Terry?'

Terry appeared next to Psyche and brought a handbook out of his blazer pocket. He quickly flipped through the pages. 'Nope. Psyche killing your Dad's hologram is allowed. You failed, Gracie.'

I lunged towards Psyche. I wanted to slap her, or hit her, or do something, but Kai held me back. 'Why are you doing this to me?!' I shouted at her. 'You had to complete trials to be with Eros. Why are you making me do it, too, when you know how horrible it is?!'

Psyche slinked towards me with a grin on her face. 'I never had to do that. I was asked to, but I never completed any trials. I made others do them for me. And that's what I've been doing to you, Gracie. It's fun watching you do trials. I like watching you cry.' She laughed and I tried to run towards her again, but Kai tightened his grip on my arms.

'Let go of me!'

Gracie, calm down—

'No! She killed him!'

He wasn't real. That wasn't him.

'But she killed him…' I choked on the tears that were rising up in my throat and I started sobbing. My body went limp in Kai's hold.

Shush, it's okay.

Kai took me into his arms and turned me away from Psyche. 'She killed him, Kai…'

It's alright, Gracie. It's okay. It wasn't him. He was just a hologram. Your Dad is fine, I promise.

I cried into his chest, wanting nothing more than to just stay there for the rest of the night. Psyche and Terry started to laugh. 'Well done, Kai. I never expected her to fall for you this quick. You manipulated her well.'

Kai let go of me and stood up. *Shut up. It's not like that.*

'Aww, did little Gracie Thracie not know that I was getting Kai to beguile you so we could control you even more?'

'I know, Psyche,' I said, wiping away some of my tears but my voice still shook as I spoke. 'Kai's not trying to control me by being kind anymore. We really like each other.'

Psyche's blue and white face turned red. She screamed and rushed towards me, her hologram disappearing just before it passed through me.

'You didn't tell her I knew?' I asked Kai, and he shook his head.

Before he could reply, the front door opened and Mum walked in with Macy. 'Gracie?'

I got up and ran to my room, locking it with my Hourglass so Mum couldn't get in. I jumped in bed and curled up under the covers, then wrapped my pillow around my head to try and block out anything my Mum said. It didn't work.

'Gracie?' Mum shouted from outside the room.

'Go away!' I replied, my words muffled by the pillow.

'Gracie, this is ridiculous! Just let me in! I need to talk to you properly about Andy!'

I held the pillow even tighter around my head and Kai got into bed with me. He wrapped his arms around me and started to sing something in Japanese in my ear to drown out my Mum's voice. I just wanted my Dad to be home.

CHAPTER 21

After I had played the scenario for the evening, which involved a weird hostage negotiation situation and convincing a hologram version of Macy to not rip out her circuits, I got a call from Dad. I fell off my bed when I saw his name light up my Hourglass' screen and I scrambled to press the green phone icon before it rung out.

'Dad!'

He chuckled and the boom of his voice sounded so warm and familiar. I could imagine him so clearly sat in the barracks, smiling at his Hourglass. 'Hey, Gracie.'

'I thought your Hourglass was deactivated?'

'It was. We've moved to Cyprus for a bit of a break whilst other squad groups take over in Egypt. The technicians have reactivated all of our Hourglasses for ten minutes so we can talk to our families.'

'Have you rung Mum?' I asked.

'I couldn't get hold of her. She must be in a meeting or something like that. How have things been at your end?'

'Absolute hell.'

'What's been going on?'

I sighed. 'Just Mum. She keeps making me cry.' I decided to miss out everything about the affair and the Voices.

'Oh, Gracie. She doesn't mean to upset you.'

'Really? Because it seems like she's doing it on purpose to me. When are you coming home?'

'I don't know exactly. After Christmas. I promise you'll be the first to know once a date gets given.'

I slumped back on my bed. It was so good to hear Dad's voice but it made me realise how much I missed him being around. 'I want to come to Egypt.'

'No, you don't,' he said, switching from calm "Dad" to tough "Captain Thrace".

If I went to Egypt, yes, I would be in danger. A lot of danger. I knew I wouldn't survive for more than ten seconds without a lot of help, but I would have my Dad, I would have Kai and I would be away from this hell hole, so what would it matter how much danger I was in?

'You. Are not. Coming. To Egypt. Do I make myself clear?'

'Yes, Dad.'

'Good.' He went back to "Dad" voice and I could sense him smiling. 'Have you met any boys at uni?'

I laughed and nodded. 'Yes. I have a stalker.'

'Just tell him that your Dad's a Captain in the army and he'll leave you alone, I'm sure.'

'Don't worry, Izumi's already threatened him for you.'

'Speaking of which, how was his party?'

I shrugged, not wanting to think about everything I found out from my short trip to Tower 142. 'Boring. Ichigo was flirting with Freddie Tilson. That was about it. There's not much to tell.'

Dad laughed. 'That's usually how it goes with her. Wasn't she trying it on with that actor Daniel Readson last year?'

'She tries it on with everyone.'

'I know. Did anyone try it on with you?'

I laughed. 'In my dreams.'

'I'm serious, Gracie.'

I fiddled with a loose thread on my jumper. Joe and Kai were the only boys to ever show any interest. I knew Joe had been faking his attraction in order to get close to me for his reports, and Kai had been doing something similar for a while. At least his feelings were genuine.

'So am I. No one came near me. I briefly spoke to the driver of the limo Izumi arranged for us, then to Izumi when we got to the party, then my stalker from university, then Ichigo, then...' I trailed off, remembering my dance with Jack Howard, the Defence Secretary. So much else had happened at the party that I'd completely forgotten about my strange conversation with him. 'The Defence Secretary was there. He said he knew you.'

Dad paused on the line for a moment before he chuckled. 'What?'

'Yeah, he said he knew you and that he was impressed with the little stunt we pulled off at my university. I had no idea what he was talking about.'

He laughed again. 'Me neither. I don't even know the name of the Defence Secretary. He was probably just mistaken. I wouldn't worry too much about it.' He paused again. 'I'm really sorry, Gracie, but I have to go now. The technicians have just come back to deactivate all of our Hourglasses.'

'But you said we had ten minutes.'

'I know, I'm sorry. If I get a chance to ring you again, I'll stay on the line for the full time. Bye, Gray.'

My Hourglass' screen turned black. 'Kai-chan?'

He appeared beside me, already dressed in his pyjamas. *You okay?*

I shrugged. 'Dad just rang.'

I told you he was alive. The Dad you saw in the scenario was just a hologram and wasn't real. Psyche was just accessing your memories to get a reaction out of you. And she won.

'I know. I won't let it happen again.'

Good, because I can't have you being so distraught that you're unable to ask Macy to make me some rice.

I just smiled, trying not to think about what he'd just said about my Dad's hologram not being real. What if, after all this, Kai's hologram wasn't real either?

CHAPTER 22

Iliana and I were studying in the library between lectures and our shifts at the café. I was working on a couple of poems and Kai was playing with my hair, whilst Iliana kept sighing as she doodled in the notepad she reserved for her Japanese class. She had a dreamy smile on her face.

'You look happy,' I said.

She giggled and sat back in her chair. 'Chris brought me some flowers this morning.'

'How are things going?'

'Great. He's taking me out for dinner tomorrow night. We're just, you know, trying to take it slow... Have you seen Joe lately?'

I carried on writing and avoided looking at Iliana. 'Nope. He's a nasty piece of work and I don't want to talk about him.'

'It wouldn't hurt you to be a bit more open-minded?'

'Why should I just go for the first person who shows an interest?'

'I didn't say that –'

'That's what you meant. Just because I'm…' An experiment? A freak? Tears welled up in my eyes. I couldn't tell her. She would stop talking to me. She would tell someone about the Voices and Kai. I couldn't let that happen. Not after all the months I had been fighting against the Voices. A few tears rolled down my cheeks and Iliana wrapped an arm around me.

'Gracie… is there something you're not telling me? You hardly ever cry in front of me.'

I held a hand over my mouth as a sob threatened to escape. It had been hard with only Kai to talk to about the Voices. Which I suppose didn't help, since he was one of them. I looked up at Iliana. I could tell her everything, right now, and then it would all be out in the open.

Gracie?

Kai's face was full of concern. I wiped away my tears. If I told Iliana, then that would mean no more Kai and I couldn't bear that. 'I'm fine. Joe's just so horrible to me.'

Iliana hugged me. 'Alright, okay, I won't talk about him again.'

I managed to smile at her, then picked up my notepad. 'I'm just going to find a book I need for screenwriting.'

'Want me to come with you?'

'I'm fine, I promise.'

I gave her another smile then went upstairs. I looked around briefly. When I was sure no one else was nearby, I slumped against the wall and let my tears fall. Kai manifested in front of me and brought me into his arms straight away.

Just ignore Iliana. She doesn't know what she's talking about. I'm interested in you.

I wanted to scream "you're not real", but instead I just nodded. 'I know. I'm fine. Go back downstairs. I just need a moment to myself.'

He nodded, and once he left, I started trying to find the bookcase I needed. I spent ten minutes traipsing up and down the rows of shelves, refusing to ask any androids for help, until I found section 808. I grabbed the screenwriting book I needed off the shelf and turned around to find Joe standing opposite me. I started to walk away, but he pinned me against the bookshelf before I could even take two steps.

'And where are you going?'

'Downstairs.'

'To do what?'

'Study.'

Joe laughed and tightened his grip, almost making me whimper. 'I don't think so. You haven't apologised for kicking me in the crotch after Izumi's party.'

'Why would I? You deserved it.'

He laughed again, quieter this time. The look in his brown eyes was feral. 'You'll regret it.'

He leant towards my lips, but I turned my head, reluctantly letting him kiss my cheek. He tutted and let go of me, but stood close enough that I could feel his breath on my nose. 'Tomorrow night you will pay for what you've done to me. Just you wait,' he whispered into my ear. He took a step back, eyes still glinting and wild. Then he walked away calmly, as if nothing had happened. I was left alone, shaking, with the screenwriting book clutched to my chest.

Iliana looked up when she saw me return and her brow furrowed in concern.

'Gracie? What happened?'

'Nothing. I'm fine.' I smiled at her and swallowed down the lump in my throat.

'Right… I'm just going to nip to the toilet. Back in a second.'

I nodded, watching as she went, only letting my shoulders slump down once she was a safe enough distance away.

Gracie? Kai asked, crouching down next to me. *What happened upstairs?*

'I'm not really sure. I got the book and Joe was stood there when I turned around. He told me that tomorrow night I'll pay for what I did to him.'

What's happening tomorrow night?

'I don't know. It's just Tuesday night. I'm not doing anything. I don't even have a shift at the café.'

Then why are you shaking?

'I'm not sure. It was just… the look in his eyes…' Just the thought of Joe's angry face made me tremble even more and Kai wrapped an arm around me.

Come on, let's get you home.

'As much as I would love to, I still have one more class and a shift at the café.'

Maybe you should go to work, but you're skipping class. Message Iliana later. Come on.

He kissed my cheek and packed my things away for me, then pulled me out of the library. He held my hand tight all the way home.

CHAPTER 23

I jiggled my leg up and down as I watched the hands on my Hourglass swivel round to show ten o'clock and I nearly started to cry.

It's okay.

I shook my head with a sniff. 'It's not. Can you go and check again please?'

He nodded and disappeared back into my head, while I sat on the bed holding my breath. Sunset happened hours ago but neither Eros, nor Terry, nor Psyche had appeared with my scenario. There was nothing. My head felt completely clear, but the silence seemed wrong and dangerous. I was sure they were going to manifest any minute and give me the worst scenario yet. I jerked at every little sound. I was petrified and exhausted from wondering when the scenario would come and how Joe's threat would be carried out. Kai reappeared looking concerned.

I can't find them.

'But they can't have just left, can they?'

No. Even when we didn't talk for the three weeks before Izumi's party, I was still inside your head. I just wasn't watching

265

what was happening on the outside, but I could tell if the other three were there.

'So, does this mean I won't have to play any more nightmare scenarios?' I asked, trying to keep the hope out of my voice. They couldn't have just disappeared for good, could they?

I'm not sure. It's odd. They might come back. Don't get your hopes up.

My Hourglass started ringing and I jumped.
Who is it?

'Iliana. I thought she was on a date with Chris.' I answered the call and held my Hourglass close to my face. 'Iliana?'

'Gracie!' she cried, panting a little.

'Are you okay? What's wrong?'

'It's Chris!' she shouted. 'And Joe!' What she said next was muffled, as if someone had put a hand over her mouth.

'What?! I can't hear what you're saying. What's happened? Where are you?'

'It's a trap!' she screamed, then the line went dead. Kai and I looked at each other. I tried to call her back. No reply. I tried to call Chris. Again, no reply.

What do we do now?

'She mentioned Joe. We need to find her.' I stood up and shouted for Macy.

The android walked into the room. 'How may I be of assistance, Miss Thrace?'

'Is Mum in?'

'Mrs Thrace is currently out of the house.'

'Good. Lie on the bed and take off your top, Macy.'

'Yes, Miss Thrace.'

What are you doing?

'When I was at IrukaTech, I found the blueprints for the trackers that the Police use. Macy's circuits are more sophisticated than my Orca, so I need to link her up to my Hourglass and find Iliana's tracker code so I can get her location. Hopefully.'

Ermmm… okay. You sound like you know what you're doing, so I'll just sit and watch.

'Thanks for the support, Kai.'

'Who are you talking to, Miss Thrace?' Macy asked, staring up at the ceiling.

'No one. You're imagining things.'

'I do not have an imagination.'

'Whatever.' I grabbed the scalpel from my toolkit and sat down next to Macy on the bed. 'I'm sorry about this, but I'll repair you later, okay?'

Her chest was the same as Maida's – leather pink skin, two lumps for breasts, and a Jangmi rose logo stamped into her navel. The only difference was that Macy had been cut open and re-stitched about 50 times for repairs or Dad's experiments. I cut the stitches running down the centre of her torso and moved the leather to one side, then unclipped the I/O shield to reveal Macy's inner wirings. The motherboard looked like a city, the resistors like houses, the capacitors and PCI slots like apartment buildings and the processor like a football stadium. The two slits where Macy's optical drive was meant to be were jammed with two slices of burnt, mouldy toast.

'Macy, how long has this toast been inside you?'

'I do not remember, Miss Thrace.'

I took the toast out and threw it in the general direction of my bin, then I lifted up the latch on Macy's processor. It was like Maida's – small and white, but a little dirty since Macy was much older.

What are you going to do now?

'Well, I can't disconnect the processor, because that'll probably destroy Macy...' I had to be careful. Macy was an old android and one wrong move could send her rouge. But I wasn't sure what I needed to do. I thought back to what I had done when Maida malfunctioned and remembered the cable I used when Professor Long tried to get her BIOS setup screen up on the computer.

I went over to where I kept my toolkit and rooted through it until I found my cable. I plugged one end into the tiny hole in Macy's hip, then I unclipped the case from around my Hourglass. I winced involuntarily at the sight of the surgery scars. I loaded up Iliana's contact details, then inserted the other end of the cable into my Hourglass. Macy's head started to make a whirring sound and the face of my Hourglass changed to lines and lines of numbers and letters. I had no real idea what I was looking for since I knew next to nothing about computer coding, but I found a line that read, "ISL0000927".

'I think I've got her tracker code.'

Now what? You don't have an Hourglass tracker.

'No. But if I type the code into the maps app, it might give me her coordinates, and then I can use those to find her.'

Just do whatever you think is best.

I wrote Iliana's tracker code down, disconnected my Hourglass from Macy, and then typed the code into my Hourglass' map app. As I hoped, it gave me her coordinates, so I switched on my Orca and typed them into the internet search bar, praying that Iliana wasn't somewhere far away. A map popped up on my Orca. Tower 142. Iliana was at Tower 142. She had said it was a trap. It probably was. But I couldn't just leave her there. 'Go and get your shoes on, Kai-chan.'

Tower 142 somehow looked bigger than usual. The tall, triangular prism was lit up, but the top two floors were dark.

Be careful.

I tried to laugh. 'I don't even want to go in there.' Kai took my hand in his and gave it a squeeze. Nothing good seemed to happen when I went to Tower 142. I took a deep breath. The fear I'd been feeling all day had vanished as soon as Iliana rung, but now that we stood outside the imposing building with my best friend possibly in danger, my anxiety was back. 'Stay with me?'

Of course.

We passed through the automatic doors and into the foyer. The cafeteria was shut and there were no staff around apart from service user and security androids. It seemed strange and too quiet. All I could hear was the faint hum of the lights. A security android rolled out from behind the front desk.

'Please present your Hourglass.'

I held out my Hourglass and one of the androids scanned it.

'Miss Gracie Thrace, daughter of Mrs Sharon Thrace. You are not permitted to enter the IrukaTech UK Headquarters after it has closed. Please leave or the Police shall be alerted.'

'Yeah, I thought so.' Despite my shaking hands, I punched the security android hard in the neck and he fell to the floor. A few sparks fired from his blue wire and he began to splutter. We stepped over the broken android and pressed the button to call the lift.

You really need to be less violent.

'Says the one who punched Joe in the face.'

I'm a hologram. He's a human. It's alright.

'He's an android. I'm a human. It's also alright.'

The lift doors opened and we got in.

Which floor?

'138.' I didn't know which floor Joe and Chris were holding Iliana, since the tracker coordinates weren't that accurate, but I thought we should start with a floor I was familiar with. Kai pressed the right button and we waited in silence. As we got higher, I grabbed his hand.

You okay?

'No. I'm nervous.'

Everything will be fine.

I nodded, really wanting Kai's words to be true. The lift doors pinged open and we stepped onto the 138th floor. The room was eerie now it was empty. There were no dancing couples or android waiters or a live orchestra. Just a dark room. After only taking two steps, the buzzing started and Eros, Psyche, and Terry manifested in front of us, all three grinning like maniacs.

'Scenario: save Iliana. If you fail to save her, you lose. Do you accept the scenario?'

I squeezed my eyes shut. This was why the scenario hadn't started at sunset. This was what they had been waiting for. They had known what was going to happen tonight. And it was real. Like the cement in the shower and the android clown's body I had buried. They were using my real life for their sick game, somehow finding out what was going on and waiting for me to play it out for them. I knew there would be no holograms this time. This would be Iliana, my Iliana, in real danger. I wasn't sure if I could do this.

I re-opened my eyes. Eros, Psyche, and Terry were waiting for my answer with frenzied smiles plastered on their fake faces.

'I accept.'

'Please confirm your choice.'

The yellow buttons popped up in front of me. I raised my hand to select "Yes" but I couldn't press it. Iliana was in trouble, but to the Voices, especially Psyche, this was all just one big game and they were using what was happening tonight to their advantage. They didn't care who got hurt, but I did. I couldn't play with my best friend's life just to get some XP and to satisfy Psyche's sick enjoyment of watching me cry.

What's wrong? Kai asked, still holding my hand.

'I can't play this scenario,' I whispered. 'What if Iliana gets hurt? This won't be like the scenario in Egypt, where everything is a hologram. It's like the one in the shower. What if I can't save Iliana and something happens to her?'

It won't come to that. I promise that it won't. I won't let it.

'You can't promise that, Kai.'

I can. You need to trust me on this. Do you trust me? He squeezed my hand and I nodded without a moment of hesitation. *Good. Everything will be fine. We can handle this.*

I gulped, then selected "Yes" and the buttons vanished, along with Psyche, Terry, and Eros. Kai and I were left alone again and I switched on my Hourglass' torch. Part of me wanted to hurry and find Iliana, in case she was hurt, but another part of me wanted to take things slow. I took a long-anguished breath. I couldn't get this wrong.

'I have a feeling she'll be on the 141st floor, considering what happened the last time I was here. We'll use the emergency stairs.'

I led Kai through the 138th floor. The marble pillars and fake ceiling domes looked less impressive in the light of my Hourglass. Something crunched underneath my foot and I focused my torch light on the floor. There was a partially hidden piece of paper under my shoe. I let go of Kai's hand and picked up an "Irukian Rising" leaflet with the Jangmi logo stamped in the corner. It was the same as the flyers we'd collected during the Il-gob scenario.

Is it a hologram? Did Psyche put it here?

'No, it's real. Someone before us must have dropped it.' It could have been anyone. I put it in my jeans pocket and continued to the emergency stairs.

'We'd better keep quiet now,' I said, one hand holding Kai's, the other on the door handle.

It's okay. I'll be with you the entire time. He kissed me on the cheek and gave my hand one last squeeze. *You've got nothing to worry about. I'll step in if you need help.*

'So will we,' Psyche said from inside my head. 'We've waited ages to see this. It's like a movie premiere. We've got popcorn ready and everything. I really want to watch you cry again. Can you just imagine what they're doing to Iliana up there? Oh, I can't wait to see!' The three of them cackled and Kai turned to glare at my ear.

Shut up, Psyche.

She gave the inside of my skull a good flick and I groaned in pain. 'Please, stop.'

Psyche just hummed. 'Maybe your boyfriend should be nicer to me. He doesn't know about the sorts of things I could do to you when he's not around. Or maybe I could make things worse for Iliana...'

Ignore her. She can't do anything.

I wanted to ask them why they had waited until after sunset to give me the scenario, how they had known what was going to happen tonight, but I knew they wouldn't give me a straight answer. I opened the door and we tiptoed up to the 141st floor. As we ascended, my mind drifted back to what happened the last time I was in this stairwell. I'd never shouted at Izumi before, or my Mum for that matter. But now wasn't the time to get pre-occupied. I had to focus on Iliana.

Once we made it up the stairs, I peered through the window in the door. The room was completely dark, but I could see there was something moving inside. I shone my light on the window and saw Iliana, tied to a chair. Without hesitation, I pushed open the door and ran towards her, but as soon as she saw me, she started crying.

'No! Go! It's a trap, Gracie!'

Watch out, Gracie!

I skidded to a halt, but it was too late. Two security androids waiting on either side of the door grabbed my arms and secured them in their titanium grip behind my back. I struggled in their grasp and I watched as Kai tried to pry me free from their fingers, but it was no use. A man started to laugh and for a moment I thought it was Eros, but then Joe stepped out of the shadows.

'Took you long enough,' Joe said with a smirk.

'What's going on?!'

'You already know. I told you yesterday that you would pay for what you did to me. Don't you ever listen?'

'Where's Chris?' I asked, ignoring Joe. 'Iliana said he was here.' Iliana whimpered at the mention of her boyfriend, her face stained with tear streaks.

'You'll see him later.'

I glared at Joe, despite how scared I was feeling. I really had no idea what was going on. 'You better not have hurt either of them or –'

'Or what?' Joe interrupted, regaining the vicious look I'd seen yesterday in the library. 'You'll get your imaginary boyfriend to punch me again?'

'How did –'

'I know? Because you were right. I *have* been watching you ever since you started hearing the Voices. What a coincidence.'

'What…?' Iliana asked, still crying. 'What's he talking about?'

'I'm sure that she'll explain everything to you once it's all over,' Joe leered. 'But for now, Gracie's mother wants a chat with her.'

CHAPTER 24

I struggled as the two androids forced me further into the room. Iliana's sobs became quieter and I sucked in a breath when I saw that we were heading for Mum's office. It was no surprise really. Mum was sitting behind her desk when we entered, scribbling something down in the dim light. She looked up and frowned. Her desk was still as messy as the last time I saw it, but the C.I.A. folder and Joe's file were missing from the top of the papers.

'Why did it take you so long to get here?'

'The security androids at reception held me up. If you wanted to bring me here, I thought you would at least let me in.'

Mum gave Joe a stern look. 'I thought you had that covered?' Joe looked embarrassed.

'I also had to track Iliana's Hourglass which took a bit of time.'

Instead of Mum ripping into Joe again, she looked taken aback. 'And how the hell did you manage that?'

'I saw the blueprints for the Hourglass tracker at the party, so I used Macy's processor and my Hourglass to find her.'

Mum nodded and let out a little chuckle. She looked unusually impressed. 'I told you that you should have done Electronic Engineering at university.'

I ignored my Mum's comment which I had heard a thousand times before. 'What do you want with Iliana? She hasn't done anything wrong.'

Mum just shrugged as if it was no big deal. 'That was just to get you here. Joe's arranged for some androids to take her downstairs. She'll be heading home. I expected her to tell you where she actually was. Then again, the stupidity of that girl should never surprise me.'

'And Chris? Where is he?'

Mum chuckled again. 'I'm afraid we'll have to keep him here for a while longer. He's the brain behind Hydrobliss. I take it you know what that is by now.' I shook my head and my Mum sighed. 'You always were short-sighted. Hydrobliss is a drug that induces some symptoms of schizophrenia, developed here, at IrukaTech,' she said with a smile. Joe came to stand at her side.

'Why do you want to give people schizophrenia? That's ridiculous!'

'Keep your thoughts to yourself,' Joe snapped.

'You've kidnapped my best friend just to get me to come here! Don't tell me what to do!' I shouted. I looked around for Kai and saw that he was next to Joe, glaring, his fists at the ready. I shook my head and he lowered his hands. This would get ten times worse if Kai started fighting for me.

'Anyway,' Mum continued, giving Joe a stern look for interrupting, 'we want to be able to control people more and the most effective way to do that is through fear. The nightmare scenarios that the Voices from your strain of Hydrobliss create are exactly what we're looking for. Just a little more tweaking and we'll have it.'

'But why do you need to control people? You already know where everyone is at all times of the day. Why do you need to control their behaviour too?'

'Why wouldn't you want to control everyone? There's very little crime in the country because of the tracker and if we can control everyone's thoughts and feelings, then there will be no crime at all. We can live in a paradise, in a utopia. Can you imagine how brilliant that will be? To not have to worry about anything? We'd control every aspect of people's lives. Isn't that freeing?' She smiled as she spoke and her eyes seemed to enlarge slightly. Did she honestly think she was doing a good thing, the right thing?

'So, Izumi knows about this?'

'Some of it. Not everything. He loves me, he trusts me, so there are no questions asked.'

'He'll find out everything eventually. He created the Hourglass. He's not stupid.'

'I know. When he does find out, he'll be okay with it. Andy's a revisionist. He wants to make this country as safe as it can possibly be. That's why he made the Hourglass. For everyone's sake. Andy hasn't been happy since his wife and son died. By making this country into a utopia, he'll have more opportunity to be happy again. To see his utopian vision become reality. That's all I want for him. To be happy. Everyone else will be too. This will benefit everyone.'

I couldn't believe what I was hearing. 'You'd do all of this for your boss and the rest of the country, but you'll barely talk to your own husband and daughter? You're delusional.'

Instead of glaring at me like I thought she would, she gave me a dozy smile. 'Precisely. You and your father have done nothing for me. All this time you have both held me back. I never wanted children – your father pressured me to have you. Why would I want a child when my career could help me to bring happiness to the world? Why would I want to stop that, to stop my mission?'

I stared at her, completely dumbfounded by her honesty and hatred toward me. Dad had said that she loved me. How could he be so wrong? How could he have not seen the truth? I had always thought it was pretty obvious how she felt about me, regardless of what Dad said. 'Do you honestly think that what you're doing here is justification to hate me? I've done nothing wrong. Except being born, apparently. As soon as Izumi finds out about this, he'll put a stop to it.'

Mum shook her head and her smile widened. 'He won't. He'll understand that I'm doing this for him. Andy's given us all so much. The Hourglass has changed my life... everyone's lives, in fact. We need to repay him. When the drug has been perfected, it will be administered through everyone's Hourglass. Once it's in the blood stream, it becomes permanent. Then the fear that the Voices cause will make people conform to our rules and once they do, no one will step out of line. Don't you see what kind of paradise we can make this country if everybody conforms?'

'What about the Irukians?' I asked, thinking of Hayden and Daisy in the Underground. 'They don't have Hourglasses. How are you going to control them?'

'More and more Irukians are being found every day,' Joe said with a shrug. 'Once they're captured, they will be given the Hourglass by force.'

'You can't do that!' I shouted. 'We shouldn't have to wear these stupid things!'

'Shut up, Gracie,' Joe said, glaring at me.

You shut up.

I looked back at Kai, whose fists were ready once more. I shook my head at him, but this time Joe noticed.

'What are you shaking your head at?' He smirked then. 'Oh, is Kai here?' I looked at the floor, not wanting to reply.

'Kai's the boyfriend, right?' Mum asked.

'He's not my boyfriend,' I muttered, feeling myself blush despite the situation I was in.

'Yeah, he is. They're always holding hands.'

It's none of your business what we do together.

Kai came over to me. He started trying to pry the metal hands off my arms, but it made the androids tighten their grip this time. 'Kai, don't, it hurts!' I shouted, no longer caring that my Mum and Joe could hear me talking to someone no one else could see.

'You really believe you can see him, don't you? I'm surprised how well the hallucinations have taken effect. Anyway, tell him that I'm sorry, but he won't be in the next participant's strain of Hydrobliss. We wanted to experiment, to see if a love interest could manipulate and control you even more but it has clearly backfired.'

I can hear, you bitch.

'What about the other participants?' I asked. 'When I found my file, I was called "Participant 1". Someone called Elena Cassidy is "Participant 4". Who are "Participant 2" and "Participant 3"? Are there more than four of us?'

'I can't tell you that. I have no idea who they are. I'm only in charge of the British participants.'

My eyes widened. Were they were planning to do this in more than one country? 'Where are they all?'

'Don't you listen? I don't know. It's a blind trial. But I do know that their results are good. Much better than yours. This Elena, she's absolutely frightened for her life and you couldn't even do that right.'

I shook my head as I closed my eyes, not wanting Mum to see my tears forming. She had volunteered me for a drug trial that gave me schizophrenia. She hated me. She *really* hated me.

'Why me? Why did you experiment on me?'

'I needed to keep an eye on the first participant, so you were the obvious choice, plus the drug had to be administered to you orally. But why didn't you ever tell anyone about the Voices? That's what I find the most strange,' she said, a light smile creeping on to her face.

'Because I felt like a freak. Because I thought there was something wrong with me. Because I'd be locked in a hospital.' I looked up at my Mum. 'Is that what you were aiming for? To have me locked away?'

'Au contraire. I wanted to see the Voices degrade you and put you under extreme stress. Clearly, the Voices and scenarios weren't scary enough for you. Maybe I should have picked a different time to first administer the Hydrobliss instead of just before your A-Level exams… I'm still not sure how you managed to pass and get into university.'

Kai glared at my Mum, then placed a hand on my shoulder, the only place he could really reach while the androids were holding me.

Don't let her words get to you, Gracie. You're strong. You're the strongest person I know. It'll be over soon. Then we'll go straight home to bed for a cuddle and spend all day tomorrow together. We'll be completely fine. I'll make you forget about tonight.

I nodded. He was right, this would be over soon, but I had no idea how this could end with a good outcome. My Mum jerked her head and the androids restraining me took me over to the door in my Mum's office, the one with the porthole that had been locked the last time I was here.

'Sit her down in there. We have more questions for her.'

CHAPTER 25

Tuesday 26th November 2047
Level 65: 101 XP
Time to sunset: 16 hours 32 minutes

One of the androids opened the door and pulled me inside. The lights were bright, but once my eyes adjusted, I saw that we were in a lab. There were lots of worktops with microscopes sitting on them along with other bits of equipment that I didn't know the names for. On one table, at the furthest end of the small lab, was a rack full of Hydrobliss vials. Were they going to give me more drugs?

The androids sat me down in a chair in front of a computer desk but held me still. I glanced around again. The desk was like my Mum's – full of paperwork and no personal effects on it. I had no idea who it belonged to.

'Kai-chan?' I whispered.

Yeah?

'What are they doing?'

Your Mum and Joe? Joe's gone. I'm not sure where…

A moment later, Mum came into the room, then Joe, and behind him was Chris. I tried to stand up when I saw him.

'Chris…?'

He gave me a forlorn look but then sat behind the desk and powered up his Orca. 'How are you this evening, Miss Thrace?'

I glared at him. I didn't know Chris all that well, but I didn't think he would be involved in this experiment. I didn't think he'd be capable of putting me through this pain. How could he do this? 'What do you think?'

He fiddled with something on his Orca then shot a quick glance towards my Mum. 'Was Iliana okay?' He mumbled the question quietly and sounded concerned.

'Like you care about her.'

He gave me another mournful look then turned back to his Orca. 'Like Mrs Thrace said, we just have a few questions about your drug trial. There aren't many and this information won't be made public. Firstly, how was your experience on Hydrobliss?'

'You're seriously asking me that?'

Gracie. Kai said as he came to stand in between me and the desk. *The sooner you answer the questions, the sooner we can go.*

I gave him a little nod. 'It's been awful.'

Chris typed the answer down. 'How could it have been made better?'

'My Mum could have told me she was volunteering me for this in the first place. Secondly, it was incredibly scary and I'm probably going to have nightmares about it for the rest of my life. Thirdly, you shouldn't be subjecting anyone to this. What kind of monster are you to agree with my Mum that this is what's best for people?!'

My Mum tutted and she moved over to one of the worktops. I watched as she snapped on a pair of rubber gloves and began preparing something in a shallow silver tray. I was at the wrong angle to see what she was doing.

'Would you recommend Hydrobliss to anyone?'

'No.'

'If you had known from the start that you were taking Hydrobliss, would you have done anything differently?'

'Stayed with Iliana so my Mum wouldn't poison my food. These questions are so stupid. Do you honestly expect me to give positive answers?'

Chris ignored my comment and he took a moment before he read out the next question. 'Finally, what can we offer you in the way of aftercare?'

'Aftercare?' My eyes widened in alarm. 'No! I don't want the cure!' The cure meant no more nightmare scenarios, but it also meant no more Kai. I would play five scenarios every day for the rest of my life if it meant that Kai could stay. Although I had told him repeatedly that I wasn't going to be like this for the rest of my life, now that I was faced with never seeing him again, I suddenly realised that I didn't want to be cured. I could deal with Eros, Psyche and Terry as long as I had Kai by my side. I didn't know how it would work, being in a relationship with someone that wasn't real. Would it last? *Could* it last? I didn't know. But I had to try. We had to try. I couldn't let anyone take that away from me. From us.

I watched as my Mum brought over the silver tray with a syringe filled with a pale yellow liquid, along with several needles wrapped in sanitary towels. She placed it down in front of Chris, then she turned to me. 'I'm going to enjoy this, Gracie.'

Chris put on a pair of rubber gloves and attached one of the needles. I started struggling once more. I managed to stand up and Kai pulled on the robotic hands holding my arms again, but it was no use. The androids were too strong for us.

Come on, Gracie! We have to get out of here!

'I'm trying!'

Joe laughed and came to stand right in front of me, leaning down with his hands fixed on the arms of the chair. 'I said you would pay for what you did to me! Say goodbye to your "boyfriend".'

Kai turned and kneed Joe in the face. But this time, my Mum was there to help Joe.

'Chris, give her the cure before she hurts anyone else.'

'Yes, Mrs Thrace.' Chris stepped over to me, looking timid despite his build. 'I'm sorry,' he mouthed. 'Androids, keep her still. Joe, can you hold her head so she won't move?'

Joe spat blood onto the floor and he grinned at me, teeth red. 'It would be my pleasure.' The androids tightened their grip and I struggled again as Joe came towards me. He grabbed my chin, holding it tight in his large hands. I couldn't go anywhere.

Gracie!

I whimpered when I felt something cold on my neck. I tried to jerk away from the slick sensation of Chris disinfecting my skin but it was no use. I couldn't move at all.

'I told you that you would regret it, Gracie Thrace,' Joe said. Then the needle was inserted in my neck and I whimpered as I felt the new drug in my bloodstream.

'Kai!' I shouted, glancing at him.

He was looking right at me, trying to smile. *It's okay! I'll still be with you!*

'You said you wouldn't leave me again! You promised!'

I started to cry as Chris pulled out the needle and Joe let go of my head. He gave commands to the androids but I wasn't listening as they dragged me away. I stared at Kai, who was standing still and fading fast. He turned from technicolour to blue and white.

His feet disappeared first...

Then his legs and chest...

Then his face...

Then finally, his incredible blue eyes.

CHAPTER 26

Numb. My head felt numb. There was nothing there anymore. Empty. I was empty. The buzzing had stopped. My head was clear. I could finally breathe. But Kai had gone.

I let the androids drag me back into the lift and they kept holding me as we went down to the ground floor. What was the point struggling now? They pulled me across the foyer and out of the building towards a parked black car that hadn't been there earlier. They opened one of the back doors and threw me inside, locking it behind them. Immediately, I tried the other passenger door, but that was locked too.

'I wouldn't bother trying.'

I looked up and saw Geoff sat in the driver's seat. He was staring at me in the rear-view mirror, a sympathetic look on his face.

'Why are they locked?' I asked, my voice quieter than a whisper. I felt so detached.

'To stop you from running away.'

I leant forward and grabbed his headrest. 'Please, Geoff. I know you don't want to do this. Please, just let me out.'

He shook his head, still staring at me in the rear-view mirror. He couldn't even turn around and look at me. 'I'm sorry, Miss Thrace, but I can't do that.'

I sank back in my seat. There was nothing I could use to open the door or threaten Geoff with – if I even wanted to sink that low. I couldn't think straight. The front passenger door opened and Mum climbed in. 'Get out,' I muttered weakly and kicked the back of her chair but she didn't even flinch. My arms and legs felt like they were made of lead. Whatever strength I'd possessed before was even more useless now.

'Drive us home, Geoff.'

'Yes, Mrs Thrace.'

I glared at the back of Mum's seat as I felt my head roll against the window. What had the cure done to me? Kai still wasn't there. 'Kai-chan?' I asked, but there was nothing. No buzzing, no arms wrapped around my waist, no kiss to my cheek. Nothing. He was still gone.

'Get out of the car, Gracie.' I glanced up at my Mum. She was standing on the pavement and my door was open. How long ago did we arrive home? I didn't even notice. I did as she said, my hands shaking as I shuffled out of my seat. Mum grabbed my arm and hauled me along the path. She unlocked the front door and shoved me inside, then pushed me down the hallway.

'Go to bed.'

'No,' I said, finding my voice again. I turned around and glared at her. 'Why should I do anything you tell me to?'

She rolled her eyes as if I was throwing a petulant teenage strop and the last few hours hadn't happened. 'You need rest while the cure takes effect. Go to your room.'

My legs were trembling and I was struggling to focus. I hated her, but she was right. I needed to lie down for a bit. I turned in the direction of my room.

'He wasn't real, you know.'

'Who?'

'Kai. We made him up.'

I shook my head. I couldn't have fallen for a hallucination. 'He's real. He is. Just because I can't hear him anymore –'

'Gracie!' she said firmly. 'He was *never* real. We created him.'

'But he has memories! And a life! He gave his second button to his Aunty and he hates water and –'

'And what? He loved you?'

I looked away from her, blushing. 'No. We haven't known each other that long.'

'You didn't love him anyway.'

'You don't know anything about my feelings!' I shouted, tears welling up in my eyes. 'No, I don't love him, but I feel *something* for him'.

'When I gave you the new strain of Hydrobliss, you started to feel sick, didn't you? You felt sick when your heartbeat sped up. Joe said in one of his reports that you threw up at his party. That was your body rejecting the forced emotion.'

'What?'

'Your strain of Hydrobliss included the chemicals that react together to make love. I bet that every time Kai smiled at you, or gave you a compliment, or touched you, you felt your heartbeat speed up and then felt sick because your body was rejecting the forced "love" emotion. You never felt anything *real* for him. Nothing natural, nothing organic.'

I leant against the wall and held a hand to my head. No. I felt something for Kai. I did. Even now, when I thought about him, I could still feel my heartbeat quicken. I could feel the butterflies in my tummy and my face heating up. I may have initially fallen for Kai under the influence of Hydrobliss, but then I fell for him properly. I'm sure I did.

'I don't believe you.'

'Fine. Don't. I'm going back to IrukaTech to sort some things out.' She went over to the front door, but I called out to her.

'Is that what you tell yourself? That love is just a chemical?'

'That's what love is. Just a chemical reaction.'

I stepped forwards then and grabbed my Mum's arm, turning her around to face me. 'You don't love Dad?'

'Not anymore. I haven't done for a long time. I knew as soon as someone else came into our lives, he would love them more than me. I was right.' She looked like she was trying to hold back tears, but I didn't move to comfort her. 'He always wanted a daughter. He loves you more than he could ever love me. You can do no wrong in his eyes. I tried to get rid of you. Did you know that? I wanted an abortion but he stopped me. Your Dad vowed to protect you for the rest of his life. But he'll realise one day. Then you'll finally be all alone. It's what you deserve for ruining *my* life.'

I took a step back feeling as if I had been slapped by the barrage of hatred. 'For the record, don't think about going to the Police with this, or anyone for that matter. You have no evidence, no witnesses that will support your story and no one will believe what you claim. That is, of course, if you want to tell anybody about this because no-one will believe you. Not even Iliana. Where will that leave you? Your friendship with her ruined by suggestions you heard voices in your head? What would you say? "Don't worry Iliana, I did hear voices but they've gone now". Good luck with that. You are alone. Very much alone.'

Then she pulled her arm free and left, slamming the front door behind her. I sunk down onto the hallway floor. She had never wanted me. Ever. She wanted to get rid of me. None of us were important to her. My hands shook again and I started to cry.

I just wanted Kai. He was all I needed. But he wasn't here. How could I get him back? I jerked up, remembering the vials in the basement, the ones I had found when I had played a scenario. Mum had changed the basement door lock to an electronic one, but I had to find a way to get in.

I stumbled down the hall and I let out a sob of relief when I saw the basement door was ajar. It hadn't been like that before. Someone had been here whilst I had been out. With shaking hands, I pushed opened the door and almost fell down the stairs in my hurry. I put the basement light on and cried out when I saw that all of the vials had gone. Mum had probably got one of the IrukaTech androids to remove them whilst we were at Tower 142.

I grabbed the table the vials had been on and pushed it to the other side of the room. I got down on my hands and knees, searching for any vials they may have missed. Something smashed under my knee and I scrambled to get up, finding a vial of Hydrobliss, shattered on the concrete floor. I tried to scoop up the liquid in my hands, but there wasn't much, so I pressed my fingers to my mouth feeling two drips of the drug slide down my throat.

I sat on the floor and waited for what seemed like hours. I wanted to hear one of the Voices – or even the buzzing – but there was nothing. No Kai. No Eros. No Psyche. No Terry.

'I want to play!' I screamed, my knee bleeding and tears falling down my face. 'I want to play a nightmare scenario! Please!'

My plea was met with silence. I curled up on the basement floor, gasping and whimpering. I wrapped my arms around myself as if Kai was holding me, promising me that he wouldn't leave me, that everything would be okay, that we would be together again someday. But it was a lie. He had no Aunty or housekeeper, no second button. He didn't even know what rice was. He wasn't real.

'Are you satisfied now?!' I screamed and slapped both of my hands on the concrete floor. 'You got what you wanted, Psyche! Just come back! I want to play... Please...'

CHAPTER 27

When I woke up, I was lying on the basement floor, the smashed Hydrobliss vial was next to my head. A moment later, bile rose up in my throat and I threw up. Clear liquid splattered over the glass shards. I sat back when I had finished, my lips wet and my breath shuddering.

Eventually, I made myself stand up. My legs shook but I forced myself to walk over to the stairs. Climbing them felt like crawling in treacle, but when I finally got to the top, I went into my bedroom. I wanted to lie down and sleep. To sleep properly, but my shoulders sank when I saw that Macy was still on my bed with her chest open. Tears welled in my eyes at the sight of her. When I had opened her up, he had still been here. Kai had still been here.

'Good morning, Miss Thrace.'

'Is it?' I murmured. I considered asking her if she would be able to get off my bed and lie on the floor until I had enough energy to put her back together. Instead, I found my toolkit and began to repair her. I hoped it would distract me from how numb and cold I felt. I cleaned the processor and got rid of the mould residue, then screwed everything tight, shoved the I/O shield back in place and stitched her up.

'There. You're done,' I said, my voice hoarse. I clenched my eyes shut and ran a hand over my face as I swallowed. I could feel the bile rising up in my throat again.

'Thank you, Miss Thrace.' She rolled her top down then rose from my bed. 'Miss Thrace, you don't look very well. Would you like me to call a doctor for you?'

Instead of replying, I stumbled from my room into the bathroom. I knelt in front of the toilet and threw up into the pan. I flushed the chain and brushed my teeth, hoping to remove the taste of bile from my mouth. I spat out the toothpaste and stared at myself in the mirror. I looked a wreck. My eyes, usually an emerald colour, were glassy and looked too bright under my tears. My hair hung down my cheeks and shoulders, curling at the ends with grease. The circles under my eyes screamed for sleep. I was in dire need of a shower.

Macy walked into the bathroom balancing something on a trowel. My shoulders sagged lower. I had obviously made a mistake and would need to open her up again to fix her. I should have waited before fixing her. I was clearly not in the best frame of mind or focussed enough to have done it correctly. She wondered into the shower cubicle and knelt down.

'What are you doing Macy?'

'I am putting more concrete in the plughole, Miss Thrace, to stop the spiders from coming into the bathroom.'

'Why are you doing that?' I asked aghast.

'Mrs Thrace said I had to get rid of the spiders "by any means necessary" and after you made me remove the previous concrete, I have made this new batch.' All remaining energy seeped out of me. I just stared at her blankly and then turned away. That was something to sort out another day. 'You don't look okay, Miss Thrace,' stated Macy as she followed me into my room.

I shook my head with a sniff and climbed under my bed sheets. 'I'll be fine.' I faced away from the android and grabbed the pillow that Kai had slept on. I pressed my nose into the fabric and inhaled deeply. My pillow didn't smell of Kai. He never had a scent.

'Can I not interest you in a banana milkshake?' Macy's voice almost sounded sympathetic.

'No, thank you.'

'Is there anything I can do for you at all, Miss Thrace?'

I held Kai's pillow tighter. 'Actually, yes. Could you lock my door electronically and not let my Mum in?'

'Certainly, Miss Thrace. Please do not hesitate to shout if you need anything.'

As soon as I heard the lock click, I got up from my bed and pushed my desk chair under the handle, then retreated back under the covers. I cuddled Kai's pillow again and I squeezed my eyes shut as I began to cry. He wasn't here. He wasn't coming back. Why was I crying? He wasn't even real.

I tried to picture him. I didn't know if it was because I'd been given the cure but I was having trouble remembering his face. I scrambled out of bed and went over to my desk. I tore a blank page from one of my journals and started to sketch a portrait of Kai. The more I thought about him, the less I could remember what he looked like, what he sounded like, how he smiled at me.

I grabbed every blue pen I had in my room and began to colour in his eyes, but nothing looked right. Every colour I had was either too dark or too light, so I scribbled harder, eventually tearing the paper. Why couldn't I remember what his eyes looked like? My tears changed from sadness to frustration. I *had* to get this right. I started again, taking time to recall what Kai had looked like. I wasn't the best artist, but the drawing came out well enough for me to remember how his eyes crinkled whenever he laughed, how his forehead creased when he called me racist, how his face softened when he slept. I hoped that if I forced myself to remember him, then Kai would come back to me.

He didn't.

CHAPTER 28

I finally left the house. I didn't want to. I didn't want to leave my room. The room where Kai had held me as I slept, where he'd protected me from the Voices, where he'd kissed me on the cheek. It was our room.

But everything was so quiet in the house. My Mum was, thankfully, permanently out. I wasn't expecting to see her again for some time, since her clothes were gone. Macy stood alone in the kitchen, expecting me to give her an order. It was even quieter inside my head. I kept glancing at my Hourglass, waiting for it to hit sunset and for the buzzing to start. The silence gave me a headache.

I needed to get out. I rang in sick to work. I didn't bother to notify the university. I pulled on the first clothes I could find – a hoodie. I yanked it over my head and gathered my hair up. It was greasy and tangled. My face was still a mess. The skin under my eyes was purple, but all of my tears had finally dried up. I didn't think I could cry anymore even if I wanted to.

I left the house and started to walk. I had no particular destination in mind, but I kept on wincing as the cars sped passed me on the road. Had the world always been this loud? My house was too quiet, but outside was too noisy. I needed to find a medium.

Ten minutes later, I was on Iliana's doorstep and I knocked without hesitation. I'd been too absorbed with my own problems to even check up on her. I was a poor friend. Mrs Lopez answered the door and she gave me a small smile. I hadn't seen her in a while and she looked tired. 'Gracie. How are you?'

I shrugged. 'Fine. I was wondering if I could speak to Iliana.'

She sighed. 'You can try, but she won't talk to anyone.'

'What do you mean?'

'Come and see for yourself.' She opened the door wider and stepped to one side. I went into the house and followed Mrs Lopez upstairs to Iliana's bedroom. My best friend was sat on her bed, Orca poised on her knee, and wearing the same clothes from that night at Tower 142. Even though she'd never been on Hydrobliss, Iliana looked worse than me. Or at least, I assumed she hadn't been on Hydrobliss. Could she have been? Could she have been one of the other participants? Had Mum been lying about whose trials she had control of?

'Hi, Iliana.'

She didn't reply, just kept on typing. I turned to look at Mrs Lopez who just shrugged.

'I don't know what's wrong with her. She came home really late on Tuesday night. She was crying and shaking but she wouldn't tell me what happened. She's been in her room most of the time. Just typing and typing.' She sighed and I saw tears in her eyes.

'Mrs Lopez, you look really tired. Go and sleep. I'll look after Iliana for a bit.'

She hesitated then smiled and squeezed my shoulder. 'Thank you, Gracie.'

She left and I sat on the bed next to Iliana, my eyes scanning the screen as she typed and I shook my head. She was trying to find some trace of Chris. I watched as she logged onto various websites, one showing that the house that he had shared with Joe was now up for sale, and then another, her university email. The emails were all from student services, telling her repeatedly that there were no students at London University called Chris Phillipson or Joe Armstrong. Maybe their first names had been real, since my Mum had referred to them, but their surnames probably weren't. They had just been placed at the university by IrukaTech to get close to me. Maybe also close to Iliana. They did a good job.

'Oh, Iliana…' I wrapped an arm around her shoulders. Had I dragged her into all of this? I tried to keep her out of harm's way, but IrukaTech still managed to use her. Maybe if I'd told her about Chris not being at IrukaTech's party, or asked her to speak to Chris about Hydrobliss as soon as I found out about it, all of this could have been avoided. Maybe that was just wishful thinking.

She went onto a newspaper website and began to hash out an email explaining what happened on Tuesday night. Going to the press was a good idea, one I'd not thought of, but we had no evidence. I stayed with Iliana and watched her furious typing for an hour before her eyes drooped closed. Her hands left the keyboard and she slumped back onto her bed. Her breathing deepened. I put her Orca on the desk, deciding against hiding it in case that made her worse, then pulled the covers over her. 'I'm sorry for getting you involved in this,' I whispered, then kissed her cheek before laying down beside her. Luna trotted into the room and curled up on Iliana's other side letting out a whimper.

'I know, girl,' I said, then reached around to scratch the dog behind her ears. I held Iliana tight. 'I'm so sorry,' I whispered, but my best friend stayed slack in my arms as she slept.

CHAPTER 29

Friday 29th November 2047

I spent the night at Iliana's, then showered in her bathroom before I went home to get changed into slightly fresher clothes. I had class today. I didn't want to go, but the university would be louder and brighter than my house, or Iliana's, and quieter than the rest of the city.

I sat on my own, at the back, ignoring the looks the rest of my classmates gave me. Despite having washed my hair, I knew I still looked like hell, but I didn't care what they thought. I didn't even know any of their names. They were just faces in a room of a university that I had never wanted to attend.

Miss Dyna talked about the importance of footnotes in our critical essays and I could hear the soft tap of fingertips on tablet screens as students hung on her every word. But I closed my eyes, not interested in paying attention to anything. I just felt empty, like there was a hole somewhere inside me that couldn't be filled with food or medicine. I stayed in class, though. I needed to occupy myself, but I had no motivation for anything. My assignments were due in soon. I had barely started them.

As soon as the class was over, I trudged back to Iliana's. Mrs Lopez opened the door for me again, looking even more tired. 'Gracie.' She smiled and ushered me inside, out of the cold.

'Is she any better?' I asked.

Mrs Lopez shook her head. 'No change.'

I nodded then made my way upstairs. Luna was lying outside Iliana's bedroom door, whining, but she sat up when she saw me. 'Hey, girl.' I tried for a smile, but I could only manage a grimace. I stroked under her chin, then sidestepped the dog and entered Iliana's room.

'Class was boring. You didn't miss much,' I said.

There was no response. She didn't register that I was in the room.

'Have you eaten today?'

The sound of her typing was the only reply. Mrs Lopez came into the room and sat on the bed next to her daughter. 'I managed to get her to eat a handful of grapes this morning, but that was it. And you? Are you eating properly? You don't look like you are.'

I nodded, not wanting to worry Mrs Lopez any further. 'I'm fine. My… Mum's in charge of cooking.'

Mrs Lopez nodded. She had no choice but to take my word for it. She'd never met my Mum. She didn't know my Mum. It seemed like none of us truly did.

'This came today.' Mrs Lopez handed me a letter from the bedside table and I read it quickly. It was from the university, informing Iliana that they had noticed her "multiple periods of absence" and her failure to complete any assignments. It was a warning notice. 'What happened to her on Tuesday night?' Mrs Lopez asked. 'Do you know anything, Gracie?'

'No, sorry,' I said as I handed the letter back. She stared at me; her eyes narrowed slightly. She must have known I was lying but she didn't push me for the truth.

'I really want to make her have a shower today, you know, clean her up a bit, but I don't think I'm going to have time. Luna gets in the way and I need to walk her as well and I can only do that when Iliana sleeps and… there's so much I have to do…'

I wished for a moment that Mrs Lopez could be my mum. She wasn't around a lot because of her job, but she made up for it tenfold with how much she cared for Iliana when she could. She was just like my Dad. 'Why don't you wash Iliana and I take Luna for a walk?' I offered.

Mrs Lopez's furrowed brow softened. 'Are you sure?'

I nodded. 'Of course.'

She smiled. 'Thank you, Gracie. I'll just go and get her lead.'

I turned back to Iliana and rubbed a hand up and down her back. 'We'll get you sorted. Don't worry about that,' I whispered.

She continued to type, her fingers not stopping, and Mrs Lopez came back into the room with Luna on her lead. 'Here you go.'

I took the lead from her. 'I'll take my time so you can get Iliana sorted.'

I guided Luna downstairs and outside. I shouldn't have agreed to this. I didn't want to wander around London. Everywhere reminded me of Kai – New Oxford Street, Marble Arch, Trafalgar Square, Covent Garden, Tower Hill, Marylebone Station, Baker Street, Charing Cross… walking by the Thames was almost too much for me. Holloway wasn't much better, so I walked Luna down to the Arsenal football stadium. Neither Kai nor I liked football. We never came here. I went around the outside of the stadium until Luna looked like she was getting tired.

'You want to go back, girl?' She barked and I stroked her head. 'Okay, time to go back then.'

Not too far away, a young man was walking towards us and my heart landed in my throat. He had black hair, pale skin… I couldn't see his eyes yet. I tugged on Luna's lead and we began to walk quickly in his direction. My heart started to beat faster as we got closer. The man had his head down, so I still couldn't see his eyes, but he was the right height, the right build. Was it him? Could it really be him?

'Excuse me? Are you…' He looked at me with a confused expression.

'Can I help you?' he asked.

'I-I'm sorry,' I said, trying to hold back tears. 'I thought you were someone else.' He smiled at me and continued to walk past. I darted over to the nearest car in the football stadium's carpark and crouched down next to it as I started to cry. It wasn't Kai. It couldn't be him. He wasn't real. Luna nuzzled into my side and I sniffed as I held her close. It wasn't quite a hug, but it was close enough. I wouldn't be getting a real hug any time soon.

CHAPTER 30

On Christmas Day, Dad rung. 'Gray!' he shouted through my Hourglass.

'Hi, Dad.' I managed a smile, my first real one since Kai had gone.

'Your presents are under my bed. I put them there before I left just in case I couldn't be home for Christmas.'

'Alright. One second.' I abandoned the cranberry sauce I was helping Macy make and went upstairs into my parents' bedroom. I ignored my Mum's empty part of the room and sat on the floor next to my Dad's side of the bed, which was by the floor-to-ceiling window that looked out at the garden. I rooted around for a moment before pulling out two packages. They were wrapped in the same shiny purple paper that Dad had used in May for my birthday gifts. A few of the corners were sticking up which made me smile. He was always bad at wrapping presents. I opened the smaller present first which was a notepad. It had blue lines etched across the white cover, which looked like wires. I traced my finger over the embossing. I put it to one side and opened the larger present next. It was a dress that I had seen when we had gone shopping together. I was surprised Dad had remembered me saying I liked it. It was green, the same colour as my eyes, and full-length. The bodice was tight with a lace mesh over the shoulders and the cool material of the skirt pooled around my feet. 'Thanks, Dad.'

'That's alright, Gray. What did your Mum get you?'

'Good question. I have no idea. I haven't seen her today.' I hadn't seen her since she had slammed the door in my face.

'What?! Where is she?'

'I don't know,' I lied. She was more than likely at IrukaTech. Or with Izumi, but I didn't want to find out.

'When is she coming back?'

'I don't know that either. But it's okay. Macy's here. She's made Christmas dinner and she hasn't offered me a banana milkshake in ages.'

'That's good.' He sighed. 'Okay, I have to go now, but when your Mum gets back from wherever the hell she is, tell her I'll be having words with her as soon as I can, alright?'

'Alright. Merry Christmas, Dad. I love you.'

'I love you, too. And a Happy New Year, Gray!'

The line went dead as Dad's Hourglass was deactivated again. I curled myself up in a ball on the floor of my parents' bedroom and stared out at the garden. I really missed Dad today. I wanted him home. He would listen to me and take me away from this mess. My Dad loved me, and he would believe me when I eventually told him everything. He had to.

CHAPTER 31

Two days after Christmas, I was working at the café, serving customers as usual, but never cracking a smile. 'What's wrong with you?' Miss Leyshon asked as she dumped a plate and mug into the sink.

'Nothing's wrong. I'm just tired.'

'Yeah. Just tired. If that's the reason, then you've been "just tired" for about a month now.'

I shrugged, obviously not wanting to tell my boss the real reason. No one missed hearing voices. 'It's just my Dad. This is the first Christmas I've had without him.'

Miss Leyshon nodded, her face softening slightly. 'I'm sure he's fine. Did he ring you?'

'Yeah.'

'I am sure that was a treat for you and your Mum at Christmas.' I finally saw Mum on Boxing Day. She happened to be passing on the other side of a street, loaded with shopping bags. All from exclusive designer stores. 'Things will work themselves out, I am sure your Dad will be fine. Now, please, smile. You'll put off the customers. This is a café, not a funeral parlour.'

She went off to clean an empty table. I started washing up, blinking away the tears in my eyes when I thought of how Kai and I used to do this together. Someone cleared their throat behind me. I dried my hands on my apron and grabbed a notepad from the Welsh dresser. I didn't look up at the customer and focused on the flickering fairy lights reflected in the cake case while I composed myself.

'Hi, welcome to Leyshon's Café. What can I get for you today?'

'A green tea, please.'

I went to write down the order, but my hand froze just before the pen touched the paper. That voice. The way it moved over the words like water, but still sounded broken. I knew that voice.

I looked up. Pale skin, black hair, blue eyes.

Those amazing blue eyes.

'Kai-chan?'

He smiled.

To be continued...

SALAD
PAGES

A NEW AGE OF BOOKS

Enjoyed Nightmare Scenario?
Visit www.saladpages.com/books to discover
more books by Hazel and Salad Pages.

INTERVIEW WITH HAZEL

Q: Tell us a bit about yourself?

A: I'm a Scriptwriting Masters student with a Degree and Masters in Creative Writing. I like writing novels, screenplays, and spend far too much of my time writing neither of those and writing fan fiction instead!! I also listen to an unhealthy amount of kpop and know next to nothing about songs sung in my own language. I live in Preston, Lancashire with my mum and three brothers. I also own a rabbit and two guinea pigs.

Q: How old were you when you wrote *Nightmare Scenario?*

A: 19

Q: What inspired you to write *Nightmare Scenario?*

A: I have psychosis, and even though mental health is more freely talked about now, I feel that psychosis and schizophrenia still have a lot of stigma attached to them, so I gave my main character schizophrenia so it could open up the conversation more.

Another thing is the too rapid development of technology. Ever since I was a child, I've grown up witnessing how quickly technology has developed. Whilst I realise some of it has been for the better, like better medical equipment to help save people's lives, some new technology has taken people's jobs and even killed some people.

Q: What do you enjoy most about writing?
A: When I started my undergraduate degree in Creative Writing, my lecturer read out some quotes, and one has stuck with me: 'Write so you'll always have something to read'. This has always been the reason why I write.

Q: When you are not writing, what do you enjoy doing?
A: I love listening to kpop and learning the dance routines for the songs. I'm also taking extra classes at university to learn how to speak Korean. I'm a fan of playing video games and I love going clothes shopping.